The State of America

The State of
AMERICA

Trevor Fishlock

faber and faber

LONDON · BOSTON

First published in Great Britain in 1986 by
John Murray (Publishers) Limited
This paperback edition first published in 1987 by
Faber and Faber Limited
3 Queen Square London WC1N 3AU

Printed in Great Britain by
Mackays of Chatham Ltd Kent
All rights reserved

British Library Cataloguing in Publication Data

Fishlock, Trevor
The state of America.
1. United States—Social life and
customs—1971-
I. Title
973.927   E169.04
ISBN 0–571–14873–5

for my mother

Preface

This is a slice, or perhaps several slices, of the American pie. I have examined the crust and ingredients mostly during my time as a foreign correspondent based in New York; though I hasten to say that part of my brief on this enjoyable, absorbing and revealing adventure is to leave New York fairly frequently to visit America. People everywhere have been generous in giving me their time, showing me their country and talking of their hopes and ambitions as well as their disappointments and misgivings. I owe thanks to Roger Hudson for his encouragement and editing skills; and, most of all, to Penny. In a particular way this book shipped a crew of two.

NEW YORK
January 1986

Contents

I   The Inside

Alaska

Can you forget those days of vast daring,
There with your soul on the Top o' the World?
ROBERT SERVICE – 'MEN OF THE HIGH NORTH'

THE TWO BIRDS flew imperiously and purposefully, wing strokes synchronized in deep and steady rhythm, like the dipping oars of a trireme. I watched them swing towards me over the brilliant rubble of sapphire ice boulders at the foot of the glacier. The mountain air was dagger-sharp and cold and numbed my face. I was alone and felt exhilarated. The high ramparts of the mountains formed a spectacle of stunning grandeur. The snow scintillated in the early morning sunshine and the slanting light had a glowing quality. There was profound silence, a sense of the primeval, of limitless and untrodden land.

The birds dropped low over a brake of spindly leaning trees and there was a flurry, as if someone had shaken a tablecloth, as they flared their long wings, extended their talons and settled on the body of a deer lying in blood-spattered snow. They were bald eagles, splendid specimens of the symbol of the United States, the fierce and regal raptor which appears on the national seal, clutching thunderbolts in the form of spears. A couple of crows, who knew their place, retreated from the carrion and hung about at a respectful distance, hopeful beggars at the gate. The swaggering, bossy eagles tore into the flesh like glutton Vikings at a feast, their yellow bills and bad-tempered faces growing bloodier with their butchery. At my inexpert approach, snow crunching underfoot, the younger of the two flew off; but the other only glared into the lens of the camera for a few seconds, his eyes hard chrome yellow under his feathery white war bonnet; and then, dismissing me, bent fearlessly to his feasting, king in his Alaskan domain.

For certain Americans this wilderness land is alluring and enchanting. To many of those who participate in its adolescence, or dream of doing so, there is, in the sheer vastness, tracklessness and majesty of the 49th state, an abundance of what they believe America has always stood for: unfenced possibility and challenge, a chance for people to reinvent themselves, a fresh start; the prospect of profit. Alaska is seen as a frontier where men can still be as free as eagles and dispense with convention's impediments while staking energy, brawn, acumen and hope in a new land of mostly young people, a vigorous society where men are thin on the icy ground and grandfathers are scarce. In more than one respect Alaska is an immature land; and its immaturity, romance, assertiveness and independence are summarised in the slogan on the state's vehicle registration plate – 'Alaska The Last Frontier.'

The frontier vanished over a century ago in most of the United States. The west, the wild west, had largely gone by the time novelists, journalists and showmen began to idealise and mythologise it. Custer made his last stand and entered American legend as a frontier hero just in time. The telephone was invented the year he died. Buffalo Bill, impresario, made himself a millionaire in the 1880s and 1890s with a wild west show that presented the frontier in defanged theatrical form, a curio, a circus suitable to be taken to London and shown to Queen Victoria. By the end of the century Sitting Bull was betrayed and dead, Geronimo in an alcoholic haze in government custody, a freak remnant from a bygone age, posing for tourists' snapshots. Butch Cassidy and Harry Longbaugh, the Sundance Kid, decided in 1901 that the old western game was up and that they were anachronisms in the settled United States. They headed for South America where there was still some frontier left. Owen Wister's novel *The Virginian*, the exemplar of western tales in which cowboys were chivalrous knights in Stetsons, was published in 1902 at a time when the range had mostly been tamed. When Marion Morrison, later to frontierise his name to John Wayne, was born in 1907 the frontier was to a large extent the stuff of old men's tales. Frontier survivors were oddities. Wyatt Earp lived on to 1929, and Emmett Dalton, who took part in one of the last of the old-time bank stick-ups in 1892, died with his boots off in 1937. As a young man of 20, in 1881, Frederic Remington, the frontier painter and sculptor, watched a train labour across the prairie, sounding its haunting whistle, and noted: 'I knew the wild riders and the vacant land were about to vanish for ever ...'

The frontier meant free and open land and at the end of the 19th century the Census Bureau defined it as land with a population density of no more than two people to the square mile. There is none in the eastern and middle states today. The remaining tracts of sparsely populated territory are chiefly in the rugged highlands or deserts in parts of Montana, Wyoming, Nevada, Oregon, Idaho, New Mexico and western Texas. Almost all of Alaska, however, is frontier by the 1893 definition. The word Alaska, derived from the language of the Aleut people and bent a little by the Russians along the way, means the great land; and it is exactly that. It covers 586,000 square miles, one-fifth of the area of the United States, and is twice the size of Texas. Its population is about half a million, so that it is both the largest and the smallest state. Outside its main population centres, back of beyond, there is, statistically speaking, less than one person to the square mile, so that Alaska is one of the most thinly peopled regions of the world. Superimposed on the contiguous 48 states Alaska would touch Mexico and Canada. Its main bulk would cover all of the mid-west. The distance from its south-east corner to Barrow in the north is the same as from New York to Denver, and the length of the Aleutian tentacle to the ultimate islands of Attu and Kiska (invaded by Japanese troops in the Second World War), would cover the distance from Denver to Las Vegas. The state has four time zones, Bering, Alaska, Yukon and Pacific.

But the frontier is more than a matter of demography, size,

open-ness and the wild west. The frontier has always been magical and it remains an engaging and potent element in American imagination. In 1893 the historian Frederick Jackson Turner gave a seminal lecture on the significance of the frontier as one of the dynamic forces of American society and democracy. This happened to be the year of one of the four great Oklahoma runs, when 50,000 settlers dashed from a starting line to grab their claims in what had once been inviolate Cherokee land: a late flowering of the good old frontier spirit. Turner's ideas were later disparaged by historians, but subsequently revisited and found to have weight. The importance of the frontier as a formative influence in the development of American society is debated, but the notion of the frontier has permeated and helps to nourish identity. It remains a catalyst, part of American vitality and romance. Pioneering, pushing west, is reckoned to be as much in the American bloodstream as seafaring is in the British.

Embedded in the American psyche, the frontier is ever evocative, a spring easily tapped, a theme constantly returned to in literature, films, commerce and politics. It stands for unquenchable optimism, for belief in the rewards of exploitation of resources. Pioneering was for dreamers and, as we know with hindsight, it was often a wretched business and ended for many migrants in the crushing of their dreams. Not much is said about the defeated who turned around and went back. Of course not: the frontier idea is primarily concerned with goals and achievement. Frontiersmen – energetic, resourceful, mobile, scornful of the rules, deeply patriotic, inventive and restless – helped to shape Americans' ideas of themselves. Frontier icons – like the westerner in his broad-brimmed hat and leather chaps, the pioneer wagon and Colt revolver, rosy-cheeked gingham-frocked Ma at the iron stove – remain staples of advertising, along with western music. Wagon trains sell cornflakes and mortgages. 'The western idea . . . with Ralph Lauren', sells high-fashion clothing. A New York investment company commercial has its chairman posed improbably on the footplate of a wood-burning iron horse, proclaiming: 'The pioneer spirit that pushed the railroads across

America drives many of today's emerging growth companies.' The lonesome cowboy minding herds in Marlboro country evokes a time and a place where no government gets on a free man's back to tell him that smoking is dangerous to health.

Frontier ideas, bootstrappery, the virtues and equalising qualities of hard work and money are commonly exploited. 'Free lunch, I never got one. Working for what you want, isn't that the American way?' – asks an advertisement. Ronald Reagan, who played many westerners on the screen, constantly invokes what he terms the old values, a certain ruggedness, standing tall and all that. Introducing his tax reform proposals in 1985 he said: 'It must be an expression of both America's eternal frontier spirit, and all the virtues from the heart and soul of a good and decent people.' Occasionally he summons up the memory of John Wayne, greatest of screen frontiersmen. On both of his presidential election eves Reagan repeated the sentimental words Wayne uttered just before his death, investing their banality with husky emotion: 'Just give the American people a good cause, and there's nothing they can't lick.' In 1979 after mobs in Iran had insulted the United States again, students in California marched with placards bearing John Wayne's image, as if calling upon an Arthurian hero to ride to avenge them. In a retrospective article on the Vietnam war, in 1985, the *New York Times* magazine interviewed an American army commander – 'the image of a tough airborne officer' – and noted that he had in his office a picture of John Wayne playing the part of a cavalry officer.

In the role of westerner John Wayne appealed to American wistfulness. Frontiersmen, of course, as settlers, forest-clearers, barbed-wire fencers, railway builders and telegraph linesmen, were dedicated to making the frontier a diminishing resource. The frontier, like youth, was brief. The heyday of the cowboy lasted thirty years. The Pony Express between Missouri and California operated for only nineteen months in 1860–1 before it was superseded by the transcontinental telegraph. The plains Indians watched the open range, the buffalo herds and their whole way of life disappear in two generations. In Oklahoma cities arose overnight on the prairie. Hard on the heels of the leatherstockings came the lawyers, preachers, politicians, manufacturers and others in the vanguard of civilisation. An epoch of such uproariousness and energy was bound to mature, leaving in the collective memory an idea of an enchanted time, of never-never land.

In Alaska there is all the ambiguity of the frontier. The Last Frontier slogan is invested with self-consciousness and sadness. It is meant to sound robustly all-American and celebratory, but it has, too, a note of nostalgic longing, regret for vanishing youth. Otherwise, surely, Alaskans would have called their land, in a more forward-looking way, the New Frontier. Men still journey here to be frontiersmen. They grow their whiskers especially for the purpose. They ransack the trading post catalogues for thick wool shirts, thermal underwear, rifles, Bowie knives and books on how to build log cabins and bear-proof larders. They buy devices to get solar electricity 'free from the midnight sun' and consider whether to invest in 'the world's most powerful hand gun, 2000 foot-pounds of raw power! Alaska's answer to bear protection.' Thus equipped they thrust their eager bushy faces towards the challenging wilderness – and are dismayed to find parking tickets on their windscreens. Anchorage and Fairbanks have traffic jams, parking congestion and severe carbon monoxide pollution. Even in distant Nome, population 2500, there are irksome regulations. The *Nome Nugget*, Alaska's oldest newspaper (the motto on its masthead states: There's no place like Nome) commented regretfully on the installation of the town's first traffic signal in 1984: 'It doesn't make us do anything we weren't already supposed to do. So, no cause for alarm yet. It just makes one wonder who will get the first ticket and how long before the first bullet hole shows up. Big city life is creeping up on us.'

One evening I went to a warm and jolly fish restaurant in Anchorage. The waitresses were also jolly, if slightly self-conscious, being dressed up as lobsters. They had pink foam-rubber costumes and yard-long claws on their feet which forced them to clomp like circus clowns with oversized boots. One girl found it more convenient to walk backwards, a reversing lobster. Although, as a newcomer, I thought all this eccentric, the regular diners took no notice.

My lobster was serving my salmon, slapping her claws the while, when, through the door and out of the penetrating cold, streamed a group of new Alaskans. There were half-a-dozen brawny young men, with cheeks as red as wine, laughing and walloping their arms, Vikings all, with bushy Paul Bunyan beards. Unzipping their parkas they revealed thick red lumberjack shirts, their trousers held up by braces. Their wives were similarly glowing and carried red-faced babies in papoose slings. They all shook the snow from their hats and from the babies' fur bonnets and settled at a large pine table, unpeeling the wrappings from their babies like so many bananas. A lobster slip-slopped over for the order and soon the table was piled with oysters, scallops, crab, shrimp, salmon and mugs of beer. The faces shone with merriment and health. Breughel would have had them for models.

Such people accord with the agreeable image that many Alaskans have of themselves. They are young, average age 27, energetic, vital, fecund, pioneers and builders of a vast area that has been a state since President Eisenhower signed it into being in January 1959. This was ninety-two years after the American Secretary of State bought it from the Russians for $7.2 million, and Prince Dmitri Maksoutoff, the last Russian governor, sailed home. Russian America, as it was then called, had become a burden because of its remoteness and the decline in the fur trade, and the Russians were relieved to sell. It was an agreeable alternative to war as a way of acquiring territory and adjusting the political map of the planet, and was the last of the real estate purchases on the grand scale. It was a bargain, although at the time many Americans thought their government mad to buy a mass of ice and tundra.

Alaska's true spiritual and cultural union with the rest of the United States did not come until 1969, the year it first received live American television and thus fastened itself securely to the national nipple. Nevertheless, Alaskans still feel ambivalent about themselves – Americans yes, but different and separate, a special people because they owe allegiance to a harsh and remote land. Alaskans call the continental United States The Lower 48, or, more graphically, The Outside.

The idea of The Outside meant more when the region was less well developed and air communications with the rest of the country were not so good. But the term retains its connotation of Alaskan insularity and the sense of distance from the mainstream. Alaskans sometimes muse that America is 'the United States plus Alaska', and feel, more strongly than people in other states, that Washington does not understand them. They certainly think that their fellow Americans do not know much about them. Alaska is a strongly conservative society, devoted to free enterprise and resource exploitation, dismissive of regulations and government interference. Its libertarian streak has led to the state government de-criminalising the use of marijuana, it being legal to possess a small amount for personal use. Similarly the state takes a liberal view on official funding for abortion. There is a vigorous sense of identity, particularly among those who were born here, or have been resident long enough to qualify as veterans, or what Alaskans call sourdoughs, after the yeast mixture with which miners and other trailblazers made bread and cakes. Veterans are a sort of aristocracy and when they retire they are known as pioneers. Obituary notices often record how long a person lived in Alaska, as if in tribute to years before the mast under an exacting skipper.

The rivalries between long-term Alaskans and newcomers, known as cheechakos, are part of the turbulence in Alaskan politics and social life. There are other aspects to it: in fewer than twenty years Alaska has experienced many events of profound consequence, the oil boom, construction and land deals, a headlong rush that has brought people pouring in.

'Alaska is ego-boosting,' Stephen Haycox, professor of history at Alaska State University, said to me.

It has always attracted individualists and self-starters, and people come here because they sense that this is a state where they can rise quickly and achieve more ... they can spread themselves and fulfil their ambitions long before their hair grows grey. They feel there is nothing they cannot do and that the class barriers and other restrictions elsewhere do not exist here. Alaska particularly suits people a little more aggressive than the average. That's what the frontier means.

The frontier is also a cruel sorter. There are many stories of men and women arriving with only a handful of dollars and clawing their way to wealth by working hard. There are also numerous failures. Alaska is around the top of the American tables recording suicide, drug abuse, child beating, mental disorder and rape. Alcohol-related deaths are three and a half times the national average and the murder rate is high. Every Sunday the *Anchorage Times* publishes notices of meetings to be held in the week ahead. A typical list includes the Suicide Prevention and Crisis Centre, Alcoholics Anonymous Sunshine Group, Survivors of Suicide, Parents United, a support group for sexually abused children and their families, Emotions Anonymous, Overeaters Anonymous, Narcotics Anonymous, Nar-Anon, for families of drug abusers, the Clean and Serene Group of Narcotics Anonymous and Alcoholics Anonymous Business and Professional Group.

In February 1984 the *Nome Nugget* carried this summary of two weeks of police work in the town:

Nome police officers responded to 1 sexual assault, 10 fights and assaults, 24 domestic violence calls, 5 threats of harassments, 2 vandalisms, 9 thefts, 1 hit and run accident, 3 vehicle accidents, 2 intoxicated drivers, 1 minor consuming alcohol, 1 run-away, 1 juvenile mischief complaint, 1 lost child, 2 curfew violations, 19 public assists, 10 agency assists, 2 man with gun calls, 1 suicide, 2 suicide attempts, 1 threatened suicide, 6 noise complaints, 13 miscellaneous complaints, 5 intoxicated persons passed out in sub-zero weather, and 24 intoxicated persons removed from various establishments.

Winter brings the awful melancholy of cabin fever. In the north the sun is not seen for about 70 days from November to January.

In the south there are only three and a half hours of daylight, the sun rising in mid-morning and setting in mid-afternoon. Temperatures in the interior fall as low as 80° below zero. An under-inflated car tyre freezes into its distorted form, giving a rough 'square wheel' ride. Frozen tyres can shatter on impact with an obstruction. The yellow pages in the Anchorage telephone directory list twenty-seven tanning studios, a substitute for the sunshine Alaskans crave. 'Beat cabin fever by taking a winter hike,' an article in the *Anchorage Times* advised. But many people feel disinclined to venture out. It is easier to sit by the television set with beer and whiskey. Bored or crazed, families slide into violence and turn on each other. Women who are newly arrived from the Lower 48 and are without friends or family support, break under the strain of being cooped up with young children. Communities set up cabin fever clinics and encourage people to take part in social activities. Anchorage runs a popular ten-day carnival and fur market every February to lure people out.

Many people do not have the emotional resources, let alone the physical ones, for life in this challenging land. One of Alaska's attractions is that it has the highest wages in the country. But people come here without any clear idea of what Alaska is like, in the thin clothing that betrays their ignorance. Wages are higher, but so are prices. Food, housing, doctors' and lawyers' services are all more expensive than on The Outside. The population is young and energetic, but also transient. About a quarter of the newcomers quit after a year and a third leave after three years. As the American frontier always was, Alaska is exciting and depressing, a magnet for the ambitious and determined and also for fugitives of one kind or another, on the run from the police, or a wife, or a way of life. Eldorado for some, it is Last Chance Gulch for others; and there are many drifters looking for luck. In 1984 one such washed-up man arrived in a small mining town in the interior and killed eight people for no reason. In an episode that might have been scripted for a television melodrama he fought a gun duel with policemen who pursued him in a helicopter and killed one of them before being killed himself.

. For many of those who settle here the weather and hardships are faced as a challenge, not a penance. People fall in love with Alaska and relish its rawness. There is an undoubted romance about the great land – I felt it myself – and its place names are evocative, reflecting the Eskimo, Indian and Aleut background, Russian ownership and mining town past: Arctic Village, Chicken, Deadhorse, Eek, Ekwok, Goodnews, Ketchikan, King Salmon, Koyukuk, Mary's Igloo, Naknek, Nellie Jean, Nightmute, Platinum, Red Devil, Russian Mission, Shishmaref, Sleetmute, Sourdough, Tin City, Tok, Woodchopper, Wales and Yes Bay.

Winifred Freeman, who runs a bookshop in Anchorage, succumbed to Alaska's spell years ago. She arrived from California in 1960 and says it takes thirty years to reach sourdough status.

At first I had a weird feeling of being on top of the globe, far away at the end of the world. But I got used to it and I won't go now. I love Alaska's beauty and the different qualities of the seasons; and Alaskans are adventurous and friendly and they all believe they are going to make money. It is a wonderful place for people who make it, not so good for those who don't. A lot of people come here to escape, leaving their pasts, but then they find they have come to the end of the line and they wouldn't make it anywhere, let alone here. Alaska has changed remarkably in my time. It used to be a strongly masculine society, but now there are more women. There is more riff-raff, too. I never locked my door in the old days, but now I do. Of course, the winters are hard and people get cabin fever, drink a lot and shoot each other, and we've had some terrible tragedies, though I think things are getting better. In the winter we hibernate. But we don't sleep much in the summer. In the middle of the summer we have daylight most of the time and the kids are out playing to midnight, and people work 18 hours a day, making the most of it. Everything is feverish but we never seem to get tired.

The great land simmers with argument. In recent times its political and social debates have turned on the matter of the land – how it should be cut up, exploited and preserved, how much the natives, oil men, the miners, the moose, the wolves and the homesteaders and hunters should get.

To dare a simplification, Alaskans are divided into two broad and conflicting streams: boomers and greenies. They can scent each other a mile off. They are locked, antler-to-antler, on the question of what Alaska means and what should be done with it. Boomers are in the majority and believe that not only is Alaska the last frontier but also that it is meant to be treated like a frontier, tamed, peopled, Americanised, hunted, dug for gold, silver, zinc, copper, lead and coal, drilled for oil, fished for salmon, paved with a web of highways. Greenies see Alaska as the last great wilderness, rather than the last frontier, and they want it mostly left alone. They think boomers have the typically American fast-buck attitude, the outlook that led, for example, to the wiping out of the bison on the great plains in the 19th century. Boomers think greenies an obstacle to progress. Greenies think boomers are live-for-today greedheads. A government conservationist said to me that he was pessimistic about the outcome of the environment battle.

I'm afraid that our attitude to wildlife is much the same as it was when the bison disappeared. We Americans live for today. More and more compromises are being forced on those fighting to keep the environment and I think the only thing that will save Alaska's wilderness will be the failure of further oil exploration. The big oil companies see this state as their salvation. If they cannot find large reserves one or two of them will go belly-up. If this happens the economy will be slowed down, but on the other hand the last true wilderness on earth will be saved.

Suggest to a boomer that Alaska's land is fragile, as the greenies say it is, and you will hear a terrible snorting. Boomers think Alaska so vast and rough and tough that it will take immense development even to make a dent in it. Boomers and greenies are robust and definite, buoyed by victories, hardened by defeats.

The first boomers were the Russians who arrived in the mid-18th century to hunt sea otter and seal. Americans came first for fish, and then for gold. Among the goldrushers was Wyatt Earp, late marshal of Dodge City and Tombstone, who arrived in 1898 and ran a saloon in Nome for three years. For two-thirds of this century Alaska mostly slumbered, far off, expensive to reach, a poor-relation colony kept by the federal government. In the bush a few whites made their peace with the forbidding land, living much like the Eskimo, Aleut and Indian natives by hunting and trapping.

With statehood in 1959 Alaskans thought they would be able to throw off Washington's yoke and subsidies and make their own independent way. But they had to wait for the pivotal year of 1968 when Atlantic Richfield and British Petroleum struck oil with their fifty-first borehole, the last shot after fifty dry ones. It was found on state-leased land at Prudhoe Bay, on the frozen and bone-bare North Slope, one of the harshest places on the planet. The reserve was estimated at nearly ten billion barrels, the largest ever found in North America. As the oil gushed an old Alaska ended.

Now a remarkable thing happened. Alaska was broke and Alaskans wanted to get the oil out and the money in the bank. But first they had to settle the question of land ownership. Without settlement there could be no development leases and no oil pipeline. In particular, there was the matter of native claims to Alaska's land. The 80,000 natives, 17 per cent of the population, had received no land provision at the time of statehood, but in the early 1960s they united and began to campaign for their share. Their politically aware leaders were able to confront the white man. They stimulated and harnessed an awakening of native people, who emerged as a political force. Under the Alaskan Native Claims Settlement Act of 1971 native people were given 44 million acres, a ninth of the state, and almost a billion dollars. It was an enlightened recognition of rights, which was remarkable. The deal stemmed partly from conscience, an American desire to compensate for centuries of cheating and destroying native people, and also from the practical and urgent need to exploit the oil.

The settlement made capitalists of native people. The money was paid into 12 regional and 200 village corporations in which native people were shareholders. These corporations have a significant role in the Alaskan economy, investing in banking, canning, oil, fisheries, timber, hotels, mining and exploration. Some have done well, but others have run into difficulties and have been exploited by outsiders, reflecting the fact that they are breaking new ground. A number of managers lack experience and business is hard. The corporations have not raised employment much. But native leaders say they are not just businesses, to be judged on profits. They also help to buttress native pride, giving people a sense of worth and involvement. Native people have not adjusted easily to changes wrought by whites, and their rates of unemployment, alcoholism and suicide are high. The corporations are meant to invigorate culture, replace despair with hope, help to support life in remote villages, and mitigate the difficulties native people have in retaining their identity and language, while being part of a modern state. Leaders set an example by returning to their villages and teaching their children to hunt and trap and prepare native food.

The essence of the land settlement is that natives own the land. Some of them regard it, sceptically, as social engineering, an attempt to assimilate them into white Alaska by imposing corporate structures and alien ideas of private property at the expense of tribal ones. But their leaders are adamant that ownership is fundamental to their survival as distinct peoples. Today, though, this principle is threatened. In 1991 natives will be entitled to sell their corporation shares, and might be tempted to do so, opening up the possibility that outsiders will move into their land, eroding a cultural, economic and political base. Leaders want the law amended to prevent sales, securing the land in perpetuity.

Having waited for native rights to be settled, the boomers had to curb their impatience while they fought a celebrated battle with the greenies over the 800-mile trans-Alaska pipeline. Greenies successfully challenged the pipeline design in court, arguing that it would damage the environment and interfere with animal migration. Litigation and redrawing of the pipeline made the enterprise more expensive and late. The boomers also lost the battle over the Alaska Lands Act which put about half the state,

159 million acres, under protection in the form of a park and forest. It was one of the last measures President Carter signed, and a victory for conservation-minded Americans. President Reagan would never have allowed it. It was vehemently opposed by big business, land developers, mining and oil concerns, and by the National Rifle Association, which believes that any attempt to pinch the freedom of gun owners undermines America itself. Most Alaskans were furious at the way the Washington government and greenies on The Outside interfered in the last frontier in this way and in 1980 expressed their rage by voting for a re-examination of the question of statehood; proposing, in their huff, to secede from the United States. Tempers eventually cooled and Alaskans grumpily concluded it was better to remain a star on the flag.

The oil pipeline, from Prudhoe Bay to the ice-free port of Valdez in the south, was one of America's historic engineering feats, ranking with the great dams and waterways of the Lower 48. The construction work created much wealth, but it was the completion of the pipeline in 1977 and the flowing of the oil at last that really made Alaska wealthy. The oilfield provides a fifth of America's oil and nine-tenths of Alaska's revenue, with the state creaming a royalty of one-eighth of the oil's value. For years the machine was jammed on jackpot and the oil revenues swelled the Alaskan exchequer by $70 every second. The oilfield has attracted crews of tough men who work long hours for high pay under gruelling conditions in the bitterest winters. Working twelve hours on, twelve off, they live in camps with strict rules: no drinking, no drugs, no fighting, no loud noise, limited gambling at cards. Drillers can earn more than $90,000 a year. A kitchen hand can get $40,000. After a two-week stint workers are flown south for a week's leave. I fell into conversation with one of them at Anchorage airport. He was a Texan, smartly dressed in western fashion, topped by a Stetson, his feet encased in Texan boots which he was having polished at the airport shoeshine stand. He left a $5 tip. 'After a spell in the north,' he said, 'I never have any doubt about what I want from Anchorage. I don't even think of

the money because I have plenty. I want a party, a drink, a steak
and a woman.' He was bursting with a certain energy. As we
talked his eyes swivelled and tracked every young woman who
passed, and to some of them he offered curious clicking, rutting
noises with his tongue.

Having become monstrously rich with oil dollars Alaska began
to enjoy and spread itself. It undertook capital investment on a
large scale and abolished both the state income tax, which had
been among the highest in the country, and the sales tax levied in
most American states. It also began to care for its pioneers, the
16,500 people over the age of 65. The state pays all their property
taxes and gives them free meals, transport, driving and fishing
licences, as well as a $250 a month grant if they have lived in
Alaska at least a year. In case anyone thinks this looks like welfare,
a paradox on the ruggedly conservative frontier, the law itself
specifically says it is not – it is called a gift. The government also
established a state nest-egg fund and decided to share the interest
among the people, an odd form of co-operativism, or Utopianism,
in such a professedly individualist society. The idea was to involve
Alaskans in the management of their economy; and certainly the
people pay close attention to the oil prices upon which so much
depends. As first proposed, the fund would have paid its dividend
according to the number of years an Alaskan had lived in the state,
reflecting the resentment that old-timers have for newcomers.
However, young lawyers from The Outside argued successfully
in court that this was discrimination, and that interest on the
cache should be divided among everyone who had been resident
six months. Some of the veterans were furious, and one of the
lawyers was lynched in effigy, so that to the rest of America Alaska
began to look a greedy, squandering, oil-rich state. Many an
Alaskan, muttering secessionist talk, said The Outside could go
hang. Still, the state government was concerned enough about
image to run a public relations drive to try to convince America
that Alaska had been lagging behind ever since it was bought from
the Russians and needed the money to catch up with the rest of
the country. In 1982 every man, woman and child received $1,000

from the state, an amalgamation of the three years of pay-outs bottled up by the residency litigation, and between $300 and $400 in the following years. The debate about the share-out endures. The oil money will not last for ever and some think it should be used to improve education, public facilities and roads; but most prefer dollars in their pockets.

Greenies say that if you want an example of bad boomerism you have only to look at Anchorage. The implication is that you would look down your nose at it. Half the people of Alaska live here, the hub of the state, though not its capital, which is modest little Juneau, nearly 500 miles away in the south-eastern Alaskan panhandle. Juneau is inconveniently sited and there has been much talk of making Anchorage the capital, or building a new one. There is, however, a sensible American tradition of having the seat of state government separate from the major cities, as a counterweight to big city arrogance and might. Anchorage would not make a handsome capital. Its people hope it will swell into a magnificent metropolis, and it is certainly swelling. It will doubtless grow uglier, for it is already an excrescence on the plain between Cook Inlet and the sublime Chugach mountains. Of another city, the architect Sir Clough Williams-Ellis said: 'By God, what a site! By man, what a mess!' – and the comment could apply to Anchorage, too. It began as a tent town for railway workers. Its first wooden building still stands, with a plaque stating that it was built in 1915, and bits of the old clapboard town remain on weedy lots near the oil companies' unimaginative glass skyscrapers. Traffic congestion in the city is often acute and because of frequent temperature inversions Anchorage has one of the most polluted city atmospheres in the United States. Being young, it might have grown with all the advantages of thoughtful planning, but it never had the luck to be managed by a hard-nosed visionary despot who might have created in it a reflection of the nobler part of the Alaskan spirit. It just grew like mould. There is nothing in its design and architecture to complement or salute the natural grandeur. It possesses little that is muscular, fine or daring, not a speck of class. It represents a lost opportunity and its ramshackle and dismal aspect might even contribute to the depression that seizes some of its citizens in winter.

Still, eyesores are sometimes removed, even here. I happened to be in town when the authorities demolished a saloon they disapproved of, a haunt of the city's hard drinkers and street girls. The outside walls of this drinking hall were painted – life imitating art – with lines from Robert Service's gold-rush poem *The Shooting of Dan McGrew* – 'A bunch of the boys were whooping it up in the Malamute saloon . . . ' and so on. I stood in the sad crowd of regulars as the demolition ball swung and the Mal fell out of Malamute onto the pavement and the whoo was knocked out of whooping. Swaying, grey-faced whites, drunk natives and gaudy girls watched in dismay as the saloon crumbled. It was as if they were witnessing the hanging of an old friend: the end of a bit of the frontier.

An insistent rumble in Alaska is the argument between well-organized hunting lobbies and environmentalists. Greenies are anxious that national parks now closed to hunting should remain inviolate. Hunters' groups chip away to get more land opened up, arguing that Alaska is so large and hunting so limited that liberating more wilderness to the guns will not matter much. Hunting, trapping and the outdoors, as well as the environmental quarrels, are of absorbing interest to Alaskans and a staple of newspapers and magazines. There is endless debate about the hunting of wolves: is it right to thin out the wolf population so that more moose, the wolves' natural prey, can survive to be hunted by man? Hunting exploits are retold at length – 'How I shot the record deer' – 'How I was treed by a bear' – and newspapers carry numerous photographs of grinning hunters with their slaughtered beasts. There are articles on woodcraft, tracking, skull-polishing, antler-cleaning and home ammunition-making. Big game hunting, for bear, moose and caribou, is a thriving business in Alaska; and while bear hunting is legal under certain conditions, the state has outlawed the sale of bear parts. Bear paw is a gourmet delicacy in Korea and China, and bear gallbladders are prized as a supposed aphrodisiac or cure for arthritis. The sums offered for bear parts have led naturally to an increase in poaching.

Names of hunting law transgressors are published along with other hunting and wildlife news. I read in the *Anchorage Times* that

Anchorage businessman Carl Brady Jr will be visiting Alaska Zoo soon. Because he shot a moose illegally Brady was ordered by a federal court judge to contribute $1000 and ten hours of his time to the zoo. He was charged with the game violation after another hunter in the Lake Clark area turned him in to National Park Service officials. Besides putting in his time and money at the zoo, Brady was ordered to pay an additional $500 fine, was placed on probation for six months and had his hunting privileges suspended for a year.

The primitive practice of hanging stuffed animal heads on walls is widespread in Alaska. No wall is imagined complete without these sad and grotesque relics. Anchorage alone has seventeen taxidermists, and I went to see one of them. His name is Hunter Fisher and he practises a more agreeable form of trophyism, being a leading fish stuffer, with an international clientele. When he arrived in Alaska in the early 1960s he worked as a federal investigator.

In those days Anchorage was only a small place. Fifty miles out of town you were in real wilderness, almost untrodden ground. I caught the Alaskan fishing fever and never recovered. I left the government and I've been mounting fish ever since. I mount a thousand a year, freeze dried mounting at $8 an inch, $9 for a king salmon, and I've done the world record king salmon and all the state records. It takes accurate knowledge to paint the fish and get the colour exactly right. If you bring a fish to me I can tell by the colour where you caught it. What keeps me here is that we have the finest fishing on earth. People come from all over the world to enjoy it and spend a lot of money. It can be expensive: a week in a lodge can cost $2700 and the plane to fly you there can cost $90 an hour. There's a big argument between commercial fishermen and sports fishermen – the sportsmen think the commercial fishermen are greedy. It is one of the debates that keeps us going. There is a parochial attitude here, and I am as guilty in this as the next man. But, as the natives say, – 'Spend a week in my moccasins before you make a judgement'.

Steak and potato is America's favourite food, but fish is the thing in Alaska – arctic char, grayling, trout, halibut, king crab, which can grow to five feet in breadth, and salmon in its various forms: pink, sockeye, chum, coho and king. King salmon is the largest in the world, averaging 50 pounds and frequently going over 70 pounds. The record is 93 pounds. The Kenai river, on the Kenai peninsula, south of Anchorage, is one of the great salmon rivers of the world. Catching big salmon by commercial net and sportsman's line is an important industry, worth about $1.5 billion a year and there is rivalry between commercial seine net fishermen and the 200 or so professional guides who operate the lucrative fishing camps and lodges for thousands of sport fishermen. The state government has shortened the commercial fishing season as a conservation measure. John Morrison, a senior official with the US Fish and Wildlife Service, said to me:

At the height of the season the fishing is so good that it is hard to find a place to park and a slot on the riverbank to fish. Men literally fish elbow to elbow. There are times when you can get a fish with every cast and the water seems to boil with salmon. But it is hardly the wilderness that many people expect. From May to September the road from Anchorage to the river is filled with traffic, bumper to bumper. Alaska's mystique is that it is the great outdoors, the open frontier. But in some places you have to wait in line just to make a cast.

Many Alaskans are urban, young and raising families, here for a while, and trying to make money before moving to somewhere warmer. But many are staying. While most remain in Anchorage and other centres, some set out to build a cabin in the wilderness and live by hunting, trapping and fishing, learning how to skin a muskrat and moose, how to survive terrible weather, how to be truly in tune with the land, taking pleasure in great silence and unpeopled immensity. To settle the frontier the state has a homesteading programme, based on the federal Homestead Act of 1864, which was a key event in the opening up of the American west. Hundreds of Alaskans are awarded parcels of wilderness land in an annual lottery and undertake to invest sweat equity, to build a home within three years and clear and cultivate the land within five. Alaskans love reading about Alaska, and two of the most popular books are a manual on log cabin building and a collection of tales about grizzly bears, of which Alaska is a stronghold. Log cabin life is for the stout-hearted few with the springs of adventure strong in them, and these wilderness Alaskans are remarkable. Some, as we have seen, are refugees of one kind or another. Several hundred are Vietnam veterans, tortured by their experiences of war and unable to fit into normal urban life, seeking solace in the wilds.

There are few roads in the bush. It is hard to build them on permafrost – permanently frozen ground – because it is unstable. There is a 470-mile railway link between Anchorage and Fairbanks, and people in the hamlets along the way can flag down the train when they want to get on. Otherwise the only practical way of reaching most of the great land is by aircraft. Nowhere else in the world is there such a high concentration of private aircraft in relation to the population. There is one plane for every seventy-five Alaskans, and one person in every forty-five is a qualified pilot. People here are as familiar with aircraft as they are with cars, and flying lore and epic take-offs and landings are favourite subjects of Alaskan conversation. Thousands depend on the pilots of small planes to deliver their groceries, heating oil, mail and medicines, and to fly them to a doctor, to the nearest town, or to a reunion dinner. This is, above all, bush pilot country, and the exploits of pilots, many of them colourful and daring men, the modern explorers of Alaska, are the stuff of legends. Alaska is an outpost of 'real flying' where seat-of-the-pants pilots set down planes on rough airstrips, beaches, frozen marshes, glaciers and lakes, often in poor weather. They modify their aircraft to cope with low temperatures and bad conditions, widening air inlets so that they do not become closed by ice, and adjusting ailerons so that their planes can leap and claw into the air from astonishingly short runs. Circumstances make them remarkable self-taught engineers and improvisers. Fractured wing struts are repaired with tree branch splints, petrol cans are cut up to mend holes made by irked bears, bent propellers are hammered back into shape on logs used as anvils, and planes make it home with vital pieces lashed together with rawhide. While many pilots are evidently skilled and resourceful there are, inevitably, numerous crashes. The weather is often foul and unpredictable and planes ice up and pilots get lost. Newspapers here publish warnings about the dangers of drinking and flying.

Americans have a fondness for symbols and emblems, and for museumising and institutionalising in some fashion the pieces of their history, natural history and environment that contribute to their identity and provide focus. Each American state was founded or evolved in a different way and each has made a collection of the characteristics that differentiate it from others. Each state has a great seal, a flag, a song, a motto and, by declaration of the legislature, a state flower, bird and tree. Alaska's motto is North To The Future, which is more hopeful than The Last Frontier, though the state song speaks of 'Alaska's flag – to Alaskans dear, the simple flag of a last frontier'. The song also extols gold – 'The gold of the early sourdough's dreams' – anchoring sentiment to money; and gold is the state mineral. The state flower is the forget-me-not, the state bird the willow ptarmigan, the state tree the Sitka spruce, the state fish the king salmon. The state sport is mushing, which is to say sled dog racing.

It is not possible to go Alaska and be unaware of mushing, any more than it is possible to go to Wales and not notice rugby football. Mushing has graduated from mere sport to being A Way of Life, constantly explored in writing for its mystical qualities, rather as bullfighting is in Spain. I was in Alaska at the time of the annual Iditarod trail race in which seventy frozen-faced mushers guided their bucking and slithering sleds for 1049 miles from

Anchorage to Nome. The newspapers and television were full of it, and the radio shouted commentaries and updates. It was impossible not to be caught up in the excitement. The Iditarod is the grand prix of mushing, carrying a $50,000 first prize, and Alaskans, with their notion that Alaska and anything Alaskans are the end of everything, call it the 'last great race'. It is certainly a remarkable test of skill and of human and canine endurance, the setting of Arctic high adventure. The weather is always an enemy, and in 1985 food had to be dropped to blizzard-bound mushers. One competitor encountered a rampaging moose which killed two dogs in his team. The record time for the race is twelve days and eight hours, but most mushers take between two and three weeks, while the slowest take more than thirty days. The race celebrates the trail-blazing of the gold rush epoch of the turn of the century when sled dogs teams were the only means of carrying mail and supplies from the south coast to remote mining camps in the interior. In particular it commemorates the heroic high-speed sled run of 1925 when serum was carried to children stricken with diphtheria in Nome and many lives were saved. Working in relays, nineteen mushers carried the serum 675 miles from Nenana to Nome in just over five days. Iditarod is one of the towns along the route.

Dog sleds were transporting mail in Alaska until 1962. (The Royal Canadian Mounted Police replaced their last dog teams with machines in 1969). But sledding skills were generally in decline before the Iditarod race was started in 1973. The breeding of sled dogs had almost stopped because of the development of motorised snow transport and the growth of aviation, but the Iditarod caused a surge of interest and nostalgia and modern mushing's take off. Alaska embraced a sport that was also an assertion of its identity.

As well as being physically tough, a musher has to be steely in other ways, for mushing requires the single-mindedness of any athlete or performer. Here, of all places, it might be reasonable to say that the race is the tip of the iceberg. First, the musher has to acquire his huskies. A dependable dog costs more than $600, and a good lead dog perhaps $3000. Established mushers breed their own to build a stock of between 30 and 50 from which to make up racing teams between 6 and 20 strong. A racing sled costs about $500 and harnesses and lines about $100. Sled dogs have to be equipped with boots to protect their feet against sharp ice and the pounding they get on the trail. Much of the skill and interest in mushing lies in raising and training dogs and fitting them into a team. Some are natural lead dogs, while others work better closer to the sled. A musher needs to understand the ability of each animal, how far it will run before fatigue sets in. The fastest dog is not necessarily the best. 'True mushers are absolutely devoted to their animals,' Dan Sisson, an Alaskan writer, said. 'They'll spend all their spare money, and a lot more beside, to build and feed a good team. They'll do a forty-hour week at work and spend sixty hours with their dogs. They'll deprive themselves of sleep so that they can train at night. I know of a musher who goes without meals because he can't afford to feed both himself and his dogs – and the dogs come first.' The diets of sled dogs are of absorbing interest to their owners, and dogs' dinners are a main ingredient of musher talk. Every musher has his formula for stamina and speed, his secret mixtures of beaver meat, fish, oil, vitamins and canned food. Some use computers to arrive at the perfect menus.

Long-distance sledding is for loners, attracting the sort of souls who go ocean voyaging on their own. The musher's satisfaction lies in being in the wilderness, self-reliant, a good navigator and judge of weather, enduring temperatures of 20° and 30° below zero, with his dogs pulling well, the silence broken only by the hiss of sled runners. It is an expensive sport, costing $20,000 – $30,000 to prepare for a major race like the Iditarod. Competitors usually need financial backing, and commercial sponsors – dog food companies, banks, airlines, hotels and stores – have their names or logos painted on a musher's dog van and on the side of his sled, a useful way of advertising in a state where billboards are illegal. Large crowds turn out for races, at the start and finish, and at towns along the way, rather as they do in the Tour de France. Leading mushers become household names, and top dogs are sometimes given the name of a sponsor's product, like Tang.

Racing is strictly controlled. The sled has to carry certain equipment, a heavy sleeping bag, snowshoes, food for musher and dogs, an axe and eight sets of boots for each dog. Dogs are checked by veterinary surgeons on the trail and teams make mandatory stops, including one of twenty-four hours. Mushers start off with large teams and drop off tired dogs which are picked up by support crews. But they have to finish with at least five.

Mushers never say mush, a corruption of the command 'marchez' used by old-time Klondike and Yukon sled men. They say 'gee' which means right, and 'haw' which means left, and other, secret, commands which they evolve in long conversations with their beloved animals. As seen on television and in the newspaper photographs, the sled dog-team pulling across the snow fields has become a modern Alaskan symbol, a reminder of an Alaskan past. Similarly, the fatigue-lined face of the musher, half-hidden by a fur hood, eyebrows encrusted with ice, eyes narrowed from seeking the horizon in the meagre Arctic light, has become a heroic emblem, a reconnection with the romance and myths of the frozen frontier and its enduring adventure. In 1985 Libby Riddles, a handsome blonde woman of 29, was the first woman to win the Iditarod race. She migrated to Alaska from Minnesota when she was 16 and now lives in a cabin in an Eskimo village of 250 people in the far west, supporting herself and her dogs by making gloves, fur hats and taking summer jobs. 'I was drawn to Alaska because I really believe it is the last frontier, and I took up sled dog racing because it represents the pioneer spirit in the best possible way. I never want to leave. Alaska is still an unspoilt wilderness. But it will not last forever. The frontier is vanishing. I want to enjoy it while it lasts.'

2 The Magic Marmalade Pudding

Florida

'Come on down!'
TELEVISION ADVERTISEMENT FOR FLORIDA

SEARCHING for words to epitomise the character of his city, the Miamian gazed out of his window at the clamorous and sticky metropolis broiling under the afternoon sun. 'Miami . . .' he murmured, drawing on a cigar large enough to have been wielded in self defence. 'Miami . . . ' The way he breathed the word through the blue smoke evoked an image of a sultry and slightly dangerous woman. Below us lay the vivid and violent Miamian tumescence, an uncoagulated society of whites, blacks and Latins, elbowing and tussling on a hot Floridian strand between the mangrove swamps and the sea; a city suffused with energy and unashamedly on the make, in the tradition of its thin history. 'No place for wimps!' the Miamian exclaimed with a short laugh and a spurt of smoke. 'No place for wimps!' And his teeth crunched down over the cigar, like an alligator's over a leg.

Regarding alligators, I was surprised that this descendant of dinosaurs does not appear on the great seal of the state of Florida. Rather than an alligator the seal bears a portrait of a gentle Indian maiden, a representative of the Seminole people slaughtered enthusiastically by settlers and soldiers in the extermination drives of the 1830s and 1840s. But the alligator surely deserves a place. He is not only the chief state beast, but also represents the opportunist spirit of many of the people who have helped to make Florida what it is today: pirates and pimps, land developers and hucksters, drug runners, sly bankers and other lurky saurians who have prospered here by force and wit. The continuing vitality of the commercial spirit was demonstrated in 1985 by a dying

Floridian who advertised his willingness to deliver messages to the dead, at $20 a time. He received many responses.

The alligator, incidentally, has shown remarkable powers of survival. Until recently there were fears that he would be wiped out by hunters and poachers and would be remembered chiefly in the form of a handbag or a socialite's shoes. He was therefore classified as an endangered species and, thus protected, multiplied splendidly. He re-established himself with such vigour that he was subsequently downgraded to a threatened species and may now be hunted within limits. About 2000 alligators are killed every year. Their hides are auctioned and the tail meat, a Florida delicacy, is sold to restaurants. In some of the sprawling resorts and developing swamp-edge towns alligators cause annoyance and even alarm by waddling through caravan parks and onto golf courses, where they gobble the balls. People demand to know whether Florida belongs to men or 'gators. But the fault often lies with the people themselves for they have made a custom of feeding marshmallows to baby alligators, eroding a natural wariness of man. Very occasionally alligators kill a human being, but they much prefer to eat little dogs who get too close and irritate them with their yapping; and they have a particular liking for those expensively coiffed and crunchy little poodles adorned by their owners with pink ribbons.

In his amphibianness the alligator is quintessentially Floridian. He lies low in the water, like the glistening and sodden half-sunk state itself, whose highest bump is only 350 feet above the dazzling sea. A land commission wrote in 1823 that southern Florida was a place of 'half-developed plains, deep morasses and almost inaccessible forests, a home only for beasts, or for men little elevated above beasts.' A vast region of the state is dense and primeval tropical swamp, of which the alligator is the proprietor and scaly symbol, and where surviving Seminoles still live, in perfect harmony with the mysterious environment. On the geological time scale Florida has but recently surfaced from the ocean, and originally it did not belong to America at all: it was borrowed from Africa. During the earth's youth, the American and African continents lay locked in tectonic embrace and Florida, then a part of west Africa, became geologically grafted to America. After 50 million years the affair cooled, the giants drifted apart and America was left holding baby Florida.

Like Alaska, Florida is an American extremity whose people like to think of it as the last frontier. The *Economist* described it as such in 1982 and called Miami the last frontier city. Both states are recent arrivals on the modern American state. Both were purchased by the United States – the colony of east Florida was sold by Spain in 1819 for the equivalent of $5 million. Young and inchoate, they erupted phenomenally after the 20th century had run more than half its course and have been transformed by people-rushes and rapacious, unregulated growth. Both are close to the communist countries that preoccupy many Americans. They have challenging, intemperate climates – Alaskans freeze, Floridians melt – and rely on modern technologies, central heating and air conditioning, to make them habitable. They are both prime battlegrounds in the conflict between plunderers and conservators.

Juan Ponce de Leon, an associate of Christopher Columbus, landed in Florida in 1513 and gave it that name because he first saw it during the Easter Feast of Flowers. The purpose of his expedition, apart from the conquistadorian search for gold, was to find the fabled fountain of youth, said to be in these parts. For most of the next four centuries Florida lay neglected, like a damp rag, in the corner of America. The real inventor of modern Florida was a multimillionaire, Henry Morrison Flagler, who had helped John Rockefeller, the sharpest of operators, establish Standard Oil. Flagler is the revered father of the Florida entrepreneurs, his life an example to the developers and salesmen who followed him. In his middle age he discovered and became obsessed with Florida: he revelled in the place, married a young woman (and, when she went mad, married another), built Miami harbour and financed churches, schools and hospitals. Miami was a palmetto-grove shack-hamlet of 250 people when he fell for

Florida. One winter a local woman sent him a sprig of orange blossom to persuade him to build the railway down to Miami, and, intoxicated by its perfume and its promise of spring in winter, he did; Miami sprouted into a resort, a playground for millionaires and sunbathers. Its offshore satellite of Miami Beach, a mere strip of sand and tidal swamp, was later dredged and cleared by another developer and planted thickly with shrubs and opulent art deco hotels. In the twenty-seven years from 1885 Flagler extended the railway, punctuated the Atlantic shore with luxurious hotels and popularised Florida as the idyllic winter haven for shivering Yankees. Like any 19th-century railway age pioneer, he was excited by the idea of laying track to the remotest places, whatever the cost, and eventually built the line all the way to Key West. He arrived triumphantly aboard the first train into the ultimate American dew drop, and died contented the following year.

In the land rush of the 1920s more than two million suckers invested in Floridian plots that resembled Mediterranean dream villages in the brochures, but in reality lay under water or in undrained bog. In the end the devastating hurricane of 1926 killed hundreds of people and pricked the land bubble. By this time even the banks had thought better of building on water. Some of the developers, businessmen to the marrow, tried gallantly to keep out hurricane relief teams, fearing that the publicity would injure the property values of paradise. Nevertheless, there was financial ruin, a drum-roll warning of what would happen in the great crash of 1929. Scenting a place after his own heart, Al Capone, the Illinois alligator, slithered into Miami Beach after the bust and found it congenial. In any case, no other burg in America would have him. More gangsters came on down and moved into racket management. Capone spent most of the 1930s out of the sun, serving a jail sentence for tax evasion, but he came back and died in Miami in 1947, owing $201,000 in back taxes.

Around the time that Scarface expired many Americans began to think of settling in Florida. Thousands of servicemen had been billeted there in the war, had been beguiled and had vowed to return. In the golden age of postwar and war-made prosperity – that most gloriously confident, conceited, cornucopian and free-wheeling of all American ages – millions had cars and money, and Florida was a wide-open frontier, promising sunshine, profit and an absence of rules: the land of the mink bikini. Construction and the pleasure industry boomed. Thousands of older people headed south to spend their retirement years on Florida's beaches and golf courses, and sales of pink shorts and deckchairs soared. As late as halfway through the century the state's popula-tion was only two million, but it doubled from 1950 to 1960 and doubled again in the next 20 years. In the pellmell pursuit of pleasure and profit cities like Miami overflowed like the magic marmalade pudding in one of my childhood fairy stories. The pudding, made by an old lady, boiled over and ran down the hill like lava to feed the hungry children in the valley below. Thus it was with Miami and its sisters – as tourism boomed they spread along the littoral, seeping into drained swamps and cleared jungle. Hotels, pink, white and yellow, were erected by the sea like closely-set fence palings. In the blink of an historical eye Florida bounded from dozing wilderness into the second-fastest-growing state in the country. By the turn of the century it will have 15 million people and will be the fourth-largest state.

There is something definitively American in this Floridian metamorphosis. Into this wild peninsula have swarmed diverse crowds of people, of differing ethnic groups and languages, ambitious second-chancers and luck-tryers, eager painters of an empty canvas. With all the desperate deadline energy of nesting birds they have raised cities, drained swamps and built roads. The sheer exuberance of it all can only be marvelled at. Americans take a simple and joyful pride – 'Ain't we great?' – in bending a landscape to their will. They have never ceased to be intoxicated by the pleasures of conquering new territory, and this exultant can-do spirit is part of the American essence.

But the idea of the onward rush, with its certainty that every-thing is possible, contains the inherent weaknesses of a belief in invincibility and a deep reluctance to accept limits. There is an arrogance to it. As skies darken and the glass falls, more sail is clapped on. The Great Florida Rush exacts a high price and is doing immense damage. Almost everyone here wishes to realise the dream of a home beside the sea or by a river and all but 15 per cent of the population lives in the coastal counties. The coastline is jammed with houses and apartment blocks and many homes are built on vulnerable barrier islands and dredged marshes. People are perfectly happy to build upon sand. One can only guess at what will happen when a ferocious hurricane strikes.

The growth of housing far outstrips the provision of ancillary services like roads and sewerage, bridges and schools. Florida puts a greater proportion of its citizenry in prison than any other state, and the jails cannot keep up with the demands as the population grows. The state constitution forbids the imposition of state income tax and consequently there is a shortage of money for public services. Large stretches of the state have become ugly and congested. Few people have wanted to stop the bulldozers. Developers have been supported by many local politicians and, in return, have generously financed the politicians' election campaigns. On the wild development frontier builders and contractors have had little difficulty in evading skimpy laws, bribing officials where necessary.

Natural rhythms have been distorted. Building projects have caused both drought and flooding, rivers have died, wildlife has retreated into diminishing refuges and the air has become polluted. Business and industry have been allowed to dump their toxic wastes willynilly and have poisoned water supplies. There is not enough water, anyway. South Florida depends for much of its supply on Lake Okeechobee, whose volume is shrinking. Underground sources are depleted as more of the state is paved and poisoned, and water has become a potent political issue, as it has in other sunbelt states. During the 1980s the damage caused by unremitting growth became clearer to many Floridians and environmental protection laws were passed. But alarms had sounded before and protective laws had been enacted without much success. While this time there seems to be a determination to make improvements and draw some lines, few doubt that Florida, with 250,000 new citizens 'coming on down' to settle every year, will continue to be under the pressures of formidable and unstoppable growth, a paradise fragmented and eroded.

As for Miami, it is one of the most compelling and repelling of American cities. Here, people say, is the future. Its dynamism is immediately evident; but there is also a sense of emptiness, a lack of heart and focus. Plenty of shine, but not much style. It lacks confidence, the necessary ingredient of style, and has a adolescent ache for recognition and reassurance. Because of its scanty history and roaring and lurid development it is inordinately sensitive about its reputation. It parades an ingratiating smile, a good suit and a diploma in civics, but it cannot hide its recidivism, the lipstick on its collar, the blood on its hands, the gun in its belt, the extortionate rent deal in its pocket, the ace up its sleeve, the laundered money in its wallet, the cocaine under its fingernails. When *Time* magazine, in 1981, ran an article about the raging crime and vulgarity of south Florida, under the title 'Paradise Lost?' thin-skinned Miami rent its clothing in rage. When *Esquire*, two years later, wrote a kindlier piece, called 'The City of the Future', Miamians pinned on large lapel badges saying 'Thanks, *Esquire*, We Needed That'. Indeed, the Chamber of Commerce gave me one.

Miami has grown into one of the major American cities. Greater Miami – Dade county – has a population of more than two million and is the Balkanised conglomeration of twenty-seven municipalities, each with a separate authority and police force. The county includes Miami, Miami Beach, Coral Gables, Golden Beach, Florida City, Surfside and Opa-Locka.

From my hotel balcony I look down and up at the banks, hotels, office towers and apartment blocks which Manhattanise the city's skyline, at panoramas of palmy avenues, tropical vegetation and millionaires' rows. There is the scent of suntan oil and cigars, petrol fumes and the sea. Out in the bays yachts dart and shoal like mackerel, brilliant against the Atlantic blue. Sleek and chromey powerboats, the lingams of Miami, are in such abundance that they are being stacked by great meachincal grabbers onto waterfront shelves, one on top of the other, like toys slotted into the high shelves of a toyshop. Around the myriad turquoise puddles of swimming pools, on blazing white beaches and decks, brown bodies glisten and turn as if spitted. In Florida, of all places, the body is a well-attended temple, exiguously clad, revealed and worshipped. Research shows, in this relentlessly and microscopically measured country, that, among women who go to plastic surgeons for breast augmentation, Floridian women choose to have breasts 25 per cent larger than those requested by women in the north.

Amid the snaking coils of Miami's highway system drawbridges admit ships to the wharves of the fastest-growing port in America. It is also the busiest cruise harbour in the world, and romantic white liners with rakishly-angled bows lie briefly berthed, loading hedonists, gin and bikinis for the Indies. Elsewhere in the waterways, by the customs quays, captured smuggling boats sit in chains. Overhead the jumbos let down into the second busiest international airport in the country, bearing tourists, honeymooners, golfers, businessmen in drip dries – and fresh supplies of grandmothers for the retirement trade. Miami is a business hot-house and commercial magnet, an international capital, the crossroads and *entrepôt* of Latin America, the way in to rich markets, a base for multinational companies, bankers and underwriters, a pool of Latin American expertise. Even into the 1970s there were few banks doing foreign business here, but now there are more than 130. Miami's journalistic institution, the *Miami Herald*, publishes a Spanish edition and is one of the important newspapers of the Caribbean and Latin America. There are no old, dirty or ailing industries in the city, for they belong to another, an older, America. Less than a tenth of Miami's income is derived from manufacturing. It is a broker, factor and *traiteur*, its money made from money-farming, service industries, tourism and property development. A large and vital part of its prosperity is built upon the immoral earnings of the drug smuggling business, for Miami and south Florida are America's golden gateway for the import of cocaine and marijuana.

Prosperity is built, too, upon the savings and pensions of America's grandparents. Far from being a drain on the state the regiments of the old have played a considerable part in shaping the economy of many Floridian cities. Social security is the largest source of personal income in Florida and pays benefits of more than $10 billion a year. Almost one person in five here is over 65 and the state is America's favourite retirement destination. Palm trees and an absence of state income tax made it hard to resist. Florida is the principal example of the way America is greying. It has the younger-to-older ratio that the rest of the country will have in thirty years; but by that time a quarter of Floridians will be over 65. The people of the Dade county municipality of Bal Harbour have an average age of 71, and Miami Beach, average age 68, has been called Heaven's Waiting Room. The local telephone directory has ten pages of funeral companies, some offering 'pre-need arrangements', 'cemetery counselling', 'rental casket available' and 'Cremations – One Call Does It All'. But the elderly do not write themselves off so flippantly. They are a large special-interest group and wield an increasing political clout. Social security payments and Medicare, the government medical welfare scheme, are their major issues. Groups like the Florida Silver-Haired Legislature keep up pressures on issues affecting the elderly; and many older people keep abreast of retirement matters through *Modern Maturity*, one of the largest-selling publications in the country with a circulation of more than eight million.

Dignified and vulnerable, the old people don their pink shorts and loud check trousers, and settle by the ocean to fade in the sunshine, talking of the old days and clicking their backgammon counters. They are the social constant, the ballast. Around their deckchairs whites, browns and blacks rearrange the social map, pushing each other out, establishing new colonies like roaming herds struggling over territory: bankers and refugees, the de-racinated and adventurous, spivs and sybarites, gamblers, place-men and the immortal prancing young. The very young ache for their 15th birthdays so that they can get a driving licence and a car to drive to school, prerequisites of the rites of courtship and serious social life. 'You ain't got a car,' a policeman notes in an observation of Miami's pre-shave society, 'you ain't goin' no-where.'

Although infant Miami was put on the map by Henry Flagler, modern Miami owes a large part of its vigour to Fidel Castro and communist revolution in Cuba. After January 1959, when Castro took power, a large part of the Cuban middle class fled to Miami, which, being close, had always had strong links with Cuba. There was a wholesale transplant of one country's educated elite to another, a sudden infusion of brainpower and expertise which changed the city, stoked its economy and put upon it a distinctive Latin stamp. At first the Cubans recreated old Cuba in south Florida and the Calle Ocho area of central Miami became Little Havana. Dr Juan Clark, an early Cuban migrant, now a sociolo-gist in Miami, said to me that as well as being educated the migrants were also strongly motivated to get out of Cuba and succeed in their adopted country. They fitted in because they had grown up in a capitalist system and knew something of American ways. Doctors, lawyers and teachers got started by serving petrol, working as janitors and packing tomatoes. Within a short time they were an established and thriving community. Turning their language, contacts and acumen to their own and the city's benefit, they consolidated Miami's status as a bridge to Latin America. Today they staff many hospitals and law firms, run a major garment industry, factories, shops, restaurants and finance houses. Within twenty years of the first exodus the Cuban community in Miami counted 200 millionaires. They had no doubt that, for them, America worked.

Miami's development in the 1960s pointed to a significant

aspect of the American future, the growth of hispanic strength. The city was an American demographic weathervane, a sunbelt city with a strong Spanish accent. The Castro catalyst was important, but even without the Cuban revolution, Miami would still have developed as an important hispanic city. Regardless of the form of government in their countries, people in the Caribbean and Latin America have always migrated to the United States to find work. Down the years many of them found the hispanic atmosphere of Miami congenial, whether they came for business or pleasure or refuge from harsh economies, tyrannies or angry proletariats. Thousands of Nicaraguans, for example, have settled in Miami since the Sandinistas overthrew Somoza in 1979. As well as being an American ladder let down into the Caribbean and Latin America, Florida has the immense virtue of being stable. Among all the uncertainties of the region it is a safe haven. No coup will ever be staged in Miami.

Quite apart from the Latin influx, Miami was destined to grow rapidly for other reasons. In the 1960s there began the great shift of commerce and people from the northern states of America to the sunbelt, particularly to Florida, Texas and California. The muscles of the industrial north grew weaker as the population moved to the new light industries and offices springing up in the warmer states. The rustbelt grew rustier, the sunbelt economically sunnier. In this respect, too, Florida was a pioneer, pointing to another piece of the American future, and has demonstrated strength and flexibility in the manner in which it has accommodated sudden surges of immigrants.

Racial and cultural collisions have been an inevitable part of Miami's expansion. Spanish-speakers form about two-fifths of the people of Dade county, and about three-fifths of the 400,000 population of Miami city. Resentful and anxious anglos, as whites are called, have moved up the coast in their thousands. But many who have remained have adjusted, learnt some Spanish, and prospered. Job-hunters have an edge if they know Spanish. The anxieties of whites are more than matched by those of blacks, who form 17 per cent of Dade county's population, for Cubans took many traditionally black jobs. Before the Cubans came blacks owned a quarter of the petrol stations; now they own fewer than one in ten, and Cubans own more than half. On the scale of average wages blacks rank a poor third to whites and Cubans. Blacks did not have the cash to move out, even if they wanted to. The black culture in Florida is not as deeply planted as it is in other parts of the south, and the black middle class is relatively new. Miami's blacks have bitter experience of what the US Civil Rights Commission called 'explicit and pervasive discrimination' in housing, jobs and education; and the black neighbourhood was fragmented by a highway driven through it in the 1980s, an action that intensified angry feelings.

More than 750,000 people fled Cuba after 1959, and in 1980 there was a sudden flood of 125,000 more, called Marielitos, because they had embarked in the Cuban port of Mariel. Many of them were criminal and insane, offloaded in a clearing of Cuban jails and asylums, and many were poor. Miami's high rate of violent crime, complicated by murderous fighting between drug gangs, was aggravated by the inrush of criminals and drifters and there was an orgy of bloodshed as rival groups fought for superiority and settled scores. Gangs obliterated each other. The trouble persuaded more anglos to move out, mostly north towards Fort Lauderdale, a resort famous, among other things, for its annual spring invasion by tens of thousands of exam-weary students determined to enjoy themselves. Blacks were dismayed to find themselves squeezed again as the Marielito newcomers sought work and took jobs for the kind of low pay that many blacks felt was beneath their dignity. At the same time Haitian refugees, many of them arriving by sail like the early pioneers, put more pepper in the social and economic stew. There was rioting as black resentment boiled following the acquittal of four white policemen accused of clubbing a black man to death. Established Cubans had ambivalent feelings about the Marielito newcomers, their countrymen. Some helped to find them a place. Others, sensitive about their image, felt they gave the Cuban community a bad name. Dr Clark, the sociologist, said:

Cubans who arrived up to 1965 were in the upper economic class, and they came to America having rejected totalitarianism. After that the immigrants were more blue collar. Marielitos were seen as lazy, as troublemakers, but many of them naturally resented having been forced to come here. They were uprooted and did not have the network of support their predecessors had, nor the skills and education. They came from a different social and political system, and the adjustments they had to make were harder.

Ethnic rivalries make Miami politics a tangle of emotions, and politicians do not shrink from exploiting racial prejudices. The city's long-term mayor, a Puerto Rican voted in in 1973, was elected by blacks, anglos and other hispanics who did not want to see a Cuban in charge. It took a long time for Cubans to take a more than perfunctory interest in local politics. For more than twenty years they were obsessed with Cuba and with ideas of returning to a free country. Their strongest political thoughts were the hatred they had for Castro and communism.

On the seafront there is a memorial to Cubans killed in the abortive Bay of Pigs invasion of 1961, which notes perceptively that 'the invasion's failure did not destroy the dream of returning to Cuba, but it did make many look at Miami as more than a temporary refuge.' As they became integrated into the Floridian economy, took American citizenship, saw their children growing up as Americans, Cubans slowly came to terms with the permanence of their migration. The militia groups they had formed to keep in training, waiting for the call to fight, declined in importance and numbers. Increasingly, Cubans began to involve themselves in politics and embrace American life in a broader way. Little Havana became less wistful and more realistic. It was, in any case, an artifical and idealized version of a Cuba that had never really existed. Symbolically, hundreds of Cubans gathered in Miami in 1984 at a mass swearing-in, taking the oath as new American citizens, no longer seeing themselves as exiles. At the end of 1985 Miami elected its first Cuban mayor, marking the inevitable arrival of Cubans as a political force.

*   *   *

On close inspection by an investigator at the docks the yams were not yams at all, but realistic fakes made of glass fibre and filled with snowy cocaine. In a large shipment of flowers from Colombia, flown into Miami to catch the St Valentine's Day market, customs officers found more than a ton of cocaine, with a street value of $600 million. Drug traders supplying cocaine and marijuana to their millions of clients in north America are as ingenious as they are ruthless and powerful. They operate one of the world's most profitable and best-organised criminal businesses, a generator of corruption, intimidation, fraud, robbery and murder. Thousands of the clients are damaged or destroyed by cocainism.

Coca leaves grow on tea-like shrubs on the eastern slopes of the Andes, mostly in Peru and Bolivia and also in Ecuador and Colombia. Colombia is the funnel, the principal exporter of cocaine, and the drug barons here buy in much of the coca crop produced by peasant farmers in the region. The leaves are rendered first into a clayey paste and then by a chemical process into cocaine powder. Cocaine and marijuana earn more in foreign exchange for Colombia than its main legal exports of coffee and flowers, and ensure that Colombia has a good trade balance, one of the best in Latin America. The business underpins widespread political and institutional corruption in several Latin American countries, as well as a crime network in the United States making many billions of dollars. In the early 1980s cocaine smuggling was regarded by American authorities as being already on an immense and alarming scale, and between 1982 and 1984 it increased by 50 per cent. In Miami it has supplied so much of the investment capital of the city and its environs that if the law enforcement agencies press too hard, it was suggested to me, they could damage the economy. The racket has made Miami a notable money-laundering centre, giving the banks embarrassing surpluses. This is a place where cool men in white suits and sunglasses do business with briefcases full of banknotes, the proceeds of drug sales. Crime was always bad in Miami and the rise of the drug trade made it worse. In 1984 it was graded the most crime-ridden metropolitan area.

I was educated in the workings of the drug trade by an officer of the Drug Enforcement Agency, which has a large and enthusiastic unit in Miami. Each of the cases he discussed with me – with its plots and sub-plots, good guys, bad guys, stake-outs, chases, bribes, pay-offs and dramatic arrests – could have been turned into a thriller. Just add sex. Southern Florida is the front line of the war waged by the DEA, police forces, customs officers, treasury agents, the coast guard and the FBI, among others; a variety of agencies which, from time to time, tread on each other's feet. Within the limits of its resources the anti-drug machinery is efficient and successful, and newspapers frequently report new records in drug seizures. Marijuana is found in such large quantities that it is burnt in power stations. Cocaine and marijuana are uncovered by the ton in aircraft, ships and fishing boats. Smaller quantities arrive strapped to frogmen's legs, concealed in swallowed condoms, secreted in suitcases and brassieres.

But the resources of the lawmen are not enough. They are piling sandbags onto a crumbling dam as the reservoir rises. As long as there is such a strong market, drug smuggling is too profitable and too widespread and well managed for there ever to be any prospect of defeating or seriously undermining it. The phrase is: we're managing the problem. The DEA told me of their gang-bustings, their difficult and dangerous undercover operations, the cunning stings they organise to catch gangsters, middlemen, drug bosses, lawyers, bankers, pillars of society and policemen – all the people drawn to drugs by the prospect of fast money. Photographs show them on their way to the cells, handcuffed and heads bowed. But drug traders are harder to eradicate than cockroaches. There are simply too many smugglers, too many boats, aircraft and vehicles engaged in the business. It is estimated that in any year 5000 boats and 5000 aircraft are transporting cocaine, marijuana and pills from Latin America and the Caribbean into Florida and other states on the Gulf of Mexico and also into California. Some of the aircraft are large transports. The authorities seize hundreds of planes, but they do not have the radar equipment and manpower to track everything. Customs officers chasing a plane over Florida discovered that it was empty and flying on autopilot. The pilot had parachuted with a load of cocaine far more valuable than his expendable aircraft. In 1985 a former police narcotics officer, carrying a bag containing $14 million worth of cocaine, jumped from his aircraft over Tennessee and was killed when his parachute failed. While the odds are against the authorities the concerted effort of recent years has made an impression; but the greater pressure put on Florida has forced drug traders to land and distribute their cargoes elsewhere. Thus a number of states which hitherto had little experience of the business have become distribution and money-laundering centres.

Cocaine and heroin use has been rising everywhere in the United States and various estimates put the number of regular users of cocaine between five million and twelve million. Women use cocaine as much as men and a drug researcher reported that when certain men date a girl they take her cocaine instead of chocolates and flowers. The *Wall Street Journal* has charted cocaine's popularity among the young and ambitious in the financial world; and by the mid-1980s the use of cocaine, steroids and other drugs by footballers, baseball players and other athletes was widespread. Cocaine use grew rapidly in private schools and local authority high schools in well-off districts where pupils could afford the drug. High purity cocaine is available for $50 to $100 a gram, but small amounts of less pure cocaine are $10 or so. Once associated primarily with the middle-class, cocaine has become cheap enough for wider use as the supplies from Colombia increase. In cities like New York it is fairly easily obtained on the streets; and so is heroin. Marijuana is widely available and New York has about 800 shops where it is more or less openly for sale.

Americans have had an affair with cocaine for more than a century. Coca-Cola owes its name to two of the original ingredients, extracts from coca leaves and caffeine-bearing cola nuts. Cocaine was part of the mixture for seventeen years after Coca-

Cola was first bottled and sold in Atlanta in 1886. It was removed when a government commission advised that cocaine in colas was habit-forming. During the late 19th century numerous tonics, potions and pills containing cocaine were sold by chemists to treat a wide variety of complaints, including piles, indigestion, catarrh, blood diseases, 'nerves' and sexual lethargy. Wine with added coca was a popular elixir which attracted excited recommendations: it was even sold through the great mail-order institution, the Sears Roebuck catalogue. For some pioneers, perhaps, it made more bearable the long winter evenings on the flat prairie. The use of opium was similarly unrestricted, and opiates were made into a variety of medicines, especially for women. Opium was banned in 1909, at a time when Americans were importing about seven tons a year; and many smokers switched to morphine and heroin. All narcotics were prohibited in 1914 and the black market opened for business. Larger profits made smuggling more attractive in spite of the risks. During prohibition, 1920 to 1933, when liquor smuggling and trading formed the basis of much organised crime, many people turned to marijuana which was legal in most states and not banned until 1937. More than fifty federal laws and hundreds of state laws have been enacted to combat drugs and stiffen penalties, but by 1971 President Nixon was calling narcotics addiction a national emergency. In 1985 Mrs Nancy Reagan headed a drive to educate Americans about the dangers of addiction. Her husband, meanwhile, halved the amount the government spent on drug abusers' treatment and prevention of addiction. There are periodic outbursts of alarm over drugs, and demands for more action, but no sustained public debate.

Cocaine has been for years a staple of sensational newspaper stories and tales of downfall. It featured both in a Chaplin film comedy and cinema dramas of degradation. It was the theme of many jazz songs and Cole Porter, in his *I Get A Kick Out of You*, originally wrote 'I get no kick from cocaine . . . ' And an American folk song, *Take A Whiff On Me*, included in the *Oxford Book of American Verse*, starts:

Goin' up State Street, comin' down Main,
Lookin' for the woman that use cocaine.
Hi, Hi, baby, take a sniff on me,
All you bummers take a sniff on me,
Take a whiff on me, take a whiff on me,
An' a Hi, Hi, honey take a whiff on me.

Although remote and small, having only a four-page telephone directory, Everglades City, population 540, sounded intriguing. I saw that it lay at the end of a long road over the subtropical swamplands of the Everglades, at the edge of the confusing confetti of islets, known as the Ten Thousand Islands, on the south-west coast of Florida. Big-city reporters unfailingly called it sleepy, painting a picture of a fishing village where men tinkered with outboards, baited their hooks, caught crabs and mullet, and sat on their verandah rocking chairs, drinking beer and raking the conversational coals. The city called itself 'The Gateway To The Last Frontier, but the citizens now squirmed under a damning label lately applied by a law enforcement officer, who, perhaps with an eye to a delicious headline, had described it as A Town Gone Bad.

From Miami I drove across the Everglades along the shimmering Tamiami Trail, otherwise US Highway 41, which connects the Atlantic to the Gulf of Mexico. On the way I passed the post office at Ochopee, which is like a sentry box and is advertised as the smallest post office in America; though it seems unAmerican to boast of something being the smallest. The Everglades are a seven-million-acre sponge, a low-lying wilderness of marshland and immense stretches of sharp spiny sawgrass rippling like savanna in the wind. It is relentlessly exotic, clogged, dripping, mossy and teeming, with tenebrous pools and oozy sloughs, estuarine mangrove forests, pine woods and cypress clumps, and choked sargassos of amphibious jungle intricately reticulated with creeks. In natural demarcation, alligators hold sway in the freshwater marshes, while the last of the American crocodiles make their final stand in the salt waters.

The laying of the Tamiami Trail across the Everglades in 1928 opened up the region to white hunters, prospectors and other visitors, ending the old secret way of life of the Seminoles who had lived almost forgotten in the marshes, by hunting, gathering and agriculture. Today they sell craftwork to tourists.

I drove into Everglades City past stucco houses, pulling up outside The Captain's Table. Every small American town has one of these places, a restaurant or café which doubles as an information exchange and meeting place, a crossroads everyone passes through, like a village pub in England. While you wait to meet people at The Captain's Table you can watch fish jumping in the brown water and pelicans standing like sentries on the top of posts by the jetty, and hope to see an alligator or a manatee – what sex-starved sailors used to think were mermaids.

Mrs Reba Wells Rupsis, the editor of the weekly *Everglades Echo*, came in, a jolly and bustling woman who is not only editor, but also the founder, publisher, reporter, photographer, designer, advertising seller and wholesale deliverer of the paper which has a circulation of about 1500 and serves Everglades City, Chokoloskee, Ochopee, Copeland and Plantation Island. She is also the editorial writer – 'But I only write an editorial when things get bad, like the time they tried to take our high school away from us. Then I go to town.'

It's all a bit of a rush, running the newspaper, she said. I might think it dead around here, but even in a city of 500 or so people there is a lot going on, and people expect to have their achievements in the paper.

I turn up at a baseball game and a kid says: 'I made a home run and you weren't there to take my picture.' So I take the picture – photography is squeeze-and-pray with me – and Joe, my husband, processes the film and I write up the game. And then someone calls up and says: 'Hey, I've caught this big fish – are you going to put it in the paper?' Ours is a real Ma and Pa operation. Joe does the phototypesetting and I take the negatives to a printer ninety-three miles away in Cape Coral and I wait while he runs off the copies, eight or sixteen pages, and then I bring back the papers.

In the issue of the week before she had inserted a prominent notice saying: 'I have declared a three-day holiday this Friday, Saturday and Sunday so that I can go on my first fishing trip in five years. My friends tell me it's about time.'

I asked how people felt about A Town Gone Bad, and she cast around for a word. 'Embarrassed,' she said at last. 'The whole country heard about it. This is a nice town with a lot of decent folk. We feel a bit sore. We didn't deserve it.'

The sudden notoriety was the biggest thing in the city's history since Hurricane Donna swamped it with a tidal wave in 1960. At five o'clock on a July morning in 1983 the city awoke to find itself surrounded by policemen and officers of the Drug Enforcement Agency who had arrived by car, boat and helicopter, had their pistols drawn and carried arrest warrants for forty-one people. Doors were knocked, and doors were kicked down, and seventeen people were taken away in handcuffs. Not all the wanted people were in town. One of those absent was a former judge of the Florida Supreme Court who had already had some bother up in Louisiana, had jumped his $1 million bail and was a fugitive from justice. The lawmen also confiscated two aircraft, several vehicles and a dozen fishing boats. Eventually Operation Everglades spread over three states and the authorities reported a haul of 200 arrests, the seizure of more than 200 tons of marijuana and the impounding of boats, cars and airplanes worth $5 million.

'I have to say I felt a fool,' Mrs Rupsis said. 'Here I am, editor of the local paper, and I didn't know a thing about it until I saw the helicopters landing. The big-city reporters had been tipped off and were on hand. But even the local sheriff didn't know what was happening until just before the raid.'

Some of the people in Everglades City wore an injured air, feeling that the town had been unfairly tarred. It had been characterised in the newspapers and on television as a closely-woven community, where everyone was everyone's cousin or in-law, up to its neck in drug smuggling. That just wasn't so, people said, and in any case being related does not make you crooked. Still, the fact that smuggling went on in a big way was well known, and people acknowledged that smart cars, diamonds, gold necklaces and lavish home improvements were not bought with the proceeds of selling mullet and stone crabs. 'You used to wonder,' Mrs Rupsis said, 'when you saw someone with a new car – is he a smuggler or isn't he? It was quite well known that it was going on, a sort of suspicion. But I always had enough to do with the weddings and bits of local news without going into investigative reporting. It's not that sort of paper.'

Some people in the town were pleased with the round-up. They objected to their fellow citizens prospering by crime and said it set a bad example to the children. On the other hand there was undoubted resentment at the way that outsiders, particularly Yankee outsiders, had interfered in a private business that didn't need any lawmen meddling in it.

Smuggling is a tradition in these parts. The mangrove swamps and the maze of tiny islands and channels are impossible to police efficiently and provide excellent cover for men with small boats who go out to unload marijuana from ships in the Gulf of Mexico. It is called pot-hauling. During the prohibition years people around here smuggled Caribbean rum and brewed moonshine liquor on swamp islands. For many years they also supplemented their fishing income by poaching, supplying the fashion market by trapping alligators at night and skinning them.

People said to me it was a shame that Everglades City was now notorious as a smuggling capital, because it wasn't that sort of place. The editor said that Everglades City was typical of small-town America. 'You can leave you car unlocked and your house unlocked and everything will be perfectly safe. People don't steal and there is hardly any crime at all.'

I went to the sheriff's office and talked to one of the deputies. He said there were still deep feelings in the town about the raid. He stuck his thumbs into his belt and eased his holster down. 'Whatever folks say, though, it comes down to greed in the end – just chasin' the almighty dollar. Morals ain't what they were.' He asked me where I lived and I told him. 'New York, eh?' He made it sound like a remote planet. 'Ain't never been there and I can't say that I want to. I hear there's a lot of violence and crime up there.' He shook his head. 'Folks chasin' the almighty dollar, I suppose.'

I drove back across the drowsy secret Everglades to the Atlantic coast, and turned south down the Overseas Highway to the Florida Keys. Quite close to a bric-à-brac shop calling itself Junktique stood a large cracked and peeling billboard which implored in large letters: Help To Preserve This Fragile Paradise. It stood out in the ranks of billboards advertising hamburgers, pancakes and pop, motels, bars and caravan parks, which disfigure many of the Keys in a perverse rape of pretty places. Other signs urged travellers to stop at aquariums and enjoy a physical encounter with denizens of the deep: Touch A Dolphin! Pet A Shark! Kiss A Sealion!

The highway makes stepping stones of the caudate coral islands of the keys, which stretch for more than 100 miles into the Gulf of Mexico. It is an exhilarating drive, flying out over the pirates' sea towards the Spanish Main on a long thread of a road built in the spirit of American determination to make every cranny of the country accessible by car and free for billboards. Many of the keys are intensely developed, with holiday and retirement homes, boatyards and jetties, offering a snoozy life in the sun and fishing trips in search of pompano, bonito, marlin, mako, snapper, snook, swordfish and wahoo.

The end of the yellowbrick road of bridges and causeways is the speck of Key West, three miles by one, its highest hill ten feet above sea level. This is where the continental United States finally peters out in a little patch of sand, concrete, barbed wire and a sign announcing: America Begins Here. There is also a red notice pointing out over the Caribbean with the legend: Ninety Miles to Cuba. Rednecks, if they wish, can stand here and glare at the horizon.

The Overseas Highway is built on the foundations of the Florida Keys railroad which was the last project of the redoubtable Henry Flagler. He built it as a link between Miami and Havana, hoping that Key West would thereby become a great port. He was 75 when the work started, and 82 when he arrived aboard the first train, to be acclaimed a hero. His railway was an engineering epic and its construction cost the lives of 700 men. Work was twice set back by hurricanes, and the line operated for only twenty-three years before it was destroyed by a particularly severe hurricane that carried away track, embankments and a train. The state used what was left to build the umbilical road. Hurricanes are an ever-present threat to the low-lying keys, and to all of Florida, the Gulf states and much of the Atlantic seaboard. Authorities have become alarmed at the rapid growth of population and of beachfront development in places like the keys in recent years.

Like islanders anywhere, long-term residents of Key West show hauteur towards outsiders and cultivate the idea that theirs is a secret society whose idiosyncrasies and customs amount to a special quality of life and an enviable philosophy. A native is known as a conch, pronounced konk, and the island calls itself the conch republic after the rubbery mollusc abounding hereabouts which, when extracted from its lovely shell, is pounded to smithereens and made into fritters and soup. The shell's use as a dootstop is almost obligatory.

Many of Key West's 32,000 people make their living out of tourism, selling shells, jewellery, sponges, tours, artistically-torn teeshirts, ragged designer shorts, microdot bikinis and fishing trips. The island's end-of-the-line remoteness, sublime climate and easy manners have made it attractive to writers and artists. Ernest Hemingway lived here for eight years in the 1930s in a fine old colonial house and wrote at a small round table, stopping from time to time to drink at Sloppy Joe's Bar, which trades heavily on his memory. In the house Papa's bed, books and bills are on display and you can buy a teeshirt with his face on it and stroke the progeny of his cats. I was guided around by a theatrical man dressed all in black and wearing heavy chest jewellery, who called everyone 'Dear heart'.

Because of its easygoing atmosphere, the island is one of the last places where examples of the American hippy may be observed, colourful remnants of the 1960s living out their days in this most agreeable of natural reserves. The island is also a haven for homosexuals who have moved into business in a substantial way and have played a large part in the restoration of old buildings, particularly the 19th-century wooden houses.

For many years Key West earned part of its living from smuggling, piracy and wreck salvage, and smuggling has remained an important activity. 'Smuggling is more than a way of life – it's an adventure', read a teeshirt slogan. Some months after I left the island I read that law enforcement officers had driven in a convoy of thirty cars down the Overseas Highway to pounce on marijuana and cocaine smugglers. They arrested the island's deputy police chief and two other senior officers, as well as some leading citizens, and announced that the Key West police force was a racketeering criminal organisation. Fancy that, said the people of Key West, pounding their conches into fritters.

The sun-cracked board nailed to the farm gate some miles south-west of Miami bore the roughly-painted words: Warning – Keep Out Or Get Shot. A splinter of malevolence. I wondered if the bilious farmer meant it.

The citizen's gun is part of America's differentia among nations. At the United States–Canada border, where Canadian customs officers confiscated 3714 guns from individual Americans between 1980 and 1984, a customs officer said: 'Many Americans don't want to travel without a handgun. They say: "It's my Colt .45 and I don't leave home without it." '

Americans are armed to the teeth. There are more than 200 million guns among 230 million of them, including more than 60 million pistols and revolvers. If every firearms factory closed tomorrow Americans would have guns in plenty. One of the reasons gun sales declined in the mid-1980s was that the market was glutted, especially with rifles and shotguns. Sales of hand-guns, which reached a peak of 2.6 million in 1982, a rate of 296 new handguns sold every hour, fell to about 2 million two years later, or 288 an hour. There are half a million machine guns in private hands.

Like liquor laws, gun control rules vary across the country in a patchwork of local differences. In general possession is more tightly controlled in the north-east, more relaxed in the south and west. The rules are tough in New York, for example, while it is easy to buy guns in Texas: a purchaser has only to show a driving licence, proof that he is over 21 and declare he is not a convicted criminal. Florida has a free-and-easy gun market, too. The Miami business directory has six pages of gun dealers, eight of security guards and consultants, and carries advertisements for machine guns, silencers, military assault rifles and bullet-proof vests. Many weapons are bought with the proceeds of the drug trade and shipped abroad. People in cities where gun laws are strict find it convenient to buy in Florida. The state is the main assembly centre for cheap short-barrelled guns known as snubbies or Saturday night specials, a name first applied by policemen who noted how frequently these weapons were pulled from pockets and handbags to resolve disputes that erupted on Saturday nights, in an atmosphere inflamed by drink and passion. Public interest in guns, reflecting the high level of predatory crime, is so strong in Florida that in 1984 Florida International University started a ten-week undergraduate course on 'the uses of deadly force, the practical and philosophical aspects of shooting to kill.'

Every year more than 20,000 Americans are murdered and more than three-fifths of them, about 230 a week, are killed by firearms. Half of American murders are done with pistols and revolvers. More than two-fifths are the outcome of an argument. Every year 12,000 people use a gun to kill themselves and hundreds of men, women and children are killed accidentally by weapons bought for family protection. Newspapers frequently report that fathers, mothers and children shoot themselves and each other with dad's bedside pistol.

Americans are concerned and divided over the part that guns have in their lives. Many argue that the embedded gun culture is at odds with the pretension to be truly civilised; that few people need a weapon; that while guns had their place in the settling of the country, Americans should have outgrown them. They believe it self-evident that the ready availability of guns promotes a high rate of violence. At the simplest level they say that in a burst of anger, in home, bar or street, the gun dictates the outcome in a deadlier fashion than a fist or a thrown saucepan. The easy access to guns raises the level of violence and terror, and on the ladder of violence Americans start several rungs ahead. If ownership were restricted, by licensing and background checks, there would be fewer serious crimes. It is sophistry, runs the argument, to pretend that guns are innocent, made dangerous only by men.

The counter-argument is that people have a right to own guns and need them to defend themselves in a violent society. Proposals to control gun ownership interfere with this right and the ease with which bad men get guns is beside the point.

The critical battleground of the controversy is handgun control, for the handgun is the criminal's principal tool. Rifles, as hunting weapons, are outside the argument. To an extent, though the lines are crudely drawn, gun control is a quarrel between liberals who tend to favour controls and conservatives who do not. Societies like Handgun Control Inc and the National Coalition to Control Handguns, lobby for stricter regulation, confronting the issue of violence that troubles millions of people. According to polls they have the support of the majority. Their main opponent is the National Rifle Association, a skilled and well-funded propaganda and lobbying group which defends the interests of manufacturers and gun buyers and says there should be no interference with the right to buy guns. It is utterly uncompromising and has a remarkable ability to mobilise activists to pressure politicians through petitions and letter-barrages. It provides an instructive example of how lobbyists with an undistracted eye exert influence in the United States. The NRA makes a strong appeal to sentiment, the idea that God and guns made the country, and that some intrinsically American quality is at risk if gun ownership is restricted. It holds that there is a constitutional right to gun ownership. The Supreme Court, among other interpreters of an ambiguous sentence, disagrees; but the NRA makes this an angels-on-pinheads debate. All its arguments run along well-worn tracks and into thickets of figures, for the use and effects of firearms have been researched to extraordinary and absurd lengths. The NRA is an obsessive and prolific generator of statistics, and reveals, for example, that 15 per cent of rifle owners have one or more pairs of electric socks. In my visits to its headquarters in Washington I have come under a withering fire of figures. Statistics are strewn like caltrops. NRA personnel have the gimlet-eyed intensity of converts to a narrow religious creed. For them the gun is a life-giving force at the American core. I once met Harlon Carter, the NRA's chief, who became so emotional in his defence of gun rights that he ranted and thumped the table.

Once a non-political society whose purpose was the improvement of marksmanship, the NRA became a fanatical anti-control lobby after the passage of gun control legislation which followed the political assassinations of the 1960s. It monitored school text books for anti-gun bias and alienated many policemen by its vigorous opposition to a proposal to stop the scale of armour-piercing bullets, known as 'cop killers' because they penetrate bullet-proof vests. The NRA argued that stopping the sale of 'cop killers' was a blow at gun rights. But it became concerned about its redneck image and started an advertising campaign showing ordinary people holding revolvers and smiling – mom, guns and apple pie.

A gun in the house is not much of a deterrent or defence. Most burglars enter empty houses and, incidentally, often steal the bedside gun. Police say the danger a gun poses to the family far outweighs its protective value; and a gun is only useful when, at the critical moment, it is loaded and in the hand of a skilled user. But it is hard to argue these points, and the NRA plays on the fear of predatory crime. Once every two-and-a-half minutes an American is robbed at gunpoint. The high crime rate ensures a flow of sensational press reports. People justifiably fear random attack, and they think America the beautiful can also be a jungle. They buy guns for reassurance, to give themselves a fighting chance. That is why Mrs Reagan, the president's wife, once kept a gun in her bedroom. People are not persuaded that a gun is more likely to enhance the criminal arsenal or kill the baby than kill the hoodlum. Fear persuades even school pupils to carry weapons: in four months of 1985 school authorities in New York confiscated more than 1000 weapons from high school students, including 76 handguns and two rifles. A school principal said that 'everything that goes on in society is felt in school. We live in a society where feelings of physical and emotional security are diminishing.'

Quite apart from questions of defence and deterrence, guns hold an abiding fascination for many Americans. The interest often seems morbid. Guns are also part of frontier myth and, for some people, are links to their history. Several banks which offered customers pairs of Colts instead of interest were overwhelmed by the response. A commemorative Colt .45 was produced to honour John Wayne, whose statue, incidentally, stands outside a gun factory in Connecticut. In his hand is a Winchester '94 carbine – 'The Gun That Won The West'.

Gun control is part of a larger debate on crime and justice. Like everyone else Americans have strong opinions on crime control and hazy ideas of the complex nature of crime, policing and justice. The NRA's solution to the problem of the armed criminal is an armed citizenry and long prison sentences. In President Reagan's words, 'locking up the hard-core criminals and throwing away the key is the best gun control law.' Although it is likely that an increase in the certainty of punishment is more effective than increases in sentences, most Americans want severe jail terms, and anger at the high levels of crime was reflected in the

1970s and 1980s in longer sentences and the sending of more criminals to jail. The prison population doubled over ten years and continues to rise although the crime rate is falling. At the current rate more than a million people will be imprisoned by the end of the century. The United States jails a greater proportion of its people than any western country. Many jails are chronically overcrowded, forcing the authorities to pack prisoners into cells and to house overflows in tents and huts. There was uproar when a New York judge drew attention to the problem by ordering the release of men from overcrowded prisons. Two-thirds of the states were told in the early 1980s that conditions in their jails amounted to cruel and inhuman punishment. Americans are determined to put their criminals away for a long time, but reluctant to pay higher taxes to build prisons for them.

Out of this conflict sprang the free enterprise solution, jails built and operated for a profit by private companies. The attraction of the private jail is that it is cheaper. For one thing, private prisons do not have to pay their guards public service salaries and pensions. 'Incarcerations Inc' seems a good idea to a public anxious to have criminals shut away cheaply; but there is concern that society relinquishes its responsibilities by putting imprisonment out to contract for profit. Like the military–industrial complex, the private prison business might become entrenched and apparently indispensable, with a vested interest in long sentences – and the public will be helpless when the jailers demand more money for their services.

There are people in their thirties and forties living along the Atlantic seashore near Cape Canaveral who have been watching rocket launches since they were children. The ear-cracking roar and dazzling ball of light of lift-off are among their earliest memories and they learnt to say four-three-two-one before they said daddy.

The space business is growing grey hairs now. In the outdoor museum at the cape the old rockets with famous names like

Redstone, Titan and Atlas stand like old exhaust pipes planted by an outrageous artist, and seem already the relics of a bygone age. Around the elbow bend of the cape, springboard to space, are rocket gantries, evoking the old frontiering days. Here is launch complex 5, from which Alan Shepard, stuffed into his capsule like an overload of laundry into a tumble drier, was fired to a height of 116 miles in 1961 and became America's first man in space. Here is complex 14 from which John Glenn started his three-orbit flight the following year. Here is complex 34, a stark memorial to the three Apollo astronauts who died in the capsule fire of 1967. Here are the hearths from which Saturn rockets, mightiest of them all, hoisted moon missions in vulcan splendour. The remnants go back to the ape age of space when chimpanzees blazed the trail for right-stuff human heroes. The first rocket launched from the cape, a captured German V2, blasted off in 1950 when Florida was still relatively wild and unpeopled. Since then the 250 varieties of birds which live among the spaceport's dunes and lagoons, including pelicans, egrets and ibis, and other creatures like manatees, alligators, turtles and rattlesnakes, have grown accustomed to the periodic thunder of rockets as restless men have sought distant frontiers. Mercury, Gemini, Apollo, the space shuttle – the alligators have seen them all.

The towns of Cape Canaveral, Cocoa, Cocoa Beach, Merritt Island and Titusville, once cheap little shack places alive with no-see'um bugs, boomed as rocketry improved under the pressure of the cold war and the pride-stinging stimulus of Sputnik. People here have a proprietorial pride in the space business. Restaurants and bars bear rocket and space-shot names and walls are adorned with pictures and autographs of astronauts, photographs of lift-offs and bright mission badges, the heraldry of space. Space travellers used to drop in for beers and steaks after a spell on the moon, Dan Dares at their ease.

When I went to the cape to see a launching I felt an outsider of sorts, for journalists who specialise in space reporting, and officials of the National Aeronautics and Space Administration, form a coterie based on long familiarity with the trade and its argot. Like parliamentary lobby correspondents or cricket writers, they move in a herd, know the players in their respective dramas and the right restaurants and pubs to go to. Just as cricket scholars and baseball buffs know the complexities and histories of their games, so space industry followers know about fuels, distances, space walkers, zero gravity, moon-trekking and what the astronauts and ground control are talking about in their private, acronymic and laconic way.

Early in the morning, before the sun rose over the spaceport, the tribe began to congregate for the ceremony. The rocket stood in the distance, across lagoons and marshland. Lights twinkled on the gantry and launch complex constructions. Along the coastal roads crowds filled the vantage places. Many people had arrived the previous evening to be sure of a view. A space shuttle flight was routine, if such an event can ever be routine, but on this occasion the crew included Sally Ride, first American woman to travel into space, and, for the time being, the nation's sweetheart. On the roads to the cape billboards said: Ride, Sally, Ride! and Good Luck, Sally! Miss Ride was saying in her self-effacing, aw-shucks way, that she was only one of the boys; but there was no doubt that a girl in the ship was the main attraction and that she was helping to boost public enthusiasm for space travel. It was like the heyday of the space programme and a hotel room was hard to find anywhere along the space coast.

After the series of six manned moon landings ended in 1972, there was a waning of interest in space, punctuated briefly by the Skylab launches and the space rendezvous with the Russians. Budget cuts contributed to a feeling of ebb tide. But shuttle flights signalled a resurgence of interest and Americans were looking for achievement and heroes again after doldrum years. Space is a field in which the United States has a tradition of success and one of President Reagan's advisers declared space activity to be part of American machismo.

Sally Ride won a place in the shuttle under government policies opening up the space programme to women and blacks. She took the first step by responding to an Astronauts Wanted advertisement in her local newspaper. Among her attributes was the low-key demeanour, the Gary Cooper-like modesty and taciturnity, that astronauts habitually display. Her commander paid her a tribute in noting that 'she has country-boy horse sense . . . I like people who don't get too excited.' The space programme allows only minor recognition of femaleness. Nasa's clothing diagrams specify 'brassière, female only' – and the 'female unique' additions to women crew members' personal kit include a lipstick. Her space overalls, and those of Guy Bluford, the first black astronaut, were put on exhibition, side by side in the Air and Space Museum in Washington.

There was no doubting that the Sally Ride shuttle had a certain romance. It was far more exciting than a later flight which carried as a passenger a politician, a middle-aged senator who used his rank to get his jaunt. President Reagan telephoned him, White House to shuttle, to remind him to vote the right way in a coming debate, a seedy gesture that diminished the marvel of the flight.

As Sally Ride strapped herself in that morning, and the sky began to lighten, the birds of Cape Canaveral chattered and croaked. Hundreds of cameras were set up on tripods, their lenses directed at the gantry embracing the rocket. On the launching pad the shuttle, although as large as an airliner, was dwarfed by the assembly of boosters and the huge fuel tank to which it was attached. It seemed vulnerable, a cub clinging to the breast of a great bear. An avuncular voice counted away the minutes and then the seconds and we all grew quiet, attention concentrated, as if we were witnesses at a birth. Blast-off is the most dramatic of dispatchings, a physical and an emotional experience that television cannot adequately convey. There was a dazzling rush of flame, a piercingly incandescent burst of light and a rolling thunderous roar. It seemed that the rocket paused, as if drawing a great breath, and then it began to haul itself hand over hand into the sky. Suddenly it was surging up on a tower of fire, through clouds of vapour, accelerating, liberated. The ground shook beneath our feet and the air crackled. There was an explosion of whooping and clapping and I saw that all around me people were weeping, their tears and faces shining in the glare of rocket fire. The pillar of flame illuminated Mosquito Lagoon and Banana River and Indian River and the sea. They became gold. Flocks of seabirds shrieked and launched themselves and fled. Alligators, it may be imagined, sank cautiously to periscope depth as the shuttle freed itself and sought its new frontier.

3 Boss of the Plains

Texas

Texas, our Texas! All hail the mighty State!
Texas, our Texas! So wonderful, so great!

TEXAS STATE SONG

WHEN ALASKA achieved statehood Texas did not for a moment surrender its historic place in the grammar of American language and braggadocio: big, bigger, biggest, Texan. Texans argue that while Alaska is twice as large in terms of crude bulk it is Texas that remains, in more significant ways, powerful, grand and pre-eminent, the basic American metaphor for size, grossness, power, wealth, ambition, high-rolling and boasting: in a word, Texanic.

Texas is a great geographic, geological and human confluence. Its configuration, roughly that of a horn of plenty, is celebrated in Texas-shaped bathmats, fruitcakes, ice cubes, keyrings, buckles, spectacle frames, stationery, jewellery and soap. It is the dominant state of the main body of the United States. Covering 267,338 square miles, it is larger than France, larger than Spain, more than twice the area of Italy, nearly three times larger than Britain. The 800-mile length of Texas is the same distance as that between London and the Faeroes, and between Paris and Naples. The state is almost as broad as it is long and the people talk of being on Texas Standard Time.

Texans believe themselves to be both distillers and guardians of the holy American Stuff, the mystical, original raw spirit they fear has vanished in other sucked-out parts of the country – a keen devotion to the rumbustious, vigorous and unhindered pursuit of wealth. Isn't this, they ask, what America is for? Does not freewheeling capitalism constitute freedom's fortress? Isn't this what American democracy and ideas of liberty are predicated on?

Texan traditions of buccaneering and self-reliance are strong and patience with the snagging thorns of regulations is short. Committees are few. Texans scorn procrastinatory barricades and prefer to confront problems, not shrink from them. They do not haver and are quick on the draw of decision. They are can-do people, as they trumpet in their own propaganda, with an oilwell-deep belief that money makes and mends all. Money is loved well here, but is also readily risked, for men think it rusts if not kept rolling. They like to play hunches and acknowledge the import-ance of luck. It is not surprising that poker is a favourite Texan game and that Texans are poker champions. Texas Johnny Moss, Amarillo Slim Preston and Texas Dolly Brunson have brought poker fame to the state through their shrewdness and refrigerated nerves. The *Houston Chronicle* ran a front-page play-by-play report when one Texan lost to another in a world poker series, with $80,000 balanced on the turn of a card.

Texans are not hypocritical about naked pursuit of wealth and openly applaud financial ambition. They like spending and are America's champion shoppers: Houston is at the top of the league of retail sales per capita, spending one-third more than New York. Dallas is second. Houston is also top of the bounced-cheque league, with Dallas again the runner-up. More Rolex watches are sold in Texas than in any other state, and Texans call the Rolex the Texas Timex. Sales surged after President Lyndon Johnson raised his shirt at a press conference to reveal his gall bladder operation scar and newspaper photographs showed scar, wrist and Rolex.

Gusto, chutzpah, manners, dress, speech, food and attitudes combine to give Texans a distinctive and welcome identity in the American agglomeration. They play up to the stereotype of the boastful, expansive, slow-speaking westerner for they know that people outside – Yankees and foreigners – have unshakeable images of Texas and its denizens. To much of America and the world the Texan will always be a cowboy; and while the tongue is sometimes in the cheek, the playing of the role is itself a subtle element in Texan identity. But image and reality coalesce. Texans genuinely like to talk, dress, sing and eat Texan. They really do love chili, their peppery stew. A Texan millionaire had it flown to his holiday home in France; and in 1977 the Texas legislature proclaimed chili as the state dish, to take its place alongside such symbols as the state tree, the pecan, the state gem, topaz, and the state flower, the bluebonnet.

Texans concede that there are no people quite like them and they are fascinated by themselves and their legendary larger-than-life qualities. They believe it a virtue to extol their attributes, for modesty is unTexan and decidedly suspect. Texan bookshelves bend with the weight of volumes on Texas. The state has 500 museums, including a fine old institution, Miss Hattie's brothel in San Angelo, with an original peephole offering a view of a bed. Much of the colour and tradition of Texas is Spanish, the Tex-Mex flavour being part of the state's distinctiveness, and hundreds of towns and natural features have Spanish names. Some of the English place-names are curious, spiky, comic and romantic – names like Pep, Ike, Fred, Art, Ogg, Hub, Grit, Happy, Teacup, Cactus, Bug Tussle, Cut and Shoot, Jot 'Em Down, Dime Box, Deaf Smith, Energy, Ginger, Gasoline, Concrete, Noodle, Structure, Muleshoe, Gunsight, Pointblank, Lone Star, Roundup, Utopia, Tarzan, Uncertain, Maverick, Friday, Earth and Gun Barrel City. Texan towns billboard intriguing native events like rattlesnake roundups, rodeos, fiestas, bullfights, polka festivals, armadillo racing, fiddlers' reunions, chili cook-off championships, barbecued goat cook-offs, black-eye-pea festivals and slingshot tournaments.

The native speech is unmistakable. The flinty New Yorker has a Bren for a mouth and rattles out words to the point of incoherence, but the mannerly Texan stretches his vowels like pizza dough. He pronounces all right *aw riot*. He hopes, at the end of his life, to go to *hay oven*, not *hail*. He straightens his bootlace tie in front of a *meer*. The present tense of sing is *sang*, so he sings '*suede land of liberdy, of thee ah sang.*' The real thing is the *rill thang*.

Oil is *all* and business is *bidness*, hence many Texans make *dills* in the *all bidness*; and they copy *bidness* papers on a *Xayuhrox*. Henry Clay Koontz, a millionaire Texas rancher, once hired an elocution teacher to help rid him of an English accent he had acquired from an English tutor while he was growing up. Now he is happily droppin' his Gs again, talkin' Texan.

Texans have bursting pride and love attention. They also have a thick streak of shortsighted greed and, even by American standards, a noted disposition to violence. When they hear this sort of criticism they usually ascribe it to the ignorance and jealousy of stuffy Yankees who have not spent enough time in the state to understand it. For such avowedly robust people they are surprisingly sensitive. They hated Edna Ferber's novel *Giant*, which scourged Texan vulgarity, racism and the *mores* of millionaires, but they bought it in great quantities and packed cinemas to see the film. They would rather be talked about than not, and if you do not talk about them they do it for you.

In claiming special qualities for themselves, Texans have had to become reconciled to the fact that a large number of them are not native. In the last century 'Gone to Texas' was a commonplace graffito daubed on barns in other states, and in recent years 'Gone to Texas' has, figuratively, been written on the front doors of millions of Americans and also Mexicans. In the early 1980s newcomers accounted for nearly two-thirds of the state's population increase. But Texans do not believe they are being diluted. They maintain that Texanhood, or Texianism, is a matter of attitude and that Texanic qualities exist in abundance in many Americans, regardless of their birthplace: it is when these people are planted in Texas, and nourished by its atmosphere, that they flower like true Texans. A man may not be born Texan, which is unfortunate; but he can be born to be Texan.

No Texan would have said, as Henry Ford did in his libel action against the *Chicago Tribune* in 1919, that history is bunk. The emphasis on teaching Texan history contributes to the sense of identity here; though perhaps part of Texan sunniness is that the state is not burdened by too heavy a history and has no historical grievance of much consequence. The origins of Texas lie in the Spanish American empire. Every schoolchild learns that after 1821 Mexico allowed thousands of white settlers into its Texas province and that in 1836 about 187 settlers perished at the Alamo mission in the war for Texan independence. The defenders were a job lot of adventurers and their leaders were Davy Crockett, who had gone to Texas after losing his seat in the US House of Representatives; Jim (The Knife) Bowie, a former slave trader and robber; and William Travis, in exile for killing a man. Travis wrote from the besieged Alamo a message ending 'Victory or Death' which is as famous in Texas as Nelson's 'England Expects' signal is in Britain. Texas was independent for nine years, a republic with a four-ship navy, postage stamps and the recognition of several European countries, an experience it looks back on with pride.

The state's history has been one of adventure, excitement and gambling, and its climate and conditions have always sorted tough and lucky men from weak and unfortunate ones. During its 19th-century growth, in the cattle king and cowboy era, it was the classic frontier that 20th-century literature and films were to extol, the authentic wild west and open range. It was here that Samuel Colt's revolver was first proved in actions that Texas Rangers fought against Comanches and Apaches in the 1830s and 1840s, and Colt included the word Texas in the name of one of his early six-shooters. Texans were the first cowboys and taught the cowpuncher's craft to the wider American west, just as, in a later epoch, they were to take their oil drilling skills to the world. It was Texas that Hollywood embraced in its constant evocations of the frontier and in the development of the western as the great American film genre. The very word has always been saleable, a sure igniter of imaginations. Hundreds of films have been made with Texas settings and with Texas in the title, like *The Texas Trail*, *Texas Cowboy*, *The Lucky Texan*, *Texas Terror*, *Starlight over Texas*, *Texas Stampede*, *Texas Kid*, *Springtime in Texas*, *Robin Hood of Texas*, *The Lone Texan* and, a title that says much, *Texans Never Cry*.

The screen images of Texas and heroes like Tom Mix, Gene Autry and John Wayne, have combined with Texas's own ideas of identity to perpetuate and elaborate the national costume. Many men in western states wear wide-brimmed hats, jeans and western boots as a matter of practicality as well as tradition. They are sensible working clothes. But western dress is also part of Texan self-expression, a reconnection with a past that always seems, through nostalgia's prism, to be romantic, brave, simple and manly. Texans are ambivalent about western dress. Some say attitude is more important than trimmings. They disparage the hats and boots business and would prefer that Texans projected a different image, more pinstriped, less cowboy. They are like Scots who speak slightingly of kilts and tartans as folkloric accoutrements. But costume, even if fake or invented, has its subtle place in identity and is a focus of sentiment and pleasure.

'A large part of it, sir, is fantasy,' pronounced Jamie Morgan, to whom I turned for advice on the social significance of frontier threads. He is the manager of a western apparel store between Dallas and its neighbour Fort Worth and which is billed, with typical Texas understatement, as the largest boot store in the world. 'What we are doin' is caterin' to folks' fancies.'

Mr Morgan was tall and made taller by his office outfit, which included a cowboy hat and cream high-heeled ostrich-skin boots. In between were a yoked western shirt and jeans supported by a belt with a fist-sized buckle. A large ring glowed like a low-watt bulb on one of his fingers. On his desk stood a cowboy statue, a popular Texan artefact. On the wall was a large portrait of the god-king John Wayne, in the western garb of his trade and philosophy. Noting my glance, Mr Morgan said reverently: 'John Wayne was, and is, a hero. There were no frills about him. He did what a man was supposed to do. He told it like it was, yes sir.'

Outside the store a line of pick-up trucks, the Texas national vehicle, were parked like broncs at a hitching rail; and inside, inspecting the merchandise, were men with muddy boots, torn jeans, stained hats and leathery faces.

Many of our customers are ranch hands, who need good boots and hats for their work and somethin' more fancy for steppin' out [Mr Morgan said]. But a lot of folks buy western clothes because they look good and are a piece of our heritage they just ain't willin' to let die. Western clothes are democratic and we like that in Texas. In your hat and boots you are as good as the next man. On Saturday night you don't stick out. You belong. Western gear is an equalizer. Now there happen to be folks in Dallas who don't think much of all this, and I'll tell you why. Dallas has gotten to be a huge business metropolis. Folks there think they are buildin' themselves another New York, what with their high buildings and high fashion and all. What they don't realise is that as much as they want Dallas to leave the west, the west won't leave Dallas.

To emphasise the point he indicated the nine checkouts in his store. 'There have been times when every checkout has had a long line stretchin' back into the store. That shows you how popular boots and hats are. And there must be a hundred boot stores in the Dallas area alone.'

There were 60,000 pairs of boots on his shelves, made from the skins of calf, goat, kangaroo, elephant, ostrich, anteater, lizard and snake. The most expensive, $3100 reduced in a special offer to $1900, were made from alligator. A nearby shop had a $6000 pair made from crocodile trimmed with ermine. Mr Morgan himself admitted a weakness for boots and said he owned seventeen pairs. Many Texans like to have several fancy pairs in addition to their working boots, and boot-making has become an art form. Customers commission colourful designs, floral patterns and fancy stitching, and bootmaker-artists fashion cutouts and inlays into flowers, cattle, birds, oil derricks, landscapes and monograms.

Boots, of course, are not easily removed. In Texan brothels – as can be seen at Miss Hattie's – an oilcloth was often placed as protection at the foot of the bed. As Texans like to keep their hats on at most times, too, patrons must have presented a notable peephole spectacle.

'America grew up under a Stetson,' Mr Morgan's advertising proclaimed. Someone has estimated the number of cowboy hats in America at 17 million. In their various styles they are the descendants of the original 'Boss of the Plains' model perfected by John B. Stetson in the 1850s. Made of felt, it kept a good shape and was a marked improvement on the wool hats which sagged like pastry in the rain and did nothing for the westerner's image. The manly stiff Stetson gave the plainsman his distinctive adornment and silhouette, as much an American symbol as Liberty's torch and the Stars and Stripes. The president of the Texas Sheriffs' Association, who wears a tall Stetson, remarked at a sheriffs' convention in 1985 that 'wearing the hat is important because it means something to people, projects the right image.' Commenting on the hat and boots President Reagan wore at his holiday ranch a presidential aide said: 'Americans like cowboys and that is the way many people think of the president.' In Texas the cowboy hat seems to take root on men's heads and becomes part of the persona. Certainly the western hat is more stylish than its poor relation, the duckbill or baseball cap, which is slightly comical and has nothing of the authority and dignity of the brimmed hat. Policemen and service officers sometimes wear bill caps and seem somehow diminished by them.

Once booted, hatted and jeaned, a man must be shirted in a proper western shirt with snap fastenings, never buttons, so that he is not caught up on cactus as he rides the range or hurries to the bar. He also needs to be belted and buckled. Belt buckles are another native art form and men pay thousands of dollars for large gold and silver buckles, on which to rest their bellies. To complete his ensemble the Texan may have a leather bolo tie with a slide made of silver, gold or turquoise, the tie-ends finished with silver tips, and also gold or silver tips on his shirt collar points. With boot caps, heel guards, spurs, buckles, tie slides, collar points and fancy hat pins, all made of silver or gold, he glitters and jingles like an ornamented dray horse.

'There's always been an interest in the western look,' Mr Morgan said, 'but what made the whole thing go wild was that

movie *Urban Cowboy*. For a time it was crazy and we were sellin'
2000 pairs of boots a day. The movie introduced millions of
people to activities that had been goin' on in Texas for years. All
over the country folks fancied themselves in boots and hats, tried
'em on and found they were lookin' good.'

Urban Cowboy opened non-Texan eyes to the redneck blue-
collar culture which thrives in the temples called honkytonks, also
known as kicker palaces because both cowboys and their boots are
known as kickers. They are devoted to country and western
music, dancing the Texas two-step, the gentle growing of beer
bellies and the sporting of western clothes. *Urban Cowboy*, released in 1980, was a music and dancing western, an old-time
B-film in a modern Texas setting, and was filmed at Gilley's
honkytonk, south of Houston. When I visited it the car park was
full of pick-up trucks, some with gun racks, most of them
emblazoned with the lone star flag and patriotic stickers saying
Texan Native and God's Own Country. The honkytonk was large
enough to house a jumbo jet, and although it was early in the
evening there were several hundred people there. A row of urban
cowboys was berthed alongside the bar, hats tilted back as they
guzzled from the longnecked beer bottles Texans prefer. The bar
was punctuated every two feet by a glass with a note in it saying
'Tipping Is Allowed'. The barmen wore hats. One of them asked
me 'Kin ah git y'all sumtin' to drank?' I passed social muster by
ordering a Lone Star longneck, the national beer of Texas. The
band was playing *I'm a Redneck* and couples were dancing the
two-step, gliding gracefully and studiously, the men mostly
hatted. In honkytonks men are known as devils, women as angels.
The angels hooked their left thumbs into the belt loops of their
devils' jeans as they danced. Longnecks multiplied amoebically
on the tables and there was a frequent crashing of punchball
machines as men engaged in fisty trials of machismo. A whooping
crowd was gathered around the mechanical bull, a contraption
offering the supreme test of honkytonkian manliness. A rider is
meant to hold onto it with one hand, and wave his hat with the
other while being shaken like a cocktail by the bull's corkscrewing

gyration. This is how the wild west has ended – young men being hurled through the air by a grotesque robot in a beer hall.

There was no mechanical bull at a crowded cocktail bar in a luxury hotel in Houston. The clientele here seemed drawn from people who bivouac contentedly in River Oaks, the smartest address in Houston, to which arrivistes aspire, a suburb of Disneyish fantasy, where no one owns less than a mansion. It is wooded and lushly green, its lawns and azaleas tended by Mexican gardeners, its doors attended by Mexican maids. The suburb has its own police force and notices outside the houses warn that armed guards are on duty at all times. The atmosphere is of wealth solidified, and the chateaux and Palladian mansions stand in slightly preposterous and very Texan profusion.

Here in the bar the boots were classy, expensive, fancily stitched, their owners darkly pinstriped, with discreetly scintillating rings which set off their cigars. Their Cadillacs, Rolls-Royces and Jaguars had been valeted away and there was no pick-up truck in sight. The bar was wood-panelled, club-fashion, hung with hunting prints, and the waiters ghosted in and out. The talk was of oil, property and shares, and not subdued. Men were ebullient and animated, swaggerers in swagger city. Women were expensively dressed, perhaps by Neiman-Marcus, of Houston and Dallas, the store that wealthy Texas women think of as paradise. These were not women to flinch at a $15,000 price tag on a dress, or a $1000 ticket on some slacks. Whether wealthy or modestly endowed, Texan women, I think, are quite distinctive. They dress in a more determinedly feminine way than their northern sisters, with more frills, ruches and flounces, in an accentuation of form and femininity, and have a panache and southern style not seen much in the north. They have an instinct for glamour. In her relationships with men, and in marriage, a Texas woman is more likely to see herself as part of the team, not a rival, and is not the combative sex-warrior that the northern woman is more likely to be. She is more shrewd and realistic, takes equality for granted and is not to be pushed around. The important fact about Texas women is that they have Texas daddies and know how to get what they want.

I have known Houston in two of its moods. I first saw it at the height of the dizzy oil boom which lasted from 1973 to 1982. If money has a smell that smell was here, and the city seemed to be printing its own. The population was growing by more than 2000 a week. There were frostbelt Yankees, go-north-young-man Mexicans, blacks reversing history's northward trend, Vietnamese, Salvadorans and, of course, carloads of Texans. The jobs sections of Houston newspapers in those days were herniaheavy and fetched $5 a copy in northern cities where industries were shrivelling. Houston was straddled by cranes and biffed by hammers as skyscrapers burst upwards like forced rhubarb. There was no town planning and Houston said 'Let her rip!' as carte-blanche developers mobilised and mechanical diggers moved in like tank regiments. 'You could feel the city growing by hours,' a fifteen-year veteran of Houston said to me. The place was an adventure playground for architects who seemed to draw with all the exuberance of men who have just heard good news, a pencil in one hand and champagne in the other. The city's iridescent skyscraper core is an unmistakable assertion of wealth, power and conquest. Towers thrust up like fists, hard and glittering, sharp-cornered and modern-sinister, as impenetrable as Darth Vader's mask. Soaring, mirroring towers – emerald, cobalt, amethyst, coffee, black and white – reflect the light, clouds and each other in fantastic kaleidoscopic display. Houston's stunning vistas are meant to provoke the kind of admiring gasps that escape audiences at operas when the curtain rises on a stupendous set. With its explosive building and human growth Houston is an American drama. It has spilt over the plain, out of control, profligate and brazen, Fastbuckville. There is little sense of history, no stabilizing structure of tradition. On the Houston scale forty years ago was close to the stone age. Nobody has ever come to Houston for its climate or its natural attractions. 'You come here,' an Houstonian said, not without pride, 'for one reason

– to make money among money-makers in a city of opportunity.'
Houstonians are mostly young and relatively new to a city of
ineradicable optimism. They want to make their fortune, earn
admiration and leave something behind, preferably large and
concrete. People say they like the lack of stuffiness and snobbery,
though the truth is that Houston, like any society, is stratified.
People know, for example, the difference between old and new
money. You can be rich in Houston, but to gain entrance to
certain circles you have to be the right sort of rich.

By the early 1980s Houston had become the fourth largest city
of the United States, after New York, Los Angeles and Chicago, a
world city, enriched by oil, gas, construction, the space and
medical industries. It started life, in the year of the Alamo, as a
real estate speculation on the banks of the mosquito-infested
Buffalo Bayou, promoted by the brothers Augustus and John
Allen, who wrote in their prospectus that 'when the rich lands of
this country shall be settled, a trade will flow here making it,
beyond all doubt, the great interior commercial emporium of
Texas.' They wisely chose a site on a navigable bayou giving
access to the Gulf of Mexico, and named the city after heroic Sam
Houston, maker of Texas.

Modern Houston is born of Texas irrepressibility and rollick-
ing enterprise. In the beginning were the wildcatters, the oil
prospectors, wily gamblers and wide-eyed hopefuls, who scraped
up dollars, sank holes and prayed for gushers. Oil has been
America's greatest modern business adventure. It made Texas. It
became America's largest industry, creating hundreds of millionaires, what newspapers called zillionaires and jillionaires.
The first major oil strike was at Spindletop, on the Gulf coast, in
1901, but the great boom got under way from 1930 and roared to
the 1980s. The oil age made major cities of Houston and Dallas
and built a huge reserve of oil expertise and venture capital. It
spawned dynasties whose wealth, quarrels, passions, philanthropy and stinginess make television soap operas look tame. The
histories of Houston, Dallas and Forth Worth are partly the
stories of mega-rich and eccentric men. One tycoon wore $100

bills for bow ties. Jim West, who had a cellarful of silver dollars, drove around Houston in his Cadillac throwing out the coins. He spent his nights cruising with the police in one of his cars, fitting himself out with a Stetson, a gold and diamond Texas Rangers' badge, a rifle, shotgun and tommygun, a Colt on his hip and his trousers supported by braces and a belt with a big gold buckle. H.L. Hunt, probably the richest of them all, sired three families, took his lunch to work in a paper bag and crawled around his office on his hands and knees for exercise.

Many Texas institutions owe their existence to the philanthropy of Texas moguls. Hugh Cullen was one who gave millions of dollars to the University of Houston and to the Houston Symphony. The Symphony was not his private band, though at every concert he attended it would play *Old Black Joe*, his favourite piece. He once persuaded the Symphony to appear at a wrestling tournament and it played *Pistol Packin' Momma* as the wrestlers thrashed and grunted. Just as in the old west, where the opryhouse followed hard on the whorehouse, Houston's wealthy have funded the civic adornments that proclaim status and respectability, slapping down millions for the opera, ballet, theatre, orchestra, picture galleries and museums.

Modern Houston is a defiance, a triumphant assertion of the American ability to grow and create in hostile circumstances. As part of the tradition of conquest it is an imperial achievement. Earlier generations in their westering pursuit of manifest destiny subjugated Indians and brought the wilderness under their control. Here on this steamy and bug-ridden bayou Texans have applied technology to conquer the climate and create a generator of wealth. The British foreign service once classified Houston a hardship post for its sapping nine-month hot season. But air-conditioning, introduced here in 1923, now shapes everything. Air-conditioning companies occupy forty-five of the yellow pages in the local directory and Houstonians spend about $3.4 billion a year on cooling. The electricity company has to keep on building power stations to meet the demand. From air-conditioned homes Houstonians step into air-conditioned garages and air-conditioned cars to drive to cooled car parks and their work in chilled offices and stores. They cool the air around their swimming pools and patios. The mighty Astrodome sports stadium is also air-conditioned, and so are some amusement parks. Anglers fish from an air-conditioned pier. During a prolonged power failure in parts of Houston in 1983 people sought cool shelter in their cars and some moved into hotels. Houston is geared to the motor car, and parking space swallows more than three-fifths of its central area. Texans do not walk much but Houstonians do press their legs into action in the five-mile network of underground air-conditioned tubes through which they reach shops, offices, garages and hotels. Only in these warrens beneath the baking streets does the centre of Houston have the equivalent of street life. Even by day the streets are eerily deserted and skyscraper lobbies are as still as cathedrals. All the bustle and energy is contained, as if in reactors, in the tall secret buildings, the laboratory-created carapaces which form a lunar city made to withstand a hostile environment. At night a few youths roam and police sirens moan in the emptiness. The place seems a corpse from which blood has been drained.

The oozing metropolis engulfs outpost communities, spread over 600 square miles, and the high-rise core and parasite appendages are roughly lashed together by uncoordinated tangles of choked freeway, hedged by monstrous billboards. The billboards of America are almost everywhere crude intrusions, but, even by American standards, the billboards of Houston are outstandingly offensive, huge and garish, creating nightmare vistas.

Houston was a Darwinian city, hustler-built, without much thought for fundamentals like sewage capacity, water supply, access and the human factor. Of its exuberance and optimism there can be no doubt. Its architecture and development reflect them. But they also reflect its neglect of human scale. Town planning was an idea that always stuck in the Houstonian craw. In the 1930s planning proposals were rejected, criticised as manifestations of a police state and of Stalinism.

When I first arrived in Houston the morning newspapers had a brief report of a man who had quibbled over his restaurant bill and one of the staff had shot him. Houston has always had a very high murder rate, often heading the league table as the most murderous place in America. In the early 1980s, for example, the murder rate was 30 per 100,000, compared with a national average of 9.7. It was also in the top ten for rape and robbery. Life has been held cheap in Texas, something ascribed to southern, Texan and frontier traditions of lawlessness. 'How is it,' a Texas judge is said to have been asked, 'that if you shoot a man in this state you go free, but if you steal a horse they hang you?' The judge replied: 'Because we've got plenty of men who need killin', but no horses that need stealin'.' The state has always attracted a large number of restless, rootless people, looking for money, and guns are freely available. Much killing is casual and you can read of murders committed for slight reasons almost every day. One evening as I was driving through Houston in the company of a Houstonian, I stopped at a traffic light and allowed my attention to wander. 'Don't do that,' my companion said. 'In Houston you can get killed for a look. Just keep looking straight ahead. There are a lot of crazy people in this city.' It echoed the advice of a murder squad detective: 'People get shot on the roads for waving, making rude gestures or honking their horns. Don't blow your horn and keep your windows up.'

Houston, once drunk on success, was chilled by unemployment and bankruptcy when I returned a few years later. The greatest boom in Texan history had ended with the 1982 oil price recession and Houston had a hangover. Office rents in the glass towers were cheap, and in one of the leviathians there was only one office occupied. Houston's hangover was making it think more clearly about its direction and the effects of its uncontrolled growth. It had to admit that its critics were right, that in parts it was a badly polluted, congested and inefficient mess. It was reluctantly conceded that there would have to be some planning and even enforcement of planning laws. (One of the few parts of Houston that is planned, and with excellent results, is River Oaks, the mansion suburb inhabited by the rich and influential who have always been vehemently opposed to planning in the rest of the city.)

Everyone knew that the oil was dwindling fast and would not last far into the next century. There was a need to diversify. Dallas had pulled ahead of Houston economically because it had built a multiplicity of business interests while brother Houston was on the binge. Not that Houston is limited in its interests. Apart from oil and gas it has one of America's major ports, steel, petro-chemicals and food industries. It is the home of the Johnson space centre, the control tower for space flights, and the richly endowed medical campus of cool, white, sterile towers, the Texas Medical Centre. Here I once watched Dr Michael DeBakey perform one of his famous heart bypass operations. The supporting cast had done their work and the patient lay sawn open and ready when the star performer stepped into the theatre and set to work. Dr DeBakey and Dr Denton Cooley, who ride the medical frontier, are Texan heroes. Another Houston star, Red Adair, the fighter of oil fires, is so tough and all-American that he was once played in a film by John Wayne.

Houston had changed since the boom. It elected its first woman mayor, a shock to hidebound Texan men. She was strongly supported by blacks, hispanics and the city's homosexuals who, to the consternation of image-conscious Texans, made a base in Houston. One of the new mayor's first actions was to shake up the disgraceful police force, a notoriously brutal and racist body which killed citizens at more than twice the average for American police forces. She hired a new police chief, a black, to provide Houston with a disciplined and multiracial force.

The sagging of the oil boom brought trouble to the Texas mega-rich. In the mid-1980s their citadels shook when banks became nervous about the extent of the credit the millionaires had, and the value of oil as collateral had fallen. Clint Murchison, of Dallas, son of an old-time wheeler-dealer who made a fortune in the oilfields, found that his own empire was a house of cards. He extended himself in high risk property ventures and when they failed the creditors closed in with claims for $150 million. Ken and Cullen Davis, of Fort Worth, who ran an oilfield services conglomerate, seemed unshakeable until eight banks filed bankruptcy proceedings, seeking $346 million. Part of Cullen's life was pure melodrama. In 1977 he was acquitted of murdering two people during a shooting rampage in his mansion. His estranged wife said that he was the gunman and had disguised himself in a black wig. Two years later he was cleared on charges that he hired a gunman to kill the judge in his divorce case.

The greatest citadel shaken was that of the Hunt brothers, Bunker and Herbert, who saw more than two billion dollars slip through their fingers in a few years, with Bunker remarking ruefully that 'a billion dollars isn't what it was'. Their father, the remarkable H.L. Hunt, founded the greatest of Texas fortunes in 1930. He was on hand with a deal when the old wildcatter, Columbus 'Dad' Joiner, working with a makeshift drill rig and borrowed cash, hit the largest oil reserve ever found in America until the Alaskan discovery forty years later. It was the basis of the Hunt billions. H.L. believed he had a genius gene it was his duty to give to the world. He had six children with his first wife, and, during this marriage had eight children with two other women. Though generous in his fathering he was in other respects parsimonious.

His son Bunker has some of his father's flair, and also his far right views. He is a generous contributor to evangelical causes but, like his father, is not personally extravagant. He favours hamburgers and ice cream to keep his twenty-stone figure in shape, dislikes fancy restaurants, drives a well-used car and flies economy. In the 1970s Bunker, Herbert and some Saudi princes thought they could guard their fortunes against inflation and taxation by building a barricade of silver. They amassed the largest private silver holding in the world and, just as they planned, the price of silver soared. Greedy banks and brokerage houses pumped in more money until, in 1980, the bubble burst,

silver prices collapsed, Wall Street came close to panic and the
world's money markets shook. The Hunts were unable to
pay their debts and a bank consortium lent $1.1 billion to
rescue them and prevent a shock-wave financial disaster. They
had to go to their sisters, Margaret (worth $1.4 billion) and
Caroline ($1.3 billion) for help, too. Bunker, Herbert and others
were charged by the Commodity Futures Trading Commission
with manipulating the silver market to push up the price. The
Hunts also lost heavily in sugar, property speculation and oil. It
was revealed in 1985 that their Hunt International Resources
Company owed more than $295 million. In four years Bunker,
Herbert and youngest brother Lamar saw their net worth fall by
four billion dollars.

The financial storm in Texas all but wiped out the old way of
doing business. There was a time when Texan millionaires and
bankers just shook hands on a deal and left everything to trust, a
man's word his bond. Certainly a multi-millionaire's word was
thought to be as good as gold, and bankers worked on the
assumption that if one part of an empire ran into trouble, money
would be siphoned over from another. What happened to tycoons
like Bunker and Herbert Hunt showed that the old informal
handshake days had gone. The impossible had happened; you
could lend money to the Texas rich and not be sure of getting it
back.

A fifth of Houston's people are black and at least another fifth are
hispanic. The numbers of hispanics are hard to estimate because
there is a growing and fluid population of several hundred
thousand illegal immigrants, mostly from Mexico. Because of its
size and growth, Houston is a goal for migrants. They help to
build and mend roads and work as labourers, ditch diggers,
gardeners, painters, maids, restaurant hands and cleaners.
Throughout the border country of Texas, New Mexico, Arizona
and California millions of illegal immigrants are the backbone of
the economy. They are an imported working class fuelling

industries with cheap labour, enabling them to be competitive. They do the tougher, dirtier jobs that most white Americans no longer wish to do. The pay is not high by American standards, but a day's pay in the United States is often the equivalent of a week's in Mexico, and that is why *el norte* exerts its magnetic pull. For some Mexicans it is a matter of 'Go north or starve.' The flow of wetbacks, wet from crossing the Rio Grande, is inexorable. People-smuggling is a multi-million dollar business. At the bottom are the men who charge fifty cents to carry illegal immigrants on their backs across shallow stretches of the Rio Grande. Many migrants are commuters, dodging the border patrols to work in the border towns, returning to Mexico at night. At the top are the 'coyotes' who operate mass transit across the frontier with buses and lorries.

Many Americans are alarmed. They see the influx as a flood and think that migrants take jobs from Americans and create a welfare and medical burden. Fear and prejudice stoke demands for legislation to control immigration. But the inflow is not large by historical standards and, while it causes social strains, it is not economically dangerous or a threat. On the contrary, the weight of evidence is that this immigration is an economic benefit. These are people in their prime working years. They fill gaps in the labour market and stimulate manufacturing activity. Many industries depend upon them. Illegal migrants form two-thirds of the labour force in the Los Angeles clothing industry, two-thirds of the roadmaking teams in Houston, a third of Houston's building workers, up to a fifth of the labour force in Silicon Valley, California. Employers say candidly that they like illegal immigrant workers because they are willing, punctual, uncomplaining and accept lower wages. A large part of the border economy is built on the basis of a continuing flow of illegal labour. With mingling of peoples, languages, customs and currency, the borderland of the United States and Mexico is a separate community, another country, a bridge between two immense and dynamic cultures, each needing the other. It defies regulation. Indeed, the frontier itself is to many of the people who live near it an artificial line, a hindrance. The borderland is a strong, young, expanding and pliable society. But it has a shadowy and wretched side. Many illegal migrants are exploited and blackmailed by wetback smugglers, landlords and employers. They often pay high prices for forged papers and lodging in safe houses. Preyed on by criminals, they have little recourse in the law, and many live under the threat of betrayal to the authorities, and deportation.

In 1985 there were 16 million hispanics in the United States, about 6 per cent of the population, and, according to predictions, they will be 15 per cent by 2020. They are more fertile and growing faster than any other group. Three-fifths of them are Mexican Americans, or chicanos – a sobriquet once considered derogatory, now worn with pride. The next largest hispanic group, 14 per cent, come from Puerto Rico, and enter the United States freely because the island's people were given citizenship in 1917. The figure of 16 million does not include illegal migrants, mostly Mexican, who are thought to number around six million.

'Houston today is like New York at the beginning of the 20th century – a lot of immigrants coming in, wanting to make it in America,' said Dr Leonel Castillo, a Houston educator and hispanic leader, who headed the US Immigration Service in the Carter administration. 'The hispanic population here doubles every seven years, and half of it is now in school.'

He drove me through the parts of the city inhabited by hispanic migrants, legal and illegal, streets of poor housing and small shops. We went into the Fiesta supermarket, a vast hangar of a store, which sells hot dogs with chili, tortillas, Spanish-language paperbacks, papier-mâché dolls and Mexican beer. There was a cheque-cashing service, an exchange for Mexican and Salvadoran banknotes and a cable office where Mexican migrants were queueing to wire money home. In a nearby panaderia selling Mexican, Salvadoran and Nicaraguan food and newspapers, there were posters advertising weekend van trips over the border to Mexico. It costs $40 to get to Monterrey to see the family.

'Houston is extraordinary,' Dr Castillo said:

You would think that a city 150 years old would be more settled, but it is still disorganised. Maps are out of date as soon as they are printed and even if you live here you cannot keep up with what goes on, for everything changes so quickly. Go away for a while and when you return you'll find new movers and shakers and new problems. Hispanics are the fastest growing minority in Houston but we do not have a stable power structure, not enough registered voters, and this makes us politically weak. Our population is young and 30 per cent of our adults cannot vote because they are not citizens. Mexicans are the slowest of all groups to take American citizenship. It's partly pride and to understand it you have to remember the history of discrimination. People would rather be first class Mexicans than second class Americans. Also, Mexico is near and people get into the habit of working here and going home, retaining their Mexican roots.

There must be about half a million illegal migrants in the Houston area. They don't qualify for welfare and they do any work they can. They knock on doors offering to clean, paint and dig. Somehow many of them have cars because no matter how poor you are you need one. People who don't understand Houston are surprised by this. But wheels are like legs – would you ask a man to cut off his legs because he is poor? Public transport is bad and distances are great. Illegal immigrants are the last people in America to wear moneybelts. Everyone else has credit cards and bank accounts, but these people can't have them. When they are robbed they can't complain to the police, and they often try to avenge themselves. They have no legal status and are vulnerable to threat and blackmail: it is almost always an hispanic who reports an illegal immigrant and gets him deported. Still, the hispanic influx will continue to grow, and these undocumented people should be legalised. Once people are settled they form a pathway into America. Their brothers, cousins and in-laws join them. Mexicans are conquering this part of the US without firing a shot. Houston used to be a very redneck town, and, it still is to an extent. But it has become much more of an international city. It has six Spanish-language radio stations and Spanish newspapers and people celebrate the independence days of Guatemala, Mexico, El Salvador and other countries. Although the hispanic community does not have political power to match its numbers, it is gradually becoming more politicised. In about fifteen years when the hispanic kids now in school are voting, Houston will have an hispanic mayor as San Antonio has now. The use of Spanish is now at its height, and it is important, or at least useful, for anglo people in the police, newspapers, banks and hospitals to know Spanish. But as hispanics become more assimilated, as their children grow up in an American environment, I think Spanish will retreat and become a language of the home.

Hispanics and blacks know best of all how tough, unequal, illiberal and cynical Texas can be. As an every-man-for-himself society it never set itself up to be fair. It is a place where the traditional American drama is very much alive, where hopeful migrants join the struggle for a better existence.

Jacko Garrett's ranch is near Chocolate Bayou, fifty miles or so south of Houston, on the flat brown land of the coastal plain which is punctuated by hamlets, farms, oil wells and filling stations. Part of the image of Texas is that its ranches are vast, and the truth is that some of them really are. The magazine *Texas Monthly* mischievously proposed a new standard for measuring Texas ranches, the RI, for Rhode Island, the smallest of the American states, which covers 1049 square miles. The King ranch, by far the largest, is 1.23 Rhode Islands, or 823,000 acres. There are several other immense spreads owned by ranching dynasties whose intermarriages and land and oil deals have been like the alliances and manoeuvrings of mediaeval barons. There are still ranches where cowboys pursue their hard trade in the traditional manner with round-ups, branding and fence mending, a link with the roots of Texas. But the great ranches are few. Most are quite small and these days their owners often have a hard time. Jacko Garrett and his wife Nancy have 2000 acres of their own and lease another 5500. They grow rice and raise Brahman cattle, an Indian breed introduced into Texas in 1906 for their suitability to the climate. Jacko, in his early 40s, and Nancy, four years younger, have two daughters. For most of their married life they lived in a small house until they could build themselves a large ranch house with a pool. They love it. They hate cities, are devoted to the country they farm and are proud of being Texans – 'the next best thing to being American.' They are tough, tanned and lean, realistic and good-humoured.

The ranch was Jacko's father's.

There was never any doubt about my being a rancher. The only time I left the place was when I went to school. I am doing exactly what I want and I know I have to be good to succeed. These are grim times for farmers. You have to keep up with technology, visit plant breeding stations and learn marketing or you go under. Some farmers think the old ways are enough to see them through, but they aren't. In the past they just took their grain to the elevators and that was it. It isn't like that any more. Men spend thirty or forty years working their land and then they get wiped out. They sell off half their land to pay their debts and say the devil with it. It's happening a lot around here. A farmer near us had 8000 acres four years ago. Now he has 850. He had to sell his land to pay back his bank loans. After all, a combine harvester costs $80,000 or $90,000, a tractor $40,000 or $50,000. These days the average farmer doesn't have a chance of survival, given the costs of production. The dollars aren't there and a lot are getting out. People are scared and pessimistic. Now I reckon I'm a good farmer, one of the top 5 per cent, and the farm is one of the largest in the county, but I have trouble. In the rice business we've had three bad years in a row and I haven't paid back my loans for two years. But we'll pull through. We work together as a family and the kids work with us. Traci is 13 and has been working on the farm since she was 8. She knows how to work cattle and can take responsibility. Christy, who's 6, does her jobs, too. Our daughters work for their leisure and their clothes and other things. A lot of city kids don't have that sort of responsibility, then they don't have the opportunity.

When we first married we did everything together, but now I grow the rice and Nancy does the cattle ranching. We have a full-time staff of eight. We get up at 5.30 and go to bed at 10.30, although at planting and harvesting we work longer and I may get only three or four hours of sleep a night for weeks on end. This is the American thing, you know, working hard and reaping the benefits. It's our country's strength and we have to make sure we keep those incentives. We don't work much on Sundays unless we are harvesting or planting, and we go to mass as a family, and I teach Sunday school. We are conservative people, and we are suspicious of politicians. We vote both Democrat and Republican, depending on the elections and who is running: we vote the man. We take an interest in the world. We have to. As a rice grower I have to know what's happening in Thailand, and what the dollar is doing. As for the Russians, well, I think that they are just as good as you and me and I'd like to see Russians and Americans getting closer together. We should try to know more about them.

We have Mexican workers on the farm, including a Mexican cowboy to help Nancy with the cattle, and we take on more at the busy times. I speak Spanish as a matter of necessity. Farming around here needs Mexican labour. Americans won't do the work because they're spoilt. In any case we can't afford American salaries. Mexican people have to work. They put in long hours and have a good attitude to the job and they take home a good cheque. As long as farming is alive in Texas you'll have people coming across the border. That's how things work round here.

Farming isn't the settled business people imagine. It is always changing. You have to look ahead. One of the things we know is going to happen, although we deplore it, is that Houston will keep on spreading. Nancy says it's a moving monster coming towards us. In the future this area will grow houses. Nothing can stop Houston growing over the top of us. Our way of life will change. In ten years things will be very different round here. But these homes will need trees for their gardens, so we are planting 1500 evergreen oaks, which will be ready in five years. I've also broadened my base by becoming a rice broker as well as a grower. I get a commission for selling other farmers' rice. I have a rice sales office and the equipment to analyse the grain.

You're looking at a happy man. We have faith in God. There are strains but life can still be simple. We don't like going to Houston with all that hustle and bustle, dog eat dog, and standing in line to get a table in a restaurant. People just lose their sense of what they're in the world for. I love this land and I like to stay around the house. We don't go out much and everything we want is here. My main relaxation is flying. I started flying when I was a high school senior. Most farmers have an airstrip and my planes only need an 800 ft strip. I use them to inspect the crops and I go up for the fun of it, too. We may not go out much but we don't shut ourselves away. Neighbours and other people drop in for coffee. They just knock on the door and walk right in. It's easy-going and people needn't be shy. In the evening we sit on the porch and relax and look out over the land and talk about tomorrow.

*　　　*　　　*

At the Dallas press club someone asked me which I liked better –
Dallas or Houston. I said: 'Dallas, of course' – and there was a
little whoop of approval and the club president gave me a
membership card, writing on it that I was a member 'Forever'.
People understood perfectly well that had I been asked the
question in Houston I would have said: 'Houston, of course'.

Born about the same time, in the 1830s and 1840s, Houston
and Dallas are the great sibling rivals of Texas. Houston is Tom
Sawyer and Dallas is Sid. Dallas sees Houston as unruly and
feckless, the muscular hole-in-the-trousers roughneck, a cowboy
in the pejorative sense of the word. It notes with satisfaction that
Houston has made a mess of its development. Houston thinks
Dallas pretentious, sanctimonious and rather Swiss with its
emphasis on cleanliness, order and soulless piling up of money. It
says there is no honest dirt under Dallas's manicured fingernails.
Houston is oil and Dallas the oil banker, and while Houston
thinks itself more virile, Dallas considers itself more civilised. It
was irritating to Dallas that the first word uttered by man on the
moon was 'Houston . . . the Eagle has landed'. And Houston has
been piqued ever since 1978 when the first episode of the
television series *Dallas* was screened and the skyline title seque-
nce made Dallas known around the world.

Curiously enough, Dallas believes that this saga of glamorous,
back-stabbing Texas folk has played a part in the rehabilitation of
the city's image. There was a time when the word Dallas seemed
to hang in the air like a bloody dagger. A television executive told
me: 'People who were in Dallas when President Kennedy was
assassinated remember the contempt in other Americans' faces
when they told them where they came from. They felt the whole
world blamed them for the murder, that they had a big capital K,
for Kennedy, branded on their foreheads. The Kennedy thing
was their albatross.'

Dallas came to resent being made to feel guilty for the assassination: Los Angeles was not blamed for the murder of Robert
Kennedy, nor Memphis for Martin Luther King's. But Dallas
had for years been amassing reasons for America to snarl at it. It

exemplified Texan crudeness. It was full of new money, conservative, staid, churchy, self-righteous, violent and greedy. (So, of course, were other American cities.) It had also developed a streak of fanaticism, an outgrowth of its reactionary politics, and some of its religious fundamentalists were strident. Wallie Amos Criswell, pastor of the First Baptist Church in Dallas, declared that the election of John Kennedy would mean the death of religious freedom in America and that Catholics should be banned from holding any public office. (Still going strong, Dr Criswell spoke the benediction after President Reagan's acceptance speech at the 1984 Republican convention in Dallas.) Extremist conservatives spat at Lyndon Johnson and his wife when they were in Dallas in 1960, and gave a rough ride to Adlai Stevenson, the ambassador to the United Nations, a month before Kennedy's death. Such ugly events gave Dallas a bad name. After the assassination Americans raged at Dallas's arrogance, uncouthness and hypocrisy. Parts of America, contemplating Dallas, saw themselves in a mirror and lashed out. Dallas became a dirty word. The song 'I'm from Big D' was no longer heard. Even the Dallas judge who administered the presidential oath to Lyndon Johnson aboard Air Force One remarked that Dallas was 'a city of hate, the only American city in which the president could have been shot.'

Twenty years after the killing, Lawrence Wright, a Dallas resident, wrote in *Texas Monthly*:

The hatred directed at our city was retaliation for many grievances. The east hated us because we were conservative, labour because we were non-labour, intellectuals because we were raw, minorities because we were predominantly white, atheists and agnostics because we were strident believers, the poor because we were rich, the old because we were new. There were few constituencies that we had failed to offend before the president came to our city, and hadn't we compounded the offence again and again by boasting of those very qualities?

Dallas people sought to come to terms with the unexpungeable. There was always more than the drab concrete Kennedy Memor-

ial to remind them. Elm Street, Houston Street, the triple under-
pass, the grassy knoll, the Texas school book depository – all were
features of the notoriety. The place where the President was shot
is still a principal attraction. Visitors gather every day, from early
morning until far into the night, at the junction of Elm and
Houston. They stand reflectively or gather to read the historic
monument plaque on the wall of the school book depository.
Sometimes there is a hot dog pushcart on the pavement, a recent
innovation to make the streets seem less sterile, and the salesman
answers questions as he serves.

There was a time when people wanted the depository torn
down, as if that would eradicate the stain. But keeping it was part
of the way Dallas learnt to live with 1963. The county bought the
building in 1977 and made it the seat of local government,
renaming it the county administration building, though to most
people it will always be the Texas school book depository. Shirley
Caldwell, chairman of the Dallas historical commission, took me
up the creaking wooden staircase to the sixth floor. It was vast and
dusty and, apart from a pile of old furniture, was bare. In 1963 it
had been filled with books. In the far corner is the window from
which Oswald fired his mail-order rifle. From this position there
is no longer the unobstructed view of the road that he had, for the
branches of a tree have spread and cast a shadow over the place
where the bullets struck. Brickwork around the window has been
chipped and fragments taken away by souvenir hunters. The
original window frame was looted as a souvenir. As we looked
onto the street Mrs Caldwell said:

The pain lingered for a long time in Dallas and this building was part of
the emotion. It was understandable that some people wanted it demolished, but, with time, we have become more objective. We think
Dallas has an obligation to history. It is not ghoulish interest that brings
people to this spot. It is simply that we Americans are fascinated by our
history. The assassination was traumatic. People are drawn by a need to
know more, so that they can try to understand it all.

The historical commission was planning a permanent public

exhibit on the sixth floor to be called, simply, The Sixth Floor, an exhibition of photographs and text, with a diorama of the streets below as they were in 1963. The area around the sniper's perch would be boxed off and left empty. Films of the assassination would be run continuously, and film and tape would evoke the political flavour of the early 1960s, describing how John Kennedy came to Texas to mend fences in his own party. Displays were planned to show world reaction to the murder, the official investigation by the Warren Commission and the ballistic aspects of the shooting.

Dallas is a centre for assassination studies and the public library has a section with hundreds of books on the event and a large collection of report and news clippings. Large collections of assassination material are also in amateur hands. A local archivist has amassed so much that her husband has built an extra room for it. A thriving coterie of assassination buffs constantly rework the conspiracy theories, the mafia theory, the big business theory, the KGB theory, the Kennedy-survived theory, in newsletters like *Continuing Inquiry, Grassy Knoll Gazette* and *Echoes of Conspiracy*.

By the mid-1980s the place where Kennedy was killed was no longer the most-visited in Dallas. It was relegated to second position by Southfork Ranch, thirty-five miles north, the star building of the *Dallas* business western in which desks take the place of horses, high leather chairs are saddles and corporate towers are the open range. It is a curious aspect of television celebrity that so many people should want to journey to see a house famous only for being a stage set for fictional characters. But there: Larry Hagman, who plays the cruel J.R. Ewing, is a celebrity in the city as if he were a real oil magnate; and Linda Gray, who plays Mrs Ewing, and is billed as an oil queen, was once invited to a White House dinner for the king of Saudi Arabia. The ranch house, built by Mr J.R. Duncan in 1970, is just an ordinary rich man's mansion. Visitors walk around the grounds, look at the cattle installed for their benefit, and buy souvenirs. When *Dallas* started Dallas sniffed, but it is now proud of it even if *Dallas* has little to do with Dallas. It is ironic that J.R. Ewing is so popular in Dallas. With his menacing Stetson, alligator smile and membership of the Brutal Tendency, he is a character out of the bad old image of Dallas that was held up for excoriation after the assassination of the President, the image that Dallas struggled to live down.

Dallas's earnest wish to be loved was one reason why it sought and won the Republican convention in 1984. The event offered redemption as well as profit. Dallas paraded its virtues. It has no smog, no mafia and no union battles, for Texans hate unions and prohibit closed shops. It is orderly and clean and the dustmen do not spill. Large parts of the city are dry, and in those that are not the favourite drink is white wine, which hardly accords with the Texan image. Jaywalking is forbidden, and it is an amazing spectacle, in a Texan city of all places, to see people waiting obediently at kerbs, as compliant as Canadians.

Dallas is run by the business community, devoted to making it clean and decent, a sort of rule by Rotary Club, a pragmatic oligarchy which believes a good quality of life is good for business. In the early 1960s these bosses heeded the storm warnings on segregation. They noted the violence that erupted in cities where the overthrow of American apartheid was resisted, and knew that redneck revolt in Dallas would be bad for trade. The city's black leaders were called in and told that on a certain day businesses, restaurants and hotels hitherto barred to blacks would be de-segregated. The blacks' responsibility was to enter these places. The city's bosses ordered white businesses to fall into line and on the appointed day blacks and whites ate at the same lunch counters. There was no trouble: business as usual. Nevertheless, there are racial tensions. In a few years Dallas will be half white and half minority. Whites have moved to the suburbs. The heart of the city is now largely black and the growing number of Mexican immigrants, legal and illegal, compete with blacks for work.

*   *   *

Dallas is well garrisoned by churches, a fundamentalist stronghold, and is one of the most self-consciously religious cities in the
land. There are 1300 churches and, according to the official
guide, 57 per cent of the population are active church members.
The Dallas Fellowship of Christian Athletes boasts 8000 members. It can be helpful to their careers for businessmen to show an
interest in a church, for this is a city of robust mercantile views of
Christianity. Emphasising the city's devoutness, the official guide
says: 'Religious faith plays a visibly active role in the personal,
civic and business lives of many Dallasites . . . religion is an
integral part of business and civic structure . . . it is not in the least
remarkable for a businessman to start the day with a Bible study
breakfast, or to overhear a conversation in a highrise office
building about a church project.' At the Republican convention
here each delegate was given a bag containing guides, literature
and gifts and, until there were objections, it was originally
proposed that a New Testament should be included. Having
been instructed in the extent of the city's piety, it was with
surprise that I read in the *Dallas Times-Herald* that: 'Morganna
Roberts, known as Morganna the Kissing Bandit, was arrested
Thursday night at a Dallas nightclub on a public lewdness
complaint. Police said she was arrested after allegedly beating a
customer over the head with her breasts during a striptease
performance.'

Dallas reveres both God and money, and there is a certain
flexibility in its ideas, enabling men to pursue one or the other, or
both. A Texan woman told me of a member of her family who, on
the failure of his company, announced he would go into 'the
preachin' business'. Dr Criswell, leader of the largest church in
town, and a millionaire, is at heart an entrepreneur who once said
that were he not a preacher he would be a businessman – 'I would
love to make money just for the challenge of it.' Under his
stewardship his church has become the largest single landowner
in central Dallas, with an array of buildings, including broadcasting stations, parking garages – and a church – on land worth $200
million. As he has grown older and richer he has become tolerant

of Catholics and moderated his vehement line against divorce since his daughter divorced twice.

As I drove out of Dallas the vitrified core of the city, lit by sunset Technicolor, filled my rear view mirror. There were huge billboards by the highway promoting the latest country music hits – 'If today was a fish I'd throw it back in' and 'I was hung up on you till you hung up on me'. Other hoardings proclaimed We Believe In You, Dallas, as if this spreading city still needs reassurance. Enormous new buildings were coming up like a harvest. Everywhere I looked there were conquering banks and churches, pardners on the prairie.

We had lift-off. The cowboy departed the saddle of his bronc and described a high arc while the crowd whooped. He had a brief elevated view of the Texas state prison at Huntsville, the death house, the rodeo arena like a Roman stadium, the thousands of people in hats-and-jeans uniform. He fell with a thump in the red dirt. Years ago there were many real cowboys in jail and the rodeo started as a way of letting them practice their bronco-busting and bull-riding skills. These days there are fewer cowpokes, but prisoners still like the rodeo and spend months training for it. Only well-behaved convicts have the privilege of risking their necks. Death row men do not get the chance. One of the events was called 'hard money'. Prisoners entered the arena and in charged the fiercest bull in the show with a $400 prize in a pouch tied to its horns. Men were tossed like rag dolls before one of them lunged and grabbed the purse. I asked one of the prisoner-cowboys what he thought of criticism that the rodeo is dangerous and degrading. 'Dangerous, a bit. Degrading, no. We love it. It gives us something to live for. We are out in the open, people like you, from the free world, are taking our pictures, we feel we count for something. A lot of guys here have never been winners, but this gives us pride. People can see we are human, not monsters, just guys who fell off the tightrope. And it's a bit of real old Texas.'

4 Holding Out

Montana, Wyoming, South Dakota

And the thunder in the mountains,
Whose innumerable echoes
Flap like eagles in their eyries

HENRY WADSWORTH LONGFELLOW

L IKE ALL BATTLEFIELDS this is a place for reflection. It lies in rolling high plains country where there are few natural shields against ferocious winters and roasting summers. Its roughness and emptiness remind me of the less accessible stretches of Dartmoor and the Brecon Beacons, a ravined landscape of weed, sagebrush and coarse brown grass through which the wind hisses in melancholy emphasis of the desolation. From this exposed ridge in eastern Montana, across the swells of land, I can see the distant Bighorn mountains, a good seventy miles off to the south, and, far to the west, the palisades of the Rockies. It is an evocative and enthralling place, and because of its remoteness only the more serious pilgrims journey here.

From the top of the slope the view of the battlefield is clear. At the bottom, half a mile to the south, the Little Bighorn river snakes among cottonwood trees. On the far bank, in June 1876, camped the Hunkpapa Sioux, led by Sitting Bull; the Oglala Sioux, headed by Crazy Horse; and their allies, the Cheyenne, the Brulé Sioux, Minneconjou Sioux, Arapaho and Sans Arc. Their tipis and wickiups, rough shelters of sticks, were stretched along three miles of the river bank, and while no one can say how many people were camped there – estimates run to more than 12,000, including 4000 warriors – they were the last great concentration of American Indians, free in wild country, before the shadow of the civilising white man blotted out their light.

Onto this hummocky, creek-veined slope rode George Armstrong Custer, 36 years old, impetuous as always, anxious for action, certain that his 7th Cavalry could whip anything. He was by nature no man for the shrewd and appraised approach. His style was the drawn revolver and the headlong death-or-glory charge. On that hot Sunday afternoon he sought the smashing victory that would serve as redemption and make him the hero of the land. Headstrong and careless, he thrust his hand into the hornets' nest. This panorama of the undulating high plains was his last view. About halfway down the slope the warriors fell upon him and his men, forcing them up the hill and off their horses. Choking dust billowed up like pyre smoke. More Indians made their way behind the ridge, where the granite monument now stands, and closed the circle. Custer's renowned luck evaporated.

The place where his naked body was found, shot through the side and head, is marked by a small white stone inscribed: G.A. Custer Bvt. Maj. Gen. Lt. Col. 7th Cav fell here June 25 1876. Custer had reached the brevet, or temporary, rank of major-general at the age of 25 during the Civil War, having established a reputation for recklessness and bravery. On the reorganisation of the army in 1866 he became a lieutenant-colonel in the newly formed 7th Cavalry, the rank he held for the rest of his uneven and blemished career. At the time of his death he was fortunate to have a job at all. Earlier that year, at a congressional inquiry into corruption involving the sale of traderships on Indian reservations, he tactlessly implicated President Grant's brother. The furious President stripped Custer of his command. Custer, by one account, went to a senior officer and pleaded on his knees for a command in the expeditions being formed to crush the militant Sioux on the plains. The President relented and Custer was back in the saddle, looking for a coup to reestablish himself.

On Last Stand Hill, in a small space enclosed by black iron railings, are fifty-two stones. They mark the places where Custer, his brothers Tom and Boston, his nephew Auty, and other officers and men were found. Spread out over the slope are other stones, alone or in small clusters, showing where the strewn bodies of the 7th were discovered by horrified soldiers two days after the battle. There is no certainty about the number killed: accounts vary between 215 and 260. Custer and his five companies certainly died with their boots on, but the Indians took the boots, along with weapons, clothing and scalps. They left many of the cavalrymen decapitated, handless and otherwise mutilated, just as soldiers used to mutilate Indians. Custer was not scalped and some have suggested he was spared this indignity as a warriors' tribute to a brave man. More likely, because the famous cavalier locks were prematurely thinning and had, in any case, been cut short, the meagre scalp was not worth having. The Indians were not aware at the time that they were fighting Custer.

His bones no longer lie here. Remains reputed to be his were disinterred fifteen months after the battle and installed at the United States Military Academy, West Point, in New York state. As a cadet Custer had finished bottom of the class and had been noted for slovenliness. His bones were trumpeted as glorious relics of the march of civilisation and symbols of ascendant American virtue. Most of the men who died with him were buried in a grave where the monument bearing their names now stands; and some of the other relics of the fight lie under glass at the battlefield museum nearby: bullets, belts, cartridges, bugles, guns, arrowheads, spurs, notebooks, buttons, badges and boots. In 1983 a fire cleared large areas of previously impenetrable scrub on the battlefield, giving historians an unexpected opportunity to examine it with metal detectors. They found nearly 5000 fragments of bone, bullets, pieces of weapons and other scraps which enabled them to plot the paths of bullets and the places where men fell.

Headlines in the special edition of the *Bismarck Tribune*, eleven days after the battle, reported: No Officer or Man of 5 Companies Left to Tell the Tale . . . Squaws Mutilate and Rob the Dead . . . Shall This Be the Beginning of the End? America roared in rage and demanded vengeance. Reporting the 'terrible disaster' *The Times* of London said that, 'every effort will be made to put a large force in the field against the Sioux, it being feared that these disasters may have a demoralising effect on other tribes heretofore placable.' Americans were astonished that Indians had defeated white soldiers, though the truth was that the 7th Cavalry, like other frontier units, was a rough lot of men, many of them ill-trained and inexperienced.

Custer may have hoped to provide Americans with a victory as a present for the centenary of their independence on 4 July, and perhaps saw himself riding through the streets in triumph, dressed in one of the gorgeous uniforms he liked to fashion for himself. When he set off on his expedition a fellow officer warned him, 'Now Custer, don't be greedy . . .' Sitting Bull said Custer was 'a fool, and rode to his death,' an opinion shared by some army officers. President Grant, no admirer, said bluntly that the last stand was 'a sacrifice of troops, brought on by Custer himself, wholly unnecessary.'

But the people would have none of it. Custer's death was not for long regarded as defeat or humiliation. For Americans who longed for legends of their own, to help in the defining of their society, the last stand was magnificent, an epic. Imperial America knew as well as imperial Britain how to sentimentalise a bloody debacle, how to translate it into noble sacrifice, to legendise it, to deceive. Custer and the hapless 7th became as one with the Greek defenders of the pass at Thermopylae, with Horatius defending the Tiber bridge, with Crockett and the resisters of the Alamo, with the Charge of the Light Brigade.

Custer was crowned with laurel, heaped with immortelles. Sentiment gushed from the nation's poets. Walt Whitman, caught up in the fever, wrote of the battle's 'trumpet-note for heroes' and extolled Custer, the golden boy, as 'Thou of the sunny, flowing hair, in battle/ I erewhile saw, with erect head, pressing ever in front, bearing a bright sword in thy hand.' Custer and his men did not use swords at the Little Bighorn: they had no value against Indians armed with rifles and the bows with which they could shoot arrows at an astounding rate. Still, the poets' task was enshrinement. They even wrote in honour of the cavalry horse Comanche, the only survivor of Custer's force. Comanche was honoured and on his death was stuffed and now resides in a glass case at the University of Kansas.

Artists, too, composed heroic depictions of the last stand, showing Custer in the middle of the fight, beside the flag, his sabre flashing. Like the images created by the poems, the drama of the paintings etched in the public mind an impression of Custer that has endured and defied all revision. The last stand continues to be invoked and in many American minds retains its original splendour. Even in 1876 it was an element of American wistfulness for a vanishing frontier, part of the half-fantastic wild west.

As 20th-century political image-makers know, first impressions lodge like jammed anchors. Custer became a frontier icon, annihilation covering him with more glory than victory ever could. By the manner of his dying he founded an industry whose strength has not diminished. No American has been so frequently resurrected in book, painting, poem and film. His bibliography is vast, 900 books and studies, including the inevitable *Custer: a Psychoanalytic Approach*. In 1985, when visitors to the battlefield increased by a fifth, Evan Connell's Custer work *Son of the Morning Star* was on the bestseller list for much of the year. Custer himself published *My Life on the Plains* two years before the battle, and the first biography of him was out by the end of 1876, a canonisation that matched the public mood. This was followed by Elizabeth Custer's trilogy, starting with *Boots and Saddles*, that lauded her husband's memory. Shd died at 91 in 1933 and until the end was a staunch defender of her husband, an unrelenting critic of the officers she thought had betrayed him. In one of the thirteen Custer films, *Santa Fé Trail*, made in 1940, Custer was played by Ronald Reagan. That film also starred Errol Flynn who, the next year, played Custer in what turned out to be the apogee of the last stand dramas, *They Died With Their Boots On*. Members of Custer societies, like the Little Bighorn Associates, wear cavalry uniforms, name their children after Custer and his wife, hold conventions and rake over the old ground, not least the seething politics of the frontier cavalry. Custer schools of thought are as divided as ever. One holds that he was a brute and a fool, the other that he was a dashing and imperishable example to the young. The questions of Little Bighorn are still debated. Did Custer disobey General Terry's orders by leaving a prescribed route? Terry himself said he did and that Custer would have been court-martialled for disobedience had he survived. Some think there was a flexibility in the orders and that Custer wanted to strike before the Indians could move away. Why did Custer divide his force into three? Could Captain Frederick Benteen and Major Marcus Reno, his subordinates, have done anything for him? Had they tried would they and their men have been butchered, too? The last stand left a host of minor myths, but the stories of supposed survivors and white eye-witnesses have been discredited; Custer did not shoot himself, as one tale has it, and there is no reason to think he was the last to fall.

Custer was known to Indians as Long Hair the Squaw Killer for the massacre of women and children at an Indian camp. In the army he was called Iron Ass and known as a martinet who flogged soldiers for petty offences, in defiance of the prohibition of flogging. Life was bad enough in the frontier army without Custer making it worse. Troopers were badly fed and diseased, morale was low and the suicide and desertion rate high. Deserters were sometimes branded as well as whipped. Custer was hard on them, but he himself was court-martialled in 1867 for going absent without leave and for ordering deserters summarily shot. He was suspended without pay for a year and his war record probably saved him from dismissal. Many troopers and officers despised him for his cruelty and arrogance.

It took some time for Custer's darker side and record to be widely exposed. For some whites in recent times he came to represent the ugliness of white expansion, the genocidal stain. For Indians, too, he has always been a demon. During the revival of Indian consciousness in the 1960s and 1970s his name appeared on the bumper stickers which are one of the means by which Americans talk to each other: Custer Had It Coming. Custer Died For Your Sins.

Whether as hero or anti-hero, Custer serves a purpose as a national totem. He was neither a great man nor a good soldier. But nations must sometimes fashion heroes from inadequate clay. What is interesting about Custer is not so much the man himself, rather why he and the last stand exert enduring fascination. Though his reputation has been frequently assailed by historian demolition experts, he has not disappeared. On the contrary, he is a boulder of a legend lodged in the national memory. If one believes that societies derive a necessary stimulus from their myths and legends, like a secreted hormone, Custer has served his country well; better than he served it as a soldier. He is there to mean what people want him to mean: last of the cavaliers, martyr, exterminator, scoundrel, frontier hero, fool, an echo of a nation's rosily remembered adolescence, resident of the American pantheon.

The Times of London commented that the defeat of Custer was more insult than injury, that the conduct of the American government towards plains Indians had been neither kindly nor wise, and that the Indians would be driven either to death or to remote and barren reservations. Little Bighorn was an incident in the climactic collision between westering whites and the natives of the plains, particularly the Sioux who roamed from the Missouri river to the Bighorn mountains. The catalyst in this showdown was the discovery of gold in the Black Hills of Dakota. Under the treaty of Laramie of 1868 the Black Hills, which were holy to the Sioux, were ceded to them 'for as long as rivers run and grass grows and trees bear leaves'. In the event the treaty lasted as long as gold was not found. When it was discovered the government gave way under the pressure of greed and of manifest destiny, the idea that Americans had a sacred duty to develop the continent. Unable to command the tide of miners, the government tried to buy the Black Hills from the Indians it was pledged to protect. When this failed it sought to corral them under its control in reservations. Defiant and proud, some of the great chiefs refused to be penned. After Little Bighorn the Indians were rapidly worn down, killed off and confined, their leaders murdered. Little

Bighorn was called Custer's last stand; but in reality it was the last stand of the free Indians of the plains. Their descendants live today under the burden of the unresolved questions of their conquest.

Sheriff France had invited me to breakfast. I drove away from the battlefield, past the dilapidated houses of the Crow Indian reservation on which it lies, and headed west for 120 miles into the outriders of the Rocky Mountains. Bettie's Café, in the small town of Ennis, was packed with people eating eggs, pancakes and fried potatoes, healthy-looking people with pink faces, thick plaid shirts, jeans and hats. Quite soon the door opened and Sheriff France stood framed. Everyone looked up and said howdy and Sheriff France looked around and nodded and said howdy and touched his broad-brimmed hat to the ladies. He gave me his card: Madison County Sheriff – Johnny France. Here was no stomach-over-the-gunbelt lawman, not one of those slovenly and truculent gum-chewing cops one sometimes sees in America. You wouldn't catch him with a lollipop in his mouth. He was the picture of western shrieval authority, the good gun, as lean as Gary Cooper, his eyes sharp and blue. His slim-fit brown shirt was crisply pressed, his sheriff's star glinted and a pearl-handled Colt .45 rested on his hip. His belt buckle was a trophy, proclaiming him Montana's champion bronco buster. In his time he had been a ranch hand, mountain guide, policeman and rodeo cowboy. 'I blend with the country,' he said. He was soft-spoken and polite and assured. He looked a tough man and he came from tough stock. His grandfather had five children by five wives and died at 84 when he broke his neck falling out of an apple tree.

Sheriff France was on his biggest case, a manhunt, and he was under pressure to make a capture. People wanted results and one of the state senators had just written to him. There were grumbles in the newspapers. The sheriff had led an intensive search in the mountains but had found nothing. The Rockies in these parts, rising to more than 11,000 feet, are one of the wildest areas of

America, trackless, thickly forested, the haunt of mountain sheep and bears. As the sheriff saw it, his quarry Donald Nichols had become obsessed with the mountains, and had begun to see himself as a mountain man, an old-time trapper and hunter, living rough and rarely coming down to town. He became filled with the idea that he and his son Daniel could live an innocent leather-stocking existence in the forests. 'Daniel Nichols fell under his daddy's spell,' the sheriff said. 'Don was possessed by his dream and he and the boy just slipped over into this fantasy. But the boy was 19 and needed female company. The old man thought they should get a bride for him, kidnap a girl and make her live with them in the mountains.'

One morning they abducted a pretty woman of 23, an athlete on a training run through the forest in the Madison range. They sprang from the trees, carried her away and chained her to a fallen tree, and disclosed their bizarre plan that she should become the boy's mate. Don Nichols tied his son's wrist to the girl's in symbolic marriage. Next morning, two searchers stumbled across the camp and startled the men. Daniel Nichols' pistol went off accidentally and the girl fell back with a bullet in her chest. One of the searchers shouted: 'Drop your guns, you're surrounded.' But the ploy failed. Don Nichols killed him with a rifle shot through the head. The other searcher ran to get help. The Nichols men unchained the girl and fled, and she crawled into a sleeping bag to protect herself against shock. Sheriff France and a search party found her and she eventually recovered.

The sheriff and his deputies, with game wardens, foresters and ranchers, combed the forests and mountains, and the sheriff rode his four horses into weariness. He searched on foot and from the air, painstakingly criss-crossing the thousands of square miles of wilderness, pursuing hundreds of claimed sightings. 'They could be anywhere in the Rockies. But I know something of Don's mind and I reckon he and the boy are here in the country they know best, perhaps in a cave, taking care how they light fires, living like animals. Don is dominating that boy, but Daniel still has a chance of a decent life if we can catch them. Don is well armed and dangerous. It's a waiting game now. Winter is coming and it gets bitter in the mountains.' The sheriff drained his coffee cup and rose to leave. He smiled. 'The next chapter in the story is when we get them. Come back and write it.'

I went to Virginia City, and saw Daryl Tichenor, owner-editor of the local newspaper, *The Madisonian*. If anyone could crack the case, he said, it was Sheriff France – 'Johnny's a tough guy, a real hot-shot western sheriff.' He had no doubt that his paper would eventually report the fugitives' capture.

The Madisonian was founded in 1873 when Virginia City was an unruly gold mining town and the capital of Montana territory. Its files are absorbing for frontier fossickers. In an advertisement in 1874 a doctor promised to cure gonorrhea in 72 hours and syphilis in five days. Five years later the newspaper was full of advertisements for grocers, stage coach lines, railroads, bootmakers, gunsmiths, horse sellers, saloons, gold buyers, wagon builders, livery stables and saddlers. In 1879 the newspaper published letters from the commissioner of the Office of Indian Affairs to the governor of Montana about 'the roaming habits of the Indian, and the annoyance to which settlers are subjected.' He complained that 'the interchange of visits between Indians on widely separated reservations is very objectionable, especially in cases where the route of travel from one reservation to the other necessitates frequent contact with white settlements.' He directed that 'Indians travelling without permits or police escorts should be treated as hostiles and arrested and punished.' In the same edition it was reported that an Indian chief ordered to a new reservation at Fort Hall told a cavalry officer: 'I am not going to Fort Hall, and you have not soldiers enough to take me. I know how it is. For a week or two we will be fed and cared for, and then we will starve. There is no game in that country. We will not go. We will live on the Yellowstone where we can find something to eat.' For the time being the Indians stayed put.

In 1885 the paper's account of a boxing match said that 'Murphy, the Butte slogologist, defeated Harian, the Idaho 'ard 'itter, in two rounds.' For 'Private Diseases and Seminal

Weakness and Lost Manhood' doctors advertised 'The Great
English Remedy'. A report from New Mexico, headlined Apache
Devils, said cavalry were pursuing a band of Apaches who had
killed about sixty people. A dispatch from Arizona said: 'The
bodies of Col. Philips' family, murdered by Apaches, have been
brought in. All are horribly mutilated. The citizens are frantic
that such outrages should be perpetuated without check.' There
were reports that a local soldier died after a knife duel and that
'Yellowstone cowboys sent two Indian cattle-thieves to the happy
hunting grounds last week.'

When that was published, Virginia City was past its goldrush
heyday. It lost its place as territorial capital to a mining town that
had started out as Last Chance Gulch but later called itself
Helena, and is now the state capital. Virginia City might have
rotted away, a ghost town, but it was restored in the 1940s and is
now a tourist stop. Any stranger feels he knows it intimately, for
he has ridden through it in a hundred westerns. Today it has a
newspaper office, three bars, two lawyers, a courthouse, drug-
store, county office, sheriff's office and a jail. The population is
about 200 in the summer, 125 in the winter. *The Madisonian*'s
editor bought the newspaper for $2000 and runs it with his wife.
The local people, he said, are engaged mostly in ranching and
agriculture and are conservative-minded, not easily stirred up, do
not like government and do not want change. It is a quiet enough
life, he conceded, and he did not feel that the paper needed an
editorial in every edition, especially if there was nothing to write
about. 'I write an editorial if I get mad enough,' he said; and he
did not look a man who gets mad often.

As it turned out, Sheriff France was justified in his confidence.
He never relaxed his pursuit of the mountain men. He picked up
their trail in the snow, followed it for four miles on foot and surprised them in their camp. He had his gun ready and they did not
resist. They had been fugitives for nearly six months. The boy was
jailed for twenty years; his father's sentence was eighty-five years.

*   *   *

I headed south to Wyoming and into Yellowstone national park where the leaking landscape seems to be cooking like an immense pie. Steam splutters from the fractured crust and rolls in billowing cannon plumes. Geysers gurgle and whoosh and the air is filled with sulphurous smells.

Not long before, a young woman who had been backpacking alone in a remote part of the park had been dragged from her tent in the night and eaten by a grizzly bear. A few days later a grizzly entered a campsite in the park and pulled a boy from his tent, injuring his arm. A naturalist and her husband who surprised a grizzly sow with her cubs were slashed before the bear broke off the attack. These incidents intensified the argument about the survival of grizzlies and their relationship with people. Tom Hobbs, chief ranger of Yellowstone, said to me that the killing of a human being by a bear was bound to be sensational. 'Everyone has an opinion on bears, and the letters I get cover the ground between the extremes of those who say people should be kept out of the wild backcountry to give the bears a chance, and those who say bears should be exterminated to make the backcountry safe for people.' Grizzlies present the managers of Yellowstone with the controversial and difficult task of providing a habitat in which bears flourish, and also a park that people can enjoy in relative safety, aims not readily compatible. 'Whose park is it anyway?' people ask.

Grizzly bears, graded as a threatened species, are the most splendid and formidable of north American animals, up to eight feet from nose to short tail and weighing 40 stone (560 pounds) when fully grown. A bear of 80 stone was recorded in a recent survey. There are between 600 and 800 left in the lower 48 states and Yellowstone is their heartland, the home of about 200. They are remarkable feeders and eat insects, grasses, berries, roots, pine nuts, small animals, fish, eggs and, occasionally, deer. They can produce an explosive burst of speed, forty miles an hour, to bring down a deer. Sustained by tyres of fat eight inches thick, they enter their dens during the last two weeks of November and emerge after their winter torpor in mid-March.

Grizzlies rarely kill people and prefer to keep away from them. Only five people were killed by grizzlies in Yellowstone between the park's opening in 1872 and 1985. Car crashes and drowning are greater hazards, and so are bison. People get out of their cars to pose for photographs beside them, and sometimes the bison become irritable and gore them. Yellowstone staff have difficulty convincing people that wild animals are really wild. The first recorded bear victim in Yellowstone was a man who poked some cubs with his umbrella and was killed by the cubs' mother. When a man was killed by a bear in 1971 his family sued the park and was awarded $87,000. The decision was reversed on appeal, but the case raised again the question of whether parks are for people or for animals. Some think parks should be made completely safe, finding nature's rawness inconvenient. People have sued Yellowstone after falling into the hot water of natural springs. In Yosemite national park, in the 1920s, woodpeckers were killed because a hotel guest complained of the noise they made.

Part of the problem is the bear's image. The teddy bear, named after President Theodore Roosevelt, and cartoon characters like Yogi Bear and Superted, have made bears seem approachable, cuddly and clownish. For almost a century bears were an entertainment at Yellowstone: grizzlies and geysers were the park's star attractions. For years feeding was an organised spectacle, with crowds around a large table marked 'Lunch Counter For Bears Only'. The black bear, which is smaller than the grizzly, was made into a beggar. People created 'bear jams' by stopping their cars to feed and photograph the animals. Two black bears had to be destroyed every month because of internal injuries caused by junk visitors fed them. Bears grew dependent on begging and, to their own disadvantage, began to lose their natural wariness of human beings. In 1967 authorities closed the rubbish dumps where bears foraged and prohibited feeding by visitors. Of course, bears have continued to hunt for food around campsites and summer cabins for they are persistent and clever, have an acute sense of smell and irrepressible curiosity. Troublesome ones are shot with drugged darts and hauled deep into the backcountry. Some recidivists, though, have had to be killed.

Park authorities believe bears can live entirely on their own resources and, in 1984, to keep people and bears apart, they started closing large areas of the 3400 square mile park to the public. The plan was to close areas in rotation, so that a fifth of the park would be closed at a time, inevitably causing annoyance to people denied access to their favourite places. 'It's a balancing act,' Chief Ranger Hobbs said in his office at Mammoth Hot Springs.

On one hand we have to ensure that the park is as safe as possible – it is, after all, a park. On the other, we have to preserve something of what Lewis and Clark saw when they first came to this region during their exploration. It has to remain wild. We try to raise the fear level of people, to make them more cautious. We don't want to scare them, but we want them to be more aware that this is a rugged place. 98 per cent of the people who travel through Yellowstone do so by car. But we have to cater to those who want adventure and go on foot.

Travellers in bear country are advised to go in groups, to wear bells and talk, so that bears can hear them coming, for they are particularly dangerous when surprised. Campers are warned to cook some distance from their tent, to store food high in the trees and to remove the clothing they wore while cooking before turning in. Bears are attracted by cosmetics and deodorants, and by odours created during menstruation and sexual intercourse. The sense of smell and inquisitiveness are exploited by poachers to lure bears into their gunsights. A single bear claw fetches more than $300 on the black market, while a skin can be sold for $10,000. Poaching is another threat to the bear's survival. Reduced and beleaguered, the Yellowstone grizzly makes a last stand and tests the national park ideal.

Yellowstone was the first national park, a remarkable act of conservation at a time when the country was being rapidly settled. Photographs and paintings revealed a grandeur that appealed at once to romantic ideas of a wild and noble landscape. Americans were relieved to know that this recognition of nature's nobility would cost them nothing: that there was no gold there. Yellowstone was so fantastic and far away that it might as well have been on the moon. Today the park is threatened by oil and gas exploration along its fringes. Many other parks are endangered by developers, poachers and prospectors. Large tracts of countryside in the United States and Canada are being damaged by dissolved sulphur emissions from power stations, smelters and other industrial plants which are carried downwind to fall as acid rain, killing trees and poisoning lakes and rivers. Pollution fogs the air in many parks where once 'you could see forever'. The dumped-upon Canadians are angry because the Americans are bad neighbours; but the United States government does not care enough about American land, let alone anyone else's.

According to Indian legend the vertical indentations on the Devil's Tower, in north-east Wyoming, were scratched by a great bear. The tower soars 1267 feet, a hard volcanic core formed at the time the Rockies and the Black Hills were moulded, more than 60 million years ago, and stands as a singular monument to creation. Indians called it Bear Lodge, but it was named Devil's Tower by an army officer during an expedition in 1875. The expedition violated Indian rights and followed an infringement of the previous year when Custer – 'chief of all thieves,' an Indian called him – led a survey which confirmed there was gold in the Black Hills. My route from Yellowstone took me over the high plains, past the Devil's Tower, through the Black Hills and the Badlands of South Dakota, to the Pine Ridge Sioux reservation and the creek, church and memorial at Wounded Knee.

The reservation, rarely visited by whites, covers more than 1500 square miles. It is bleak and largely treeless land, and its worthlessness is what commended it as a reservation to the authorities. The Sioux were meant to end their centuries of nomadic hunting and become sturdy farmers, to bury their culture and take to the plough. But the land is mostly unsuitable for growing crops. The small reservation settlements only add to the air of desolation. Their poverty is plain. Around the shacks and unkempt clapboard houses and trailers are rusting crumpled cars and heaps of junk. Dogs mooch about in the detritus. The road across the reservation tells a terrible story, for it is etched with twisting skid marks which, here and there, converge in patches of oil and fragments of glass, or just run off into the roadside grass. A symptom of despair among many of the people who live here, drink and drunken driving are leading causes of death.

The wooden church at Wounded Knee stands upon a bluff and below it is a scratched and scruffy green notice board bearing the legend: Massacre At Wounded Knee. The word massacre is painted over the word battle, originally employed to dignify the debacle here. I was impressed by the contrast between this shabby memorial and the one at Little Bighorn where whites and Indians tend the battlefield and there is an excellent museum, a careful recording and proper popularising of history. But at Wounded Knee there is just the sign, with rubbish and beer cans beneath it. In the small churchyard a stone pillar bears the names of some of those killed in the massacre – Spotted Thunder, Shoots the Bear, Picked Horses, Bear Cuts Body, Chase in Winter, No Ears, Wolfskin Necklace, Blue American, Scabbard Knife, Bird Shakes, High Hawk, Standing Bear and Pretty Hawk. These were in the group of 153 men, women and children killed when the 7th Cavalry, whose motto was Remember Custer, had their squalid revenge on 29 December, 1890.

It was the final blow, though there had been other demoralising wounds as the people were pauperised and reduced. Crazy Horse was murdered while in custody in 1877 and his heart lies buried near Wounded Knee. There is a memorial notice to him on the reservation, near Porcupine, defaced and holed by bullets. Sitting Bull lived to witness the humiliation of his crushed people and at one time took the tattered remnant of his tribe to Canada for four years but failed to find permanent sanctuary. The last flicker was in 1890, with the spread of the ghost dance religion, a neo-Christian messianism which preached non-violence and foretold that Indians would be restored to the prairies, with buffalo and horses and the old ways they knew before white men came. It was a pathetic twitch of life.

The ghost dancers worked themselves into trances and the authorities became alarmed. They ordered the arrest of Sitting Bull and on 15 December he was murdered by Indian police at the Standing Rock reservation in South Dakota. A fortnight later a band of Sioux surrendered to the army at Wounded Knee. Almost every Indian weapon had been handed over to the soldiers when a gun went off. The soldiers panicked and started firing indiscriminately. The Indians, mostly unarmed and terrified, scattered. The soldiers opened fire with machine guns, killing not only women and children but twenty-five of their own men. The soldiers gathered for a photograph as the Indians' frozen bodies were thrown into a pit. 'God seems to have forgotten us,' Chief Red Cloud remarked on the fate of the plains Indians.

Pine Ridge reservation today covers a whole county, the poorest in the United States. Its chief town, Pine Ridge, has a sign saying Welcome to Indian Territory. It is a listless and dismal little place with rundown housing, a shop, a café and a hairdresser's salon, several churches, the Bureau of Indian Affairs building, the tribal office and the post office, the smartest building in town.

In the struggle against plains Indians General William Sherman said they would have to be killed 'or maintained as a species of pauper'. And so they are. Many Sioux have not assimilated for they believe their identity would be subsumed. The 17,000 people on this reservation are among the weakest, sickest, most vulnerable of Americans. Unemployment is at 85 per cent. Here and at similar reservations most jobs are in the Bureau of Indian Affairs, in government offices, so that job-holders form an élite and many Indians think of work as being possible only within the system that effectively imprisons them. The people are shrivelled by poverty, depression and illness, the dependents of the government. The cynical say that the plight of the reservation Sioux demonstrates the worthlessness of welfare assistance. Indians have endured various government policies – extermination, isolation, assimilation and, for fifty years, an imposed and weak self-government alien to their traditions. After all these years they are still swindled and their reservation land still taken. There remains a divide between impatient whites and a once dignified and self-sufficient nomadic people. Their plight represents a failure of imagination and an enduring shame in an affluent society. They die for want of hope.

Charles Abourezk, a large and genial man, who wears his hair in Indian braids, met me at the reservation's radio station, which broadcasts in English and the tribal language. He was once the station's news director and is also a tribal attorney. He is not an Indian, but has married into the Oglala Sioux tribe and has six children who go to school on the reservation. His grandfather migrated from Lebanon in the last century and was given a ticket to the Rosebud reservation, to the east of Pine Ridge, where he set up as a storekeeper. His son James became a US senator and a champion of Indians, and Charles was raised on the reservation and has committed his life to Indians.

Children here grow up dependent, humiliated at the government offices, getting food as if it was United Nations relief. People go hungry and few have any prospect of work. When they leave the reservation they experience racism and coldness. They have never received fair treatment and the historical injustices weigh on them. Their health and educational facilities are poor and they have been robbed of initiative and self-esteem. The story here is a long one of official mismanagement. There is some good grazing land on the reservation, but most Indians cannot get loans to stock it. Their land is rented to non-Indians, but the money, their money, is controlled by the Bureau of Indian Affairs. In spite of everything, they still have their humour, their great family warmth, and even some optimism. I would say, though, that this optimism is diminishing because of bad economic conditions and because they have no voice.

Charles Abourezk is a supporter of the American Indian

Movement which, in the early 1970s, demanded a better deal for
Indians. Its militancy, which included the occupation of Wounded Knee and an armed confrontation with the authorities, was
controversial among Indians themselves, for many felt it would
make matters worse, and that its leaders were manipulators. But
others thought it a positive blow for Indian pride and a startling
reminder to Americans that Indians still existed. 'John Wayne
didn't shoot us all,' one of the radical leaders said wryly. But the
plight of Indians hardly bothers most Americans. There are only
about a million and the majority of Americans never see Indians
or know much about them.

I had tea with Father Joseph Sheehan, a Jesuit priest who had
worked at Pine Ridge for twelve years.

There is an unhappy story here. This place is a large concentration
camp. Indians were put here, got out of the way, by people who looked
on them as inferiors. Indians have a feeling of uselessness and frustra-
tion and they think they are considered savage. But it would be hard now
to change the rules and eliminate reservations, for Indians do not want
to disappear and the reservations are all they have. The land is their only
wealth.

They are bitter because they know what has been taken from them.
Their art, for example, is always of the past, and they do not have much
of a sense of where they are or where they can go. They want the simple
things that are so hard to get: justice, respect and equality. They feel
they are treated with contempt. As an example, let me tell you about the
white girl who taught at the Red Cloud school here. She is rather
Indian-looking, and when she tried to buy a car in Rapid City she was
subjected to snide comments about her ability to pay for it. When she
made clear she was not Indian the atmosphere changed. That is what
Indians go through. They can't get loans and they are treated as a group
and not as individuals. There is no bank here and only one big store, so
money naturally moves off the reservation.

The Reagan administration hurts Indians, who live marginally anyway. If the government cuts in health and welfare continue the government will be destroying a people, taking what little they have, taking
away hope. In the white man's dealings with the Indians the wrong
people have usually been in charge and greed and hatred have prevailed.

First there were the bad traders and then the army; and once you start dealing with people through an army you become alienated and contemptuous. To this day whites have a lawyer mentality in dealing with Indians, and Indians feel trapped, unable to meet the white man on his own terms. They constantly have to deal with crafty lawyers. On some reservations people fight an uphill battle for land, mineral and water rights. There is harassment, a constant pressure, attempts to take away part of the land. The Bureau of Indian Affairs is regarded with a sense of loss. It is mostly Indian-staffed, decent enough people but innocuous. It hasn't done its job of protecting its community.

I dread winters because I know I shall witness suffering. People go hungry. The money due to them does not come on time and they are humiliated and made to wait for it. It makes them angry and it makes me mad to see it. There is a lot of pessimism on this reservation, but optimism, too. White people make the mistake of taking a monolithic view of Indians. They have beautiful character. They are very openhanded and their greatest virtue is generosity. They survive because they share. We shouldn't romanticise them, for they have their weaknesses. But it is wrong to characterise them as alcoholics. They still have great dignity and they don't want pity. They want your respect. They are not going to go away. They show us that although we have sometimes been well-intentioned, we have hurt them terribly, that we have been evil and still are.

At the Rosebud Sioux reservation, forty miles from Pine Ridge, and home to 9000 people, Dr Clark Marquart said government cuts in Indian health services were scandalous.

Even by reservation standards the rates of death and illness here are exceptionally high. Half the people die before they reach 45. Diabetes kills at three-and-a-half times the national rate, influenza at four times, and tuberculosis thirteen times. There's a denial of health care and conditions are so bad and money so restricted that we can send only life-and-death cases to hospital. We run out of vital drugs from time to time. The hospital is decaying and half the building is condemned.

Reservations get some conscientious doctors, young and highly motivated, and they also get impostors, incompetents and cranks. Many come to pay off a public-service obligation to the government and get out as quickly as they can. In a three-year period in the 1980s 200 doctors came to Rosebud, stayed a few days or weeks, and went. Dr Marquart said:

It is tough here. Temperatures fall to minus 20°F and many Indians go hungry and cold in rotting, overcrowded houses. There is no doubt in my mind that the health of these people would be better if there were jobs, hope and respect. For all the discouragement, though, Indians have qualities that help them endure. They draw strength from each other. They never had it easy, anyway. Even when they were free and following herds of game, life was hard. That historical sense and pride in independence helps to sustain them.

The Indian question is too intricate to be open to easy solution, and retrospective anger over the frontier white man's brutality is futile if it fails to promote a change in attitudes. In the American melting pot Indians, on the whole, did not melt. Some have integrated, and many Americans have Indian blood; but a large number remain on the margins. Little of the imagination and resourcefulness that built the country has been directed to making a dignified place for Indians. They lack the advantages of homogeneity and have no tradition of acting in concert. There are more than 300 tribes, many sharply different in language, traditions and outlook. About half of them live on 272 reservations, covering 52 million acres, and have their own tribal governments and police forces. It is difficult to generalise about living conditions. Some reservations have decent standards of education, health and housing; others are pits of poverty. Nothing is more dismal than the condition of the Sioux in their heartland of South Dakota.

Part of the Indian struggle today is for compensation for land swindled from them. In the early 1980s the Sioux were awarded $106 million for the 7 million acres in the Black Hills confiscated by the government in the 1870s, but they are divided over whether to accept. Some do not want the money, saying they want the land which is sacred to the tribe. Others think the possession fight is lost and that the money will help bring industry and other facilities to their poor reservations. In 1984, after a fifteen-year legal struggle, the Oneida Indians of New York state won a United States supreme court ruling that they were cheated out of their land in the late 18th century and that they were entitled to damages from the local authorities who now own it. Whites worry that such judgements will upset land values. In other parts of the country Indian insistence on water, fishing, timber and hunting rights causes friction with white communities. The lesson of the modern Indian experience is that wily lawyers and governments have to be confronted on their own ground and that Indians need better education and legal expertise, and to become politicised.

A capitalist outlook is not easy to develop among tribes which have no tradition of profit-making and have been subjugated for generations; but more Indians have become business-minded. Alaskan native people negotiated a good settlement and tribes throughout the country are exploiting mineral wealth beneath their reservations. Some take advantage of the special legal status of reservations by making big money out of bingo. Reservations are exempt from state gambling laws and whites flock to Indian bingo halls to play for jackpots unobtainable off the reservations. Gambling raises money, creates jobs, pays for roads and clinics and stimulates reservation economies. In Florida the Seminoles made $4.2 million in a year and have established scholarships and cattle herds with the profits. Still, some Indians feel that there must be better ways of rebuilding hope and dignity than running gambling saloons for palefaces.

5 Here in Delirium

New York

MORE SUNLIGHT reaches the Alaskan permafrost than pene-
trates this canyon in New York. To compose an idea of the
world and weather outside I stand at the window and stretch my
neck in the manner of a browsing giraffe, feeling comradeship
with the shrivelled shrubs and thin tree struggling to photo-
synthesise in the courtyard far below. The apartment faces north
and lies in an umbral gloom formed by the huddle of neighbour-
ing buildings whose configuration makes the sky a small patch, a
missing piece in the jigsaw of masonry, so that I sometimes
imagine I am imprisoned in a cellar, looking up at a distant
trapdoor.

Each afternoon, at certain times of the year, the departing sun
flashes a brilliant ray into my room. It does not enter directly, but
is reflected heliographically by the black glass of a distant building
and passes through an embrasure in Manhattan's ramparts to fall
into place like the midsummer's beam at Stonehenge. It charges
the walls with sudden and tantalising light, a lasered splendour so
brief that if I turn my back to put the kettle on for tea I miss it.

The prospect from the window is, for the most part, unre-
lievedly dreary. The building opposite bears an institutional or
penitentiary appearance, its brickwork the shade of a jaundiced
face, its window frames black. In my immediate gaze, as I look up
from the desk, are perhaps a hundred cell windows. I wish they
had bright or striped blinds; but the only stipple of colour in the
drabness is made by tomatoes set out to ripen on one of the black
sills, a tenuous still-life link with horticulture. Of the inmates
there is little to be seen. Occasionally there is a party – and smoke

and laughter and music drift over our crevasse. Once, in early summer, a young woman came to an open window and seemed about to rest her pale breasts upon the windowsill, as if to sun them like tomatoes. But, like the magical afternoon light, she vanished as suddenly as she had appeared. All in all, the building opposite is a continuing disappointment: in two years one bosom and several pounds of underripe tomatoes amount to meagre commons. Sometimes, feeling that I am in a surfacing bathyscaphe, I go to the roof to absorb light and the panorama of the imperial capital. If I stand tiptoe I can just spy the swirling brown East River, depository of gangsters' victims, a peeping piece of the top of the Empire State Building and a sliver of the World Trade Centre. In the theatre of Manhattan I am behind a big man with a hat.

Little that is evocative or agreeable falls on my ears from the outside. Sometimes a man shouts at the top of his voice, unleashing a stream of invective and obscenity, as if rehearsing an *avant garde* play. In the exercise yard below there is a slide for children, but I have seen no children there, nor heard childish laughter. There are few children in Manhattan, for there is not enough room or time or money for them. Disneyland is for children, Manhattanland for adults. Occasionally I hear sweet birdsong, but, more often, a corvine croak or disputatious squawk, echoing the quarrelling in the streets. There is, too, the poignant barking and wailing of dogs, imprisoned all day in apartments, enduring longing and aching sphincters as they wait for their weary masters. At dusk the windows light up in crossword patterns and I imagine these suffering dogs springing up with joy. Hands reach for leashes, for sheets of newspaper, tissues, plastic bags and patent turd-grabbing shovels, for it is illegal in New York, under pain of a $100 fine, to permit a dog to soil the pavement. It is a great leveller, this time of the day. Canine bowels move in concert and Wall Street panjandrums, real estate czars, white collar criminals, corporate molecules, showbusiness spangles, thrusting career women and fashion princesses stoop humbly to retrieve fresh faeces, each his own untouchable.

At this time, too, the entire city heaves and writhes, never more feverish than in its daily episode of disgorgement, the evening sloughing of the day shift, the bridge and tunnel folk who live beyond the glittering island's pale. As they head for outer darkness their rear-view mirrors blaze with images of the tall city in its Liberacean suit of lights. In bars this is the time of half-price drinks, the belt-loosening happy hour, or, as some call it, the attitude-adjustment hour. On the streets, though, in the tidal rush to Manhattan's vomitories, it is the animus hour, like a session of that bizarre group treatment for personality disorders in which screeching people abuse each other. Every large city has traffic thrombosis but nowhere in the world have I seen such mass tantrums as are thrown in New York. There is a concerted primal scream. Patience lies everywhere in ruins. Men bang their foreheads onto steering wheels, call upon Jesus and pound fists onto their horns. Taxi drivers, converted into fuming desperadoes and executioners *manqués*, smite their brows with the heels of their palms and cry 'It's unbelievable!' 'It's outrageous!' and 'It's unforgivable!' The vulgar fecal noun, always used freely in America, is the chief verbal currency in the uproar. Two yellow cabs grind closely together and one driver leans over and spits out: 'I kill your face!' And the other hurls back 'I kill *your* face!' Traffic oozes like glue, thousands of decent people are transformed into catamountains and the atmosphere is frantic and hostile, flecked with spittle, stinging with fumes and insults. A woman pedestrian quarrels with a traffic cop and drivers put their heads out and yell 'Book her! Book her!' – a Roman mob demanding death. Cars, jostling like penned bulls, nudge pedestrians who retaliate by bonking the bonnets with their fists like angry tympanists, and raising their middle fingers in abuse. The drivers lean out and jab their own fingers and snarl. A man pays off his taxi and the driver looks disbelievingly at the notes demanding: 'Where's the tip, buddy?' The man shouts: 'Screw you!' and the driver glistens with fury and roars: 'Screw you, bastard!' A chorus of youths chant 'Gridlock! Gridlock!' to taunt the simmering sufferers in the junction jams. A platoon of young men armed with cloths and squeegees dart into traffic and fan out to clean windscreens and say 'God bless you' and ask for 25 cents, which seems to me cheap for a clean screen and a blessing. Some drivers smile and pay, but others feel assaulted and shriek 'Get out!' and wave their fists.

Tiny old ladies with puppet-red cheeks, whose longevity testifies to the city's stimulating environment, scuttle crabbily over the crossings and drivers bawl: 'Move ya ass, lady!' and shout 'Chrissakes!' to the skyscrapers. A female traffic cop, pinkened with rage and carbon monoxide, stalks over to the innocent bystanders on First Avenue and points to her colleague, a male cop. 'I don't need this,' she announces to her audience, like an actress stepping out of a play. 'I'm a grown woman. I don't have to take this from him. He's been bugging me all day.' We think for a moment she might cry, but, of course, New York cops are like Texans, and they don't cry. With a heave of her Valkyrian bosom, she strides, like the trouper she is, back to her post in the terrible ganglion.

Ambulances whoop and implore, inching like icebreakers, looking for weak-willed drivers to give way to the sick. Majestic Stentors of fire engines demand right of passage with thunderous foghorns. Rock music thuds from car stereos. Radio news is read frantically over a distracting newswire clatter: Ten Ten WINS News – All News All The Time – Give Us Twenty-Two Minutes We'll Give You The World. The news is of fresh disasters, overturned trucks, gridlock and long delays ahead on parkways, highways, freeways, expressways, beltways, thruways and turnpikes. Oaths and blasphemy rise on the hot stink of visible air; and through all of this, wiggling their hips as they thread through the traffic, moving perversely against the tide, are young men with rock and roll in their cassette player earphones, roller-skating home. More daredevil yet are the express cycle messengers, the fastest means of moving small packages in Manhattan. Rapier-thin and nerveless, they aim themselves at the narrowest cracks, zigzagging like wing-threequarters, shrill whistles kept permanently in their mouths to clear people from their path.

Seemingly exempt from all laws, they run red lights and dart onto pavements to shave seconds, as if every letter were a last-minute reprieve to stay the executioner's hand. Though frequently unhorsed by lorry wing mirrors and taxi doors, they think the greatest danger is that of being swallowed up by the earth. New York potholes are the ultimate, so large and fearsome that casts of some of them were once made by Jaguar and incorporated in a test-track in Britain as the most challenging of suspension trials. Pavements are pitted, too, and thousands of pavement potholes are catalogued by the Big Apple Pothole and Sidewalk Protection Corporation, a firm dealing with pedestrian claims. By law the city only considers claims for damages relating to registered potholes. 'New York potholes', says the BAPSPC supervisor, 'are really something!'

There is a sudden limousine crisis. One of these black-windowed elongated monsters double parks and the driver scuttles out, runs to the boot, a fair distance, pulls out a bottle of gin and some tonic water and returns to thrust them into the gloomy interior. I glimpse the stomach of a fat man and an elegant female leg. It is part of the preposterousness of New York that it should permit these lumbering and impractical vehicles on its congested streets so that those hidden deep within can ride to their loved ones or a business conference, sipping gin and watching pornography or baseball on the video screen. They take up more than their fair share of the parking space that is one of Manhattan's scarcest resources. Parking here costs about $20 a day and New Yorkers regard double parking as a human right. There are men who make a living as car shepherds, moving clients' cars around the street all day, and there are often nasty struggles over spaces. I see, in the *New York Tmes*, that a dispute over a parking space in Manhattan is settled when one of the drivers pulls out a sub-machine gun and kills the other.

The medical director of the United Nations declares that if you can live in New York you can live anywhere in the world. The city's noise augers into skull and bones. A noise abatement official maintains that the abatement code, such as it is, is the only barrier between the average New Yorker and total insanity. Plainly the barrier has been dangerously breached. A hospital worker says he wondered why he was so nasty to patients and reasoned that noise was responsible. He bought some earplugs and now he is as nice as Nightingale to the sick and wounded. People buy earplugs at news-stands for 35 to 75 cents a pair, to help them make it through the day. Thousands shut out the city with headphones and music players, looking like radio operators fleeing the front.

Even in the deepest pools of night the city is not still: indeed, there is no dead of night, only a sense of being close to the remorseless pistons of a titanic ship. In this untranquil place there is ever an insistent thrum of vital and aortic energy. Short interludes in which tumult abates are like pauses in battle; but even these spaces are punctuated by the chilling whoops of sirens, trapped and echoing in the canyons of mirrors. And before the sun rises there is a vibration, a distant clamour, as of incipient revolution. It grows steadily more insistent, in the manner of Ravel's *Bolero*, and then ominous and thunderous and, finally, frenzied, as the invading army, trumpeting its energy and impatience, swarms in to seize the city.

New York is America's difficult child, kinetic, neurotic and self-obsessed. In some respects it is the most unAmerican of American cities, the outrageous outsider; and as a virtual city state it could send an ambassador to Washington. It revels in this separateness and wears the confidence that comes from being certain of its identity, power, superiority and central place. New Yorkers assume that they inhabit the capital of the western world and for many of them it is worth the price they pay for the privilege of wielding oily rags in the imperial engine room. No other city has so many songs written about it, and most are celebratory. Many Americans hate the city for its predominance, arrogance and cut-throat competitiveness and are pleased to note its occasional rides on a banana skin. But in the end they all have to do business with it, or measure themselves against it, or pay tribute of some kind, as New York knows. It can therefore seem insufferably pleased with itself.

Like all cities it attracts Whittingtons. It is the ultimate arena for the sharpening and testing struggle they desire. They make a commitment by moving to it to recreate themselves, to escape other, kinder, environments they think do not extract their talents. It has abundant opportunities and these are fiercely fought for: this is the heap whose summit people want to reach. Aggressive striving and overwork are normal, and people reek of midnight oil. They buy books on dressing for success, power lunching and office warfare. They really believe that working breakfasts achieve things. Their search for self-esteem and applause helps to give New York its nervous edge, its appearance, sometimes, of being an overcrowded playpen. It is part of the mythology of New York that it is the only place to find 24-carat success.

New York is favoured by history, a founding city with the advantages that well-rooted money and maturity bestow. It is innovative, constantly renewing itself, a living organism. A geographically commanding ocean city, it was built on sea-trade and the cheap fuel of immigrant labour. Its gatepost, the Statue of Liberty, symbolises its role as a goal and ideal. It is the nation's counting house, the financial and corporate capital, and the principal drum, beating out news, words and ideas from the towers of broadcasting, journalism, publishing and advertising. It is a hub of philanthropic, research, medical, educational and religious institutions, and is quite infested with lawyers. As a cultural smelter, its stages and studios run with sweat. It is the city with the most employed artists, actors, authors, dancers, composers, musicians, painters, sculptors and photographers; and the opera, concert and theatre seats are the most expensive in the world.

New York is at all times a spectacle and a drama, always self-consciously on stage. Its street life is astonishing, curious and shocking, with the physical intimacy and bustle of an Asian bazaar. The very surface of the streets, with their seeping steam, seem volcanic and alive. When I talked about the city's spirit to Edward Koch, the mayor, his eyes widened and he jabbed his finger enthusiastically. 'Diversity – did you know that mass is said in twenty-three languages in New York? It's the diversity that makes it electric, gives it its special intelligence, makes you think faster, walk faster, talk faster!' There is a staccato briskness to the New Yorker's stride – living here is like being in a street scene in a primitive hand-cranked newsreel. And there is a punchy rapid rhythm to his speech, a peremptory, saw-like speech, stripped to the bone. 'Gimme-a-slice. Gimme-a-shake,' he demands impatiently, ordering a pizza and milk shake. Television news readers talk like auctioneers, so fast that they are sometimes incomprehensible.

The mayor is a metaphor for New York, abrasive, fast-talking and ornery. He is Jewish, like two million – more than a quarter – of the city's people, and his life has been a classic American dream progress. Born in the Bronx, the son of Polish Jewish immigrants, he knew hard times in the Depression, worked in a shop to pay his way through law school, entered politics, became a congressman and, in 1977, won the top job in American municipal government. He was elected for a third four-year term in 1985 and said he wanted to be mayor forever. He once remarked that God had a hand in getting him the job and a rabbi rebuked him for such presumption.

The greatest mayor of New York, by general consent, was Fiorello LaGuardia, who ruled from 1934 to 1945, and Mayor Koch's ambition is to be judged greater. In his City Hall office he occupies LaGuardia's desk and faces a portrait of the hero, as if to remind himself of the competition. He told me that he had the best job in the world and thought he did it pretty well. 'I'm the best salesman this city has had for a long time. Even my enemies have to agree that my personality is helpful to the city.' Like LaGuardia he is a skilled and effervescent newsmaker, wearing his personality like a loud check suit. He is combative and likes to get his retaliation in first. His New York cadences are peppered with words like 'Outrageous!' 'Unforgivable!' 'Baloney!' and

'Schmuck!' He can be gratuitously rude, has an elephantine memory for slights and says that rather than forgive he gets even. He has never shared his life with anyone else and is wed and passionately devoted to New York, his first sweetheart. He would agree with one of his predecessors, Jimmy Walker, who said: 'I'd rather be a lamp post in New York than the mayor of Chicago.' Mayor Koch believes he should be more than a city manager and is delighted to be the larger-than-life representative of what he proclaims is the world's greatest city. He is mayor, prime minister, foreign secretary, jester and chief barker; and was once cartooned as King Koch, clinging to the Empire State Building. Like Ronald Reagan, he has the knack of apparently being on the side of the ordinary citizen and against the government while, of course, heading it. His mobile features, raised eyebrows and shiny pate have become as much a feature of the city as Liberty's face. Whenever he opens his mouth microphones are thrust at him like assegais. Newspapers see him as good copy and, on the whole, he gets a good press. He loves broadcasting as much as LaGuardia did. He appears on television almost every day and his favourite light is lime.

He is a cabbie of a talker, with an instant opinion on anything. No one is surprised that he is questioned about events that have not the slightest bearing on New York, for he and the reporters and citizens understand perfectly well that the city lies at the world's navel and it is inconceivable that great events could not have a New York dimension. Mayor Koch is always on the front pages, where New Yorkers know they belong. Most Americans and New Yorkers imagine New York as an independent land off the north-east coast, and certainly the Mayor thinks it proper that it should play its rôle in world affairs. As a major Jewish city it makes its feelings known about events in the Middle East; and the President of Egypt once remarked that New York had a foreign policy all its own. When the American hostages were released from Iran in 1981 Mayor Koch, who else, led them on a tickertape parade on Broadway.

Americans like a boss figure, a modern wagon train leader, to run their towns. They want to feel led, to have a focus, and they prefer to deal with and grumble about a person rather than an anonymous council; and many American mayors have wide powers and responsibilities. Mayor Koch's assertiveness, candour, chutzpah and big mouth often rub fur the wrong way, but New Yorkers on the whole approve of these qualities: they would not want a mouse for mayor. He is the sort of person many New Yorkers think they are, or what they think they ought to be: abrasive, street-smart, confrontationist and – no *l'ésprit de l'escalier* here – quick on the draw with a stinging retort. New Yorkers love their repartee. A friend of mine was sitting in a bar when a glamorous model walked in. 'Hey,' he nudged his companion, 'that's Christie Brinkley.' 'So what?' said the man, refusing to turn his head. 'She ain't gonna screw any of us.'

In politics-as-showbusiness the mayor is a strong and marketable performer. His waspish autobiography in which, in keeping with his bleak philosophy of getting even, he daggered friends and foes like, earned $300,000 in two years; and he also received one per cent of the gross of the off-Broadway musical based on it.

One of the sketches in this revue depicted the initiation of a newcomer to the city – 'never say sorry or pardon me . . . use "schmuck" on all occasions.' An American business magazine complained recently of an apparent rise of uncouthness in the country and condemned New York as rudeness capital of the world. For New Yorkers this was gratifying recognition, another medal. The brusqueness is said to stem from the demanding pace of an intimidating city full of ambitious strugglers scrabbling for space and recognition. General acceptance of the lab-rat theory enables people to feel licensed to live up to the reputation, to act the part. New Yorkers, it sometimes seems, feel they are only being real New Yorkers if they are making a scene. They are victims of their own propaganda. In 1985 the Association for a Better New York offered a weekly prize of $1000 for citizens found guilty of committing acts of courtesy, and ran courses in politeness for people who deal with the public. In the run of things, I encounter much courtesy and robust good humour, but I am not surprised by episodes of rudeness and impatience, whereas, after many visits to Canada, I was taken aback to encounter my first rude Canadian. New Yorkers like to think of themselves as tough, but really they are sensitive to slight, almost as if they have a layer of skin missing.

One evening I was in a taxi bouncing over potholes in a thunderstorm. Drenched people hurried across the road with newspapers held over their heads and the driver naturally started to barge through them. Some of the pedestrians shouted and a young woman stood in front of the taxi, turned her back, flipped up her skirt and let her knickers express contempt. 'Animal!' shouted the driver. 'Animal!' rejoined the woman, waving her fist.

'Animal', a taxi driver said a few days later, 'was the first English word I knew.' He looked up from the Greek newspaper balanced on the lectern of his steering wheel and shouted this over the raucous Greek music on his radio. He had just been yelling 'Animal!' at another driver in a 42nd Street duel. Later, while I was in a line of people waiting to pay a bill, the man in front of me suddenly lost patience and shouted at the staff. One of them told him to behave. He turned to the rest of us, his face like a damson, and cried: 'I don't believe these animals!' The clerks looked at us and said: 'The guy's an animal.'

In New York's notorious queues one confronts the myth of American efficiency. Lines are as explosive as trails of gunpowder and people punch and grapple when someone tries to jump ahead. In a train queue a musician in front of me raised the cello he was carrying as a threat to a man who tried to push in. 'Don't jump the line – it's undemocratic,' he shouted. Queues are so maddening that an agency rents out professional queuers. For $7.50 one of these stoics will wait in the driving licence line, perhaps the most torturing in the city. The queue service probably contributes to physical and mental health and is so popular that at peak times people queue at the agency to rent a queuer. The vehicle bureau and certain banks have the most testingly slow lines, but the best queuing spectacle is to be seen at Manhattan's main post office on the day in mid-April which is the deadline for posting income-tax returns. This is a festival for procrastinators, an agonizing celebration of the eleventh hour. The post office stays open until midnight and during the evening up to 20,000 people converge on it, aiming to secure that day's date stamp on the hated form and to avoid the fines imposed for late filing. They are shamefaced, scowling and anxious. At midnight an official signals the franking clerks to change their date stamps and a terrible mandrake shriek goes up. 'I know exactly what will happen because it happens every year,' the official said. 'When I call midnight people come to me and shout. They point to their watches which say twenty minutes to midnight. I can see the hate burning in their eyes. I can tell you that it is a very tense time. I've seen people arrive at fifteen minutes to the deadline and start filling out the form. They are desperate and crazy, because everyone knows it takes a long time to fill it out. But they wait to the last moment because they are lazy, or they want to hang on to their money for as long as possible, or they want to make a useless protest against paying taxes.'

Some New Yorkers join queues to be exquisitely humiliated. The gobemouches and suggestible roam the streets in herds to graze in new pastures dictated by fashion. They jostle outside newly acclaimed discotheques pleading with stony-faced door-keepers to admit them. These arbiters have cruel social power, squeezing out suspense, like sultans choosing harem girls. The grovelling of the supplicants is as pathetic as their gratitude when the contemptuous flunkeys raise the summoning finger. Egos are at stake and the bruising is terrible. Doorkeepers are threatened with guns and knives by those they condemn to social death. Rich slobs mutter menacingly about having them fired. A man who says to a woman: 'I can get you in,' and then fails, suffers a form of castration. Similarly, the craven ache to be favoured by imperious *maîtres* in fashionable restaurants and endure long waits and, as often as not, mediocre food at the end of it. As pointers to new trends and places, restaurant reviews are widely read, as tracts by the faithful. The work of preparing them is demanding: the great Mimi Sheraton, doyenne restaurant critic of the *New York Times* in the 1970s and 1980s, had to leave the job after seven years' active nosebagging, felled at last by obesity. 'I had a hard time leaving anything on the plate,' she confessed, having hit 14 stones for the second time. A restaurant favourably noticed in the newspapers is bombarded with bookings. Indeed, a small magazine for dedicated diners makes a virtue of its limited circulation, by pointing out that if the *New York Times* recommends a restaurant you may be trampled as the herd stampedes to it. The magazine tracks eating trends, reveals where film stars dine so that celebrity-hunters may observe their mastication, warns where you may feed badly for $100 a head and names the restaurants that operate a caste system, dividing their clients into 'divines' and 'peasants' – the class and money-consciousness of the city makes one think that the Statue of Liberty began to rot with tears of shame.

Restaurant-going is more than a matter of nourishment and entertainment. It is part of New York's dynamic and drama and also a recreation for people living in cramped apartments. The city is unexcelled in its diversity of eating houses and in a nation of people who love to eat out, New Yorkers are champions. It sometimes seems that half the people of Manhattan are eating in restaurants and the other half are cooking or serving in them. There are more than 7500 restaurants in Manhattan alone, and, judging by the prices, the proprietors of more than a few have the morals of extortionists. These days there is some hand-wringing about the rudeness and sulkiness of waiters. A recent review in the *New York Times* of a famous and expensive Manhattan restaurant, the Russian Tea Room, noted: 'The stale rolls with patches of mould did not whet my appetite, and the waiter offered no apology. The waiters tend to be a mirthless lot and fine points of service have all but vanished. With dessert our waiter brought a handful of forks and set them in a heap for us to distribute.'

In Newport, Rhode Island, I was once dining with some New Yorkers who identified the waiter, by his truculence, as a fellow citizen. Asked several times to bring garlic bread, he finally banged down a plate of white sliced bread. One of my companions reacted instantly to the insult, threw up a window and hurled plate and bread into the street. If some waiters and waitresses seem dramatic it is probably because they are dreaming of stage stardom, having come to New York as aspiring actors, dancers, singers and models, subjecting themselves to the cruellest of sieves. Restaurant pay is low, usually the legal minimum, and the stage-struck depend on diners' tips to pay for the rent, drama lessons, and the dreams. In a good restaurant tips can be between $100 and $250 a day and the Manhattan diner can regard himself as the patron of the struggling artist. One evening a waiter – 'My name is Leopold and I am your waiter this evening' – brought me the bill and said with a note of menace: 'Some of you Europeans think the tip is included in the bill. That's not the way we do things in New York.'

Once, having been sourly treated in a restaurant, I experienced *schadenfreude* when I saw its name some weeks later in the cockroach column, the *New York Times*'s weekly list of eating houses which have violated health regulations. New Yorkers have long had a special relationship with cockroaches and have spent millions of dollars trying to rid themselves of these almost indestructible creatures. New York is America's cockroach centre and its coat-of-arms could fittingly have a cockroach as an armorial supporter. War is waged with cockroach motels – 'roaches check in but they don't check out' – and sprays and poisons. The latest weapon is a chemical said to render male cockroaches homosexual.

This is the most alimentary of cities, its air filled with pungent, tantalising and rank cooking odours, its pavements dammed by heaped black plastic sacks of kitchen refuse, leaking and stinking. A magazine photograph shows a grim-featured security guard with a rifle, guarding racks of pig carcasses in a New York meat market. In its way it is an American metaphor: abundance, meat, macho pose and gun. It also seems absurd, a man apparently prepared to kill or lay down his life for dead pigs. But men who guard meat with guns are protectors of valuable commodities. New Yorkers eat 250,000 tons of beef every year and spend seven billion dollars a year on food, a good part of it in restaurants. There are many fingers in such a rich pie. Gangsters control much of the fish market and their cut is reflected in higher prices. In 1983 dairies which had conspired to fix milk prices were fined and ordered to refund five million dollars to consumers. The mafia, the overheads, the rents and big tips combine to make New York food expensive. In my local 24-hour greengrocery a woman was complaining to the manager about his prices:

'It's outrageous,' she cried.

'It's New York,' he said, as the till bell pinged.

Like most greengroceries in New York this one is run by a Korean family, on the well-beaten immigrant path of working relentlessly to build a business. In the past few years Koreans have taken over more than half of the fruit and vegetable stores, and they follow the tradition of the small Mom and Pop stores in a city which does not have many huge supermarkets and whose people shop daily. The shops are pictures of abundance, with bright heaped-up displays of melons, tomatoes, grapes and nectarines. Inside are salad bars which at lunchtime and in the early evening are crowded with single women in their battledress of pinstripe business suits, floppy bow-ties and thick-soled gym shoes.

Manhattan is a mosaic of small neighbourhoods. When they shop people do not venture much outside their own borders. My territory is fairly typical. It has several Korean greengroceries. It also has three Chinese laundries and I stay loyal to the same one, which has been run by one family for seventeen years. The shop is as cramped as a submarine, stacked with parcels of shirts, and the pressing iron is manned in shifts on a narrow bench. There are still 2000 Chinese laundries in New York. There was a time when laundries and the restaurants of Chinatown were the only economic scrambling net for Chinese immigrants. Newspaper shops and newsstands are also run mostly by immigrants prepared to work the long hours that give them their break and help New York to live up to its boast of being a day-and-night city. Newsstands used to be run by the Irish, then Italians and Jews. Now three-quarters of them are run by Indians and Pakistanis. They make 6 cents on each 30-cent copy of the *New York Times* and 20 per cent on the cover price of magazines. They also make money selling lottery tickets. When the prize runs into tens of millions of dollars the city is gripped by lottery fever and there are long lines at newsstands for tickets. 'I hope I don't win,' a woman said to me as we queued for a ticket for a $40 million prize. 'It would just ruin my relationship with my husband.'

The newsstand people and the Korean grocers often look tired. America's immigrant past is sometimes seen in rosy retrospect, but the reality was of grinding work and, often, failure. Many migrants turned around and went back home, seeing Liberty's arm raised in farewell.

In the immediate locality are three cheese shops, an expensive delicatessen selling take-away quail, a grocery whose proprietress sings haunting Korean folks songs as she serves, an art dealer, an antique dealer, three pharmacies, a boulangerie, an FBI office with black windows matching the dark glasses of the agents who emerge, a dog grooming salon, a couple of hairdressers, a bagel shop and an ironmongery. There is a sandwich shop which at first is intimidating because the pastrami, ham, beef and turkey are offered on such a variety of breads that it is hard to make that snap decision that New York demands; just as it is in bars where barmen reel off a list of beers – Budpabstshlitzmillerbeckscoors – and leave me floundering. There are also three fortune tellers who read palms and tarot cards and cast horoscopes. One of them, Sophia, said there are many astrologers and the like in the city. They have Wall Street brokers, bankers and lawyers among their clients, usually people in their 20s and 30s, seeking guidance in business deals and their careers. It is curious to think of these well-educated and hard-nosed professionals sitting down for a tea-leaves session. Perhaps it is a form of therapy. Many New Yorkers go to psychotherapists and, because they tend to reveal themselves readily, a lot of them can be overheard in restaurants talking about their therapy and therapists. Panic grips them in high summer when therapists go on holiday. In 1985 a psychotherapist ran a seminar on 'What To Do When The Shrink's Away'. A phone-in service, called Shrink Link, was founded by a psychologist and a psychiatrist to help people hit by a sudden anxiety attack and unable to reach their usual therapist.

My neighbourhood has Chinese, Thai, Japanese, Mexican, French, Italian and Spanish restaurants and several Irish bars, pizza ovens and hamburger counters. A biscuit shop bakes soft, sweet, chocolate-studded cookies on the premises and people emerge dipping their hands into their cookie bags. Three ice cream shops stay open far into the night. Americans adore ice cream and its consumption is part of the pursuit of happiness. It is rather touching to see intense and heavy-suited bankers in the after-work rush, briefcase in one hand, ice cream in the other. I have been in blizzards and seen women, heads down against the blast, determinedly licking their Haagen Dazs, one of the fashionable ices. Brought up to regard eating between meals as wrong, I remain surprised at the way Americans graze like ruminants, a slice of pizza there, a bagel here, an ice cream later, always nibble, nibble, nibble. In cinemas they cuddle cardboard buckets of popcorn, making the floor so sticky with the debris that it is sometimes hard to release one's shoes. When not eating they still like to keep their jaws match-fit with gum and I am appalled to see the faces of intelligent and lovely women suddenly emit a disgusting pink balloon of bubblegum.

There are two supermarkets near here, one open twenty-four hours. I like the way the black and hispanic girls on the check-outs dress. They are vivacious and wear lipstick as shiny as sports cars, large earrings and the latest hairstyle, and have names like Coochie and Angel. It is entertaining to wait in the check-out queue: I like to read the slogans on people's tee-shirts and billcaps and listen to the grumbling of the unstoical. Sometimes there are disputes at the check-out, though Coochie and Angel can handle anything. Querulous old ladies take so long groping into their purses for money that I can sense impatient queuers thinking hard about euthanasia. As well as the entertainment provided by people there are also the headlines of the outrageous newspapers sold at the check-outs: Woman Turns Into Dog After Eating Pet Food, Man Gives Birth to Baby, Dwarf Parents Have World's First Dwarf Twins, Doctors See Soul Re-enter Man's Body and Blind Man Reads with Glass Eye.

Across the road is a small and steamy restaurant with a black cook and cheerful Greek waiters in bow ties. It serves breakfast for under two dollars and large cheap lunches of meatloaf, chicken potroast, corned beef and cabbage. The helpings of mashed potatoes are so large that they seem to have been shovelled on like snow. The restaurant has a row of stools at the counter and some booths. At lunchtimes the booths are often occupied by little elderly ladies who abound hereabouts. Beautifully turned out in good quality dresses, carefully made up and bejewelled, they fork their mash and then sit and relax with cigarettes, coffee and elegant gestures, for all the world as if they were duchesses who had just paid $100 for lunch at Le Cirque. They talk about tax lawyers and their pets while salivating intending lunchers wait in the doorway to get a crack at the meatloaf. New York's population of elderly, a little island of ambitionless serenity in the swirl, has doubled in twenty years. A fifth of all apartment renters are over 65. The grandest dame in this area is Greta Garbo, who has lived in seclusion at the eastern end of East 52nd Street since the 1940s. The people in her neighbourhood are rather like the inhabitants of English villages where royalty live. They like the reflected light and they are proud, protective and loyal. The enigmatic Miss Garbo can be seen out and about, her face shadowed by a hat and dark glasses, browsing in bookshops and doing her shopping. She smiles and waves shyly at shopkeepers she knows. 'It is an honour having her live in the area,' Kal Socrates, a grocery shop manager, said. 'She is very private and we respect that.' People hang around outside her apartment block, which overlooks the East River, hoping for a glimpse; and people say she is still beautiful.

There is a riverside piazza near me where old ladies meet on sunny days and here, too, in the first sunshine of spring, a small flock of babies, the winter's crop, congregate with their minders. Curious adults, as if at a zoo, watch the infants feed and play. What would be a commonplace elsewhere is a remarkable spectacle here because New York is an almost childless city, its babies as rare as panda cubs. Nearly nine-tenths of households have no children under six years old, and seven-tenths have no children under 18. Ninety-four per cent of the people buying apartments have no young children. The low breeding rate is a reflection of the way the city is evolving. Many districts of Manhattan are affordable only by the wealthy. After winning $13 million in a lottery in 1985 a man said: 'Now I can afford to live in Manhattan.' Because housing is so scarce and expensive finding and financing a flat is a major preoccupation. With building land in the mid-1980s costing four dollars a square inch developers aim for the expensive end of the market, and they build shrunken flats. New apartments have a fifth less space than those built ten years ago. Tenants sub-divide rooms into tiny cells and even build beds over refrigerators. This is the capital of the convertible sofa-bed. There is a growing market for room-mates to help pay the rent and many young women prefer to share with men because men do not hog the bathroom and do not, as a rule, take their make-up, clothes and boyfriends.

A third of the city's renters pay at least two-fifths of their income in rent, and a quarter pay at least half of their money. But for all its high costs and squeezed living Manhattan remains the magnet for young professionals, here to try their strength. It's Manhattan or die; and thousands have two jobs to make ends meet. Costs and conditions are an effective form of birth control. People put off marriage and many career women wait until they are in their thirties to marry or have a child, balancing ambition and biology, and they often pay a price in anxiety. New York can be tough and lonely for single women determined to make careers. They work hard in Wall Street, Madison Avenue or Fifth Avenue, rise early, run and do aerobics, report for a business breakfast at a hotel, work a ten-hour day and pick up a salad at their neighbourhood Korean on their way home. They often dine alone, for one of their complaints is that when they seek companionship among men there are not enough to go round. Research indicates that for every ten eligible single women in the city there are only six eligible men. Women grumble that some men work too hard and are too ambitious to be able to include relaxation with women in their schedules. They also fatigue themselves by running and body-building, or spend too much time on the therapist's chaise longue. Match-making is an important industry, and I have seen courses offered in both kissing and learning how to meet people and find romance in department stores.

One of the difficulties for single women is that a higher proportion than average of men in New York are homosexual. This is where homosexual militancy and organisation started, in response to police brutality. During first social meetings many women ask men frankly if they are heterosexual, bisexual or homosexual. Because of its large numbers of homosexuals and drug addicts using needles, New York has more Aids victims than any other city, more than a third of all American cases; and the spread of Aids is accompanied by a strong fear of it. Since the disease was first identified in the United States in June 1981 many of its victims have found themselves regarded with loathing, untouchables, thrown out of their jobs and homes, shunned by acquaintances. For all the assurances of doctors, many people fear they could become infected by drinking from a glass used by a homosexual, or by food served by homosexual waiters. Some churches responded to anxiety by discontinuing the use of the communion chalice and serving wine in individual glasses.

Thousands of young men and women have flocked to join the new religion, the development of the lovingly sculpted American body. High class sweatshops have become fashionable, rivalling and even supplanting discotheques and bars as places of social collision and courtship. Gymnasiums, with factory-like rows of body-building machinery, have opened up everywhere. Squash players are dismayed to find that their courts are filled with more profitable muscle-stretching contraptions into which are inserted narcissists in expensive leotards. People really do say: 'I am into my body' – and this new American body, created by pain and much money, has become an end in itself, a social and sexual visa.

The perspiration industry, manufacturing treadmills, exercycles, jogging watches, work-out suits and weights to make running shoes heavier, is enormous; and so is its publicity offshoot. The body-shaping image is increasingly used in advertising, in numerous pictures of wrung-out exercisers and sweaty hunks. A cigarette company shows a girl, limp from her work-out, gratefully flushing the fresh air from her lungs with a smoke. President Reagan was photographed in a weight-lifting machine and psychoanalysts say that the bodybuilding and exercise trend is evidence that Americans are regaining their traditional sense of self-reliance. A fitness chic has emerged, and an arrogant fitness élite. Replete with newly built muscles young executives say they feel superior to colleagues who do not hone their bodies, that their fitness gives them that sharper edge in boardroom and sales war.

For all the publicity given it, however, vigorous exercise is practised by only a small minority, particularly the city strivers. Most Americans do not take enough exercise. 'We are a bunch of fat slobs,' the editor of *American Health* said. Still, many of those who exercise earnestly do so in the belief that they will be able to keep away from doctors and their monstrous bills. Medical costs in the United States are high and increasing rapidly. In the mid-1980s health care cost a tenth of gross national product, having doubled in twenty years. The strains on public and private budgets are making health care a critical social issue. Most working people are covered by insurance. If a wallet biopsy discloses that a hospital patient is uninsured he is transferred to a public hospital. Other people are covered by the welfare schemes for the poor and elderly; but insurance costs are rising steeply to meet the expense of treatment, and government has to pay more as the number of elderly increases. Medicine, meanwhile, becomes more of a business with the growth of profit-making hospitals run by corporations.

*　　*　　*

There is a woman living on the pavement outside my apartment block. To my own knowledge she has been there for more than two years. She is in her mid-thirties I would guess, dressed in jeans and a sweater, with a blanket around her shoulders in colder weather. Her possessions are piled around her in plastic bags and bundles, and more are crammed into a supermarket trolley. She is a New York bag lady. Sometimes she looks out with an enraged stare, at other times she engages in bitter soliloquy. Occasionally, at night, she screams. Although she is not a beggar people give her quarters and dollars and she buys sandwiches and wolfs them down. She moves constantly around the block, painstakingly shifting the bundles and trolleys in relays, setting up a new camp. An old man with a white beard and a thumbnail three or four inches long sits on a wall all day, gazing as if at some far horizon. An ancient mariner of a woman approaches passers-by with her housing problems. A ragged man sits on the kerb, shouting abuse, his feet in the gutter, his ankles a mass of running sores.

When we first arrived in New York, making the rounds with an apartment agent, we encountered a screaming naked man in the street and women were in nearby telephone booths calling the police. 'That's New York!' the agent said with a grin, as if pleased that his city had provided another eye-popping spectacle to live up to its reputation.

In New York the streets are the asylum. Thousands of people are plainly mentally ill, homeless and helpless, blowing aimlessly like tumbleweed among the towers of the richest city. They sprawl in gutters, doorways and subway entrances, scavenge in litter bins and lie on steps with their trolleys and bags of rags and newspapers, hollow-eyed, scabby and sour-smelling. In the 1960s mental institutions in New York State, some of which were grossly overcrowded and inhumane, released patients after it was argued that many of them were confined unnecessarily and in violation of their rights. There were 80,000 people in state mental hospitals in 1965. Twenty years later there were 21,000. It was thought that with new drugs controlling their illnesses and making them safe, patients could be looked after at the neighbourhood level and that many could even find a place in society. This has not happened. Unsupervised people do not take their medicines regularly; neighbourhood residents gang up to prevent community care centres opening in their areas; and there is a shortage of money for helping the mentally sick.

So the deranged wander the streets – hundreds of them accommodated in city shelters every night – and they are only a small proportion of the increasing army of homeless who constitute the most intractable of New York's social problems. Many lost their homes when their landlords, taking advantage of the heavy demand for apartments, moved them out to convert low-cost blocks into high-cost flats for the burgeoning professional class. As the better-off moved in to renovate blocks many poor people had no place to go but the streets; and the city was unable to meet the demand for cheaper public housing partly because the Reagan administration reduced its commitment to it. Because of the chronic shortage of low-rent housing the city quarters 3000 families in hotel rooms, one family per room. Health officials found malnutrition and disease among the 7000 children living in these hotels in 1983. Some of the hotels are squalid, but the owners have the city authorities in a vice. For the owners homelessness is good business: one was paid more than $7 million a year in rent.

No one can say how many homeless there are. Welfare groups estimated more than 40,000 in the mid-1980s, a figure the authorities said was too high; but everyone agreed the numbers were increasing. On one freezing night in 1985 more than 8000 street people were taken in to shelters, the highest number since the Depression, and about 20,000 people were in hotels and other facilities. A number of American cities provide no publicly-funded help or shelter for their homeless: their attitude is sink or swim. New York spends many millions of dollars on providing temporary shelter and food. But it is like a country running a relief operation for desperate refugees after a disaster. Homelessness is only part of the problem. About a quarter of the people in New York were living below the poverty line in the mid-1980s, including more than half-a-million children.

There are now about eighty soup kitchens, symbols of the Depression, operating in the city. I found more than a hundred men, women and children queuing outside one run by the Holy Apostles Church on West 28th Street. On this bitter December day they waited silently, sniffing the smell of cooking, stamping their feet. At the door a man called Jimmy controlled the line. Whenever a person emerged from the 58-seat canteen another was allowed in. No one was asked if he had any money or who he was. Those who run the canteen said that the sort of people who came here had had enough of being humiliated. Guests, as they are called, received a free meal, a smile and no questions. All they were asked to do was to eat and make room for another person.

Edwin Meese, then a senior presidential aide, said that some Americans were going to soup kitchens not because they were poor but because the food was free, an echo of the President's notorious remark that food stamp recipients bought vodka with their spare money. But the gaunt homeless people at this canteen certainly looked in need of a meal and warmth. They told me they were sleeping rough in stations or huddled over steam vents or in rat-infested hotel rooms. 'We see the traditional Bowery bums,' said the Rev William Greenlaw, who runs the canteen, 'but we are getting a surprisingly high number of people in their 20s and 30s, white and black, who have drifted out of the economic mainstream. We serve more than 400 lunches a day. It is the only meal many of these people get. You would think that in America we could handle things better, but the poor have a bad time with red tape. There is an adversary relationship between government welfare people and those they are meant to serve. The welfare system has become a maze – it is immoral, horrible and shaming.' A report by the Community Service Society that winter said: 'New York remains a city of gold for those at the top, a city of despair for many elderly and homeless.'

Along Fifth Avenue that Christmas there were tee-shirts on sale for nearly $100 apiece. Silver dog bowls, engraved Dog, were $2000 and gourmet dog biscuits $10. A patch of spinnaker from the losing America's Cup challenger was $1000. For $150 a patisserie sold a Christmas cake on top of which a train ran through a landscape of marzipan penises and breasts. Shopping raged unabated all day, seven days a week, the big stores closing at ten o'clock at night for the idea of early closing is unAmerican. Agencies were undertaking shopping for people too busy to do it themselves. A sporting equipment firm said it would deliver exercise machines on Christmas morning. And, there being no Boxing Day, the shops were ready to open on the 26th. Christmas in New York sees commerce and consumerism in full spate. Nothing is more clearly illustrative of the spinal importance and vitality of the business dynamic in American society.

I recall how surprised I was, shortly after I arrived in the city, by the saturation and excitement of the news coverage given to an electricity breakdown in Manhattan. No lives or property were threatened, and the reaction seemed to stem from the New York media tendency to make a gale of a Manhattan zephyr. But the breakdown was big news because it was a form of coronary attack, striking at New York's very being, its business. Newspapers and television were full of stirring accounts of heroic candlelit shop-keepers battling through.

As usual at Christmas, Santa Clauses were standing outside the stores ringing handbells. Charles Dickens, visiting the United States, wrote: 'I am getting sick of the sound of sleigh bells' – and today he would be sicker. At Macy's, the world's largest store, 22 Santa Clauses worked in shifts and suffered Santa Knee from being sat on so much, and one reported that a couple in their eighties sat on his knees and thereby fulfilled a life's dream to travel from their home in Mississippi to be in Macy's at Christmas. A woman in Florida announced that she was giving her husband his heart's desire as a Christmas surprise: she had arranged for him to be a Macy's Santa Claus.

In expensive shops where the window goods have no price tags

there were specially bred tall and haughty female assistants, their
lips coated in cruel lipstick, forever on the edge of a sneer. High
up on one of wealth's bastions, the new Trump Tower, a pillar of
decadence and extravagance, tunic'd trumpeters saluted the poor
and rich of Fifth Avenue. In the lobby and atrium far below
doormen paraded in red coats and bearskins, like moonlighting
Coldstreamers. A grand piano was played and a choir of nubile
girls carolled against the backdrop of a great wall of rose marble.
A waterfall cascaded. The effect was of a Cecil B. de Mille epic,
lacking only Elizabeth Taylor's cleavage.

Dickens himself might have invented the name of the young
developer, Mr Trump, with its smack of New Yorkian triumph
and success. New York is becoming a city for the wealthy, he says,
and notes that wealth and that indefinable 'it' get you good tables
in restaurants. The Trump Tower glisters like Liberace's trousers. And, fittingly, Mr Liberace stayed at the tower when he
marked his fortieth anniversary as an entertainer by filling Radio
City Music Hall with 6000 people every night for a fortnight. He
arrived onstage in a silver Rolls-Royce studded with mirrors and
alighted in a silver-sequinned suit and a rhinestone-embroidered
blue fox cape with a train which was sixteen feet long, weighed ten
stones and was worth $300,000. In a land lacking royalty and
craving its glamour Mr Liberace does his best to compensate.
Even Terry, the chauffeur, was got up in sequinned white livery.
The great art deco hangar of the music hall, with twin Wurlitzer
organs emerging from secret compartments to fill the hall with
sound, was a proper setting for one of the last of the great
American exhibitionists. He showed his outsize gold and diamond rings to the front row, as if his fingers were a Tiffany tray,
and projected pictures of the rings onto a screen so that they
could be admired by the wider audience. At last he played some
snatches of sonatas and concertos, a Rachmaninov stew flavoured
with pieces of Chopin, Liszt and Tchaikovsky. Some of the more
modern stuff was performed with what old warriors would
recognise as a Naafi-bass, the singalong vamping evocative of
beer-rings on the piano and cigarettes burning the varnish. But

Mr Liberace's admirers were not there only to hear him play. At frequent intervals he left the stage to slip into something more expensive, reappearing in another coruscating suit. He whirled and flashed like the mirrored ball at a dance hall. While he was absent the stage was filled with the Rockettes, the long-legged troupe of dancing girls who are a New York institution and anachronism, and a wholesome reminder of what sex appeal meant before Hefner and Guccione hijacked it. In one setpiece, Mr Liberace, dressed like a grotesque Venetian courtier, played while his decorated piano revolved, vapour rose to envelop him, coloured fountains danced in the background, an entire orchestra rose from the bowels of the theatre, the two Wurlitzers emerged from their priestholes, waltzers swirled to Strauss and the twinkling and cherubic virtuoso ascended aboard a rising stage, his audience roaring gratitude. He exited briefly and returned gorgeously caparisoned and with fresh jewels. Terry arrived in a Rolls-Royce convertible to bear him off. His face lit by joy, Mr Liberace stood in the back, his outstretched shimmering hands blessing the multitude.

Some time earlier I saw another star performer borne by chauffeur-driven car to his place of employment. This was at Yankee Stadium, during a long night of baseball. I soon saw that the baseball and the drama of rising and crashing of reputations was only the half of it. The rest was the relentless mass chewing of junk food, an anorexic's nightmare of bulging squirrelly cheeks. Within a few minutes of the start we were squirting mustard from sachets over our first hot dogs of the evening and onto our trousers. Soon our shoes were hidden in a litter of expended sachets, paper beer cups, ice cream cartons, peanut shells and ketchup-stained napkins. That evening the stadium had a record crowd of 55,000 people and I calculated that the median fan was consuming three dogs, which at eight inches to the dog, was twenty-one miles of pungent frankfurter. The reeking stadium sent up a thermal of sausage vapour. Salesmen scurried up and down the gangways bearing trays and crying: 'Hot dawgs! Beer! Soda!' Hardly had we thrown down the sachets, napkins and cups than dawg and beer men arrived like genies. Thousands of jaws champed a background rhythm as the stadium's organist responded to the action on the field in the manner of a cinema pianist illustrating a silent film. When tension rose he thumped out dramatic chords and blew a cavalry bugle call, whereupon fans opened their dawg-filled mouths and spluttered: 'Charge!' The huge electronic scoreboard flashed its orders to the mob. 'Clap!' it commanded and the people stuffed their dogs in their mouths and clapped. Even when the teams changed innings there was no time for idle reflection. Vendors swarmed, a jazz band strutted through the aisles in competition with the organ, and a video camera roamed the crowd and flashed faces on a screen twenty times lifesize. There was roared approval when the video man lit upon the face of a pretty girl and we could see the blush infusing her twenty-foot face. Cricket it was not.

Back at the match, the Yankees were faltering. Dave Winfield was not smiting too well and fans opined that a man earning a million a year should smite better. Advisers in the crowd also thought it time for a change of pitcher and started chanting: 'Goose, Goose, bring on the Goose!' After a while a pair of gates opened at the end of the stadium where relief pitchers were confined like bulls. There was exultant cheering as Rich Gossage, dubbed the Goose, emerged into the light. He did not, however, waste his carefully husbanded strength walking to the pitcher's place. He was borne in a car around the edge of the field, exiting grandly a few steps from his place of work, the pitcher's mound. As it turned out, though, the Goose did not have a nice evening. The crowd was dismayed to see that he was struck very hard in all directions. Quite soon the Yankees lost the game and the hot dogs tasted of ashes in the mouths of the fans. But the end of the three-and-a-half hour match was not the end of the evening.

Americans have an abundance complex and are unable to decide where to draw the line. They believed that if a lot is good more must be better. This evening was a double-header, and having played one match the players trooped out to start all over again. More hot dogs were sold. Belts and belches were released and paunches overflowed. As time wore on, the weight of hot dogs and beer, the stifling 90° heat and the Yankees' failure to smite induced irritability among the fans. We could feel that it would end in tears. People started disagreeing about the merits of players and began bopping each other, and security guards escorted the boppers out. Halfway through the second game we stole away, feet crunching on beer cups and skidding on mustard sachets which spurted over our shoes. From a distance the brilliantly lit stadium, throbbing with organ music amid the desolation of the Bronx, seemed like a great space ship in a fantasy film. There was a strong whiff of hot dog on the breeze. Slightly nauseated, we decided we needed a hamburger supper and caught a subway train to Manhattan.

The subway used to be New York's pride. It was what made the city work. It was founded in the early years of this century and in its heyday was a cheap and efficient transport marvel. It was one of the agreeable features in what was once a more agreeable city. Today New Yorkers call their subway filthy, horrible and crime-infested. The mayor agrees, describing it as miserable and intolerable. The city transport chairman says it is having a nervous breakdown. The New York subway has a worldwide reputation for being a labyrinth of foul, dark and forbidding tunnels, where criminals lie in wait.

In the 1930s and 1940s it reached peaks of two billion passengers a year, but numbers fell in the 1950s as people moved out to the suburbs and relied more on their cars. The subway deteriorated, stations became dirty, stinking, ill-lit slums. Ageing trains kept breaking down and carriages were covered with graffiti. Thousands of people were frightened off by subway murders, assaults, robberies and vandalism, and the spectacle of wretched people living underground amidst dirt and rats. The subway is now the object of a desperate rescue operation. It is one of the world's great mass transit systems and while there are reasons for its decline and squalor – age, decaying equipment, mismanagement, union problems – it is plain that New York has squandered a famous and vital asset. It is extraordinary that in this rich world capital of free enterprise there should have been such a catastrophic failure of civic pride, business sense, imagination and political will. New York has been saluting new soaring towers while, down below, its subway has grown rotten and shaming.

Fear and loathing of the subway helped to make Bernhard Goetz a bizarre New York celebrity in 1985 after he emptied his pistol into four black youths on a subway train. He said they were trying to rob him. His gunfire seemed to be not merely one man's resistance to the oppression of crime, but a shout of rage against the whole awful subway system. He lived out a common fantasy by hitting back at tormentors. As is often the way of things, he became the centre of a craze. In spite of his nervous and slightly shifty appearance, press, public, polls and politicians converted him into an heroic avenger. People started wearing tee-shirts with slogans supporting him. He became a plaything of the press and television. Only in such a self-absorbed and hyperactive hothouse of a city could he have been awarded such notoriety.

Piledrivers pound out the rhythms of an unparalleled building boom. The skyline of Manhattan changes weekly like a window display and postcards are always out of date. This demonstration of economic muscle is good for business and the city's reputation; and, as it happens, a side effect is that it is also good for the mobs who run the city's organised crime. Gangsters have for years had a grip on the construction industry, on suppliers and unions, and have extorted millions of dollars in rigged contract bids and in the Danegeld paid by businessmen under threat of violence.

In 1984 an officer of the Federal Bureau of Investigation remarked that, 'the finely manicured hands of the Colombo family are at every construction site in New York. You can't pour concrete in this city without paying off the Colombos.' The Colombos are one of the five major mafia gangs operating in New York, the most powerful criminal organisations in the United States. Although, strictly speaking, the word mafia applies only to the Sicilian secret criminal and terrorist society, it is widely used by law enforcement agencies to describe the long-established organised crime gangs who are also known as the mob or Cosa Nostra, meaning 'our thing'. These gangs, families as they are often called, are the inheritors of a long tradition of organised crime rooted in New York's violent and lawless past. Many Italian Americans feel unfairly smeared by the ethnic stereotype because many mob leaders have had Italian or Sicilian backgrounds, but many have not. For much of the 19th century New York crime was dominated by Irishmen, and during the first thirty years or so of this century a number of Jewish gang bosses ruled.

The five main New York crime families, Gambino, Genovese, Colombo, Bonnano and Lucchese, take their names from former leaders. According to the FBI the largest, the Gambino and Genovese groups, each have about 200 members who have taken an oath of secrecy, and about 1000 associates. The other three families have about 100 sworn members and 500 associates each. The families were first organised together in 1931 by a Sicilian, Salvatore Maranzano, who became the boss of bosses and carved the city into crime districts to avoid bloody and wasteful overlapping and competition between gangs. Shortly afterwards he was murdered in his Park Avenue office by rivals. For half a century after that the mafia was periodically attacked, but not seriously troubled, by the agencies of the law. The FBI, when it was run by J. Edgar Hoover, campaigned against racketeers but left much of the investigation to local police forces which were not efficient: they tended to be short of resources and torn by rivalry and, in some places, were undermined by the close links between criminals, politicians and the police. Organised crime prospered partly because underworld chiefs had city bosses, police, judges and prosecutors in their pay.

The FBI used to draw up a league table of Public Enemies, but for many years, and especially in the 1930s, criminal figures were glamorised and the battles between police and folk-hero gangsters seemed only an extension of the crime films. The Kefauver senate hearings of 1950–51 showed how politicians, gangsters, police officers and businessmen worked together, and how entrenched organised crime was. The public was informed, shocked and deeply fascinated by the interrogation of criminal moguls on television; but no significantly damaging action was taken and organised crime remained an affront to American society.

It was not until the late 1970s that pressure from Congress, reflecting public disquiet, made the FBI, state and city police forces, customs and tax investigators undertake what had been long postponed, a large and concerted offensive against organised crime. The law enforcers were better equipped than they had ever been. Firstly, they had new legislation aimed specifically at the mobs, and regional crime strike forces to co-ordinate investigation and reduce rivalry between the FBI, police forces and other agencies which had always hampered the fight against crime (and still does to an extent). Secondly, they had modern electronic recording equipment that made penetration of gangs easier. And they made it a central part of their offensive to round up the generals as well as the troops.

The gangs had moved with the times and extended their activities. Drug dealing, gambling, prostitution, usury, the jukebox business, cigarette vending machines, pornography and protection rackets remained the staple of their business. But they had also moved into fraud to loot banks and pension funds, and increased their infiltration of trade unions so that they could milk their funds and put pressure on business, dictating what goods, services and materials should be used. The ultimate sanction, as always, is violence. Major criminals used their extorted riches to involve themselves in legitimate businesses like construction, transport, waste disposal, clubs, restaurants and liquor shops.

In the authorities' offensive against the mobs New York's powerful crime families were a principal target. Gangs in Boston, New Orleans, Kansas City, Philadelphia, Chicago, Denver and Los Angeles were also penetrated by hidden microphones and cameras and telephone tapping. Undercover agents worked painstakingly to gain the confidence of criminals. In a typical sting operation an agent posing as a dealer in stolen goods entertained gangsters aboard a well-bugged yacht in New York. In another case the FBI set up a pasta factory in the Little Italy district of Manhattan, an ideal cover, and there conducted deals with gang leaders under the gaze of concealed cameras. The old gang tradition of *omerta*, or silence, was gradually eroded and a number of middle-grade criminals became informers.

On the evidence thus gathered about 3000 people involved in organised crime were convicted between 1980 and 1984. Many of the gang leaders arrested were elderly men. The mafia was changing and a number of younger men felt disinclined to follow their fathers' criminal example. Some ambitious young men, though, were keen to take up their inheritance. One such was Salvatore Testa who, at the age of 28, was profiled in the *Wall Street Journal*. It was not the usual sort of business biography, for Testa being the son of Chicken Man Testa, head of the Philadelphia mafia, was heir to a racketeering empire. A police officer, approached for a character reference, said: 'He gives you that look like he might rip your jugular out.' Another cop said heavily: 'He's the apple of our eye.' On the other hand, a family friend said: 'To us he's still a wonderful little boy.' Chicken Man had sent his son to good private schools and university, so that he was one of America's best-educated mobsters. Chicken Man was blown up by a bomb and, in the fullness of time, his death was avenged: a man was found in a sack, full of bullet holes and with fireworks in his mouth, a code signalling revenge for a bomb. Gangsters generally like to avoid publicity, but young Testa led an interesting life and kept getting into the newspapers. He recovered from gunshot wounds in 1980 and three years later was shot eight times, and again recovered. He had to keep looking over his shoulder because of a feud with a rival faction led by Harry the Hunchback Riccobene. Finally, some time after his *Wall Street Journal* profile was published, his luck ran out and he was found, tied in a kneeling position, with a bullet hole behind each ear, trademarks of a mafia termination.

Recently some friends in the country outside New York offered me, as a feature of a Sunday afternoon walk, a look at their neighbourhood's 'mafia house'. We walked by a substantial suburban house. There were many cars parked outside, and we imagined that behind the closed curtains gangsters were planning crimes, examining their extortion ledgers or worrying about the tightening of the police snare.

Probably, though, they were all sprawled in front of a video screen watching the *Godfather* films which depict mafia life. A detective who got close to gangsters on undercover assignments related to a senate committee in 1981 how underworld life imitates art. He disclosed that members of crime families are keen fans of these films and some have seen them many times. On one occasion, he recalled, a mobster gave a restaurant waiter a handful of coins and instructed him to play the *Godfather* theme music over and over on the jukebox while he dined. Mobsters watch the films, the detective said, to see how they are supposed to behave, and try to live up to their screen image.

The body of Count Basie lay in an open coffin amidst a blaze of red roses. People filed slowly by and the line stretched out of Abyssinian Baptist Church into 138th Street. A diminutive woman in her eighties, dressed in her Sunday-best blue suit and a white straw hat, said: 'My doctor told me, don't you go out now, you're too sick, you stay in bed. But I got up anyway. I never met Count Basie, but I love him. We all did. He made us dance.'

Basie illuminated the history of both Harlem and jazz. In Harlem's expansive period he learned much of his music watching Fats Waller play a cinema organ. Now, in its most handsome church and bastion of its spirit, Harlem honoured and mourned both a hero and itself. There was an underlying wistfulness to the Basie tunes played on a piano during the service. Basie had grown up when Harlem was young, when this teeming five-and-a-half square mile section of Manhattan was America's black capital, a cauldron of creativity and a place of hope. In its heyday it was a new frontier, and blacks streamed here in thousands, especially from the south. Adam Clayton Powell Sr, pastor at Abyssinian Baptist Church in the 1920s, and father of the politician who became a local hero, called Harlem a symbol of liberty, 'the promised land to negroes everywhere'.

The incandescence was relatively brief. The sheer vitality of its best years has made its decline all the more painful. In the 19th century New York blacks lived mostly in slums on the middle west side of Manhattan. Few lived in the predominantly white middle-class neighbourhood of Harlem. The collapse of a building boom in the early 1900s left rows of empty and affordable homes, and blacks took the chance of a better life and moved uptown. Churches set up cultural and spiritual fortifications, and political and social organisations, newspapers, professionals and businesses moved in. In the decade after 1910 Harlem became almost completely black. In the 1920s it was alive with jazz, dancing and poetry, and its ballrooms and theatres were thronged. Duke Ellington beckoned Americans to *Take the A Train* to a Bohemian Harlem which nurtured stars like Ella Fitzgerald, Billie Holiday, Bessie Smith, Paul Robeson, Scott Joplin and Dizzy Gillespie. It mirrored white society with a rich élite, smart set and bourgeoisie; and, of course, its humble and hard-working majority who did not stay out *Stompin' At The Savoy* all night. Its church leaders had large congregations but were dismayed by the spread of saloons, whorehouses and gangs.

Harlem was so much a magnet that it became chronically overcrowded; and then it was devastated by the Depression, unemployment, low wages and extortionate rents. Much of its fabric crumbled into slums, the bright lights flickered out, and the dance halls fell silent. In the 1950s a large part of its middle class moved to other suburbs; and in the 1960s, like other broken-backed black ghettoes, it became a symbol of unrest. Unemployment and the rates of crime, tuberculosis and infant mortality are high. It is blighted by violence and drug trading.

Many people in Harlem think the police are oppressive and brutal. The mayor is accused of appeasing the affluent by being tough on blacks, who form nearly a quarter of New York's population, and Puerto Ricans and other hispanics, who are nearly a fifth. In Harlem one day I watched the mayor arrive at a hearing to defend the police against allegations that they had a down on blacks and Puerto Ricans. The room was packed and hot and people were as sticky as fudge. Someone pleaded: 'Cool it, brothers and sisters, cool it' – but the noise and the press of people made it impossible for the hearing to start. It was postphoned and the mayor was booed as he climbed into his car. Later he partly quietened the grumbling by appointing a black police chief; but there was a furious outcry among blacks when a fat, sick old black woman in the Bronx, who was behind with her rent, was killed by police when they went to evict her. They broke down her door and four men with riot shields burst in. When the woman picked up a knife in her fright they killed her with two blasts from a shotgun. A coffee and a coaxing chat might have solved the problem. The police were later cleared and appeared smiling in a newspaper photograph.

Some of the black resentment lies in the way New York is changing. The city booms as more expensive flats go up, but affordable housing for average people is hard to find. The number of poor and homeless increases and the gap between rich and poor widens. New York grows more lopsided. While some of Harlem has the appearance of having been struck by a storm, it also has many quiet and tree-lined streets of handsome brownstone buildings which look increasingly attractive to middle-class people squeezed by Manhattan's high apartment prices. Whites are beginning to move in, renovating houses and staunching decay. Many poorer blacks feel that they will be gentrified out of their homes as newcomers move in and prices go up; and black leaders are anxious that their political base will be further eroded.

Many New Yorkers, though, never see Harlem. 'You crazy?' taxi drivers say. 'It's the combat zone up there. Wanna get killed?'

'Oh, no,' said a driver when I gave him a Harlem address. 'No one goes up there. It's a bad place.' I hailed a cab in Harlem to return downtown and the driver said: 'How'd ya get lost up here, feller?'

Black-operated tour companies make a business of taking visitors into Harlem, narrating its history and showing off its fine old houses and commenting sadly on the dismal slums where furtive drug peddlers sell to the addicts who move like trembling marionettes. A guide told me that some tourists are seeking a frisson. 'They think they are going to see the worst, the chamber of horrors, crowds of barbarians. They can't imagine that this is a district where thousands of ordinary people live. I had a group of people once who demanded their money back because they saw no one fighting or dying or naked or crazy with drugs.'

Many of its people are deeply attached to Harlem and hope, in spite of the seemingly irremediable poverty and long background of failed panaceas that there will eventually be re-building and renaissance. 'I have no illusions about Harlem – life is tough, but I was born and raised here, so I won't leave,' a shopkeeper said to me:

Only a few years ago parents were still bringing up families in the old way and children had some stability. Now there are a lot of one-parent families. Kids drop out of school and don't get the skills they need, and they find themselves figuring out ways to beat the system and they go into crime to get those $50 sneakers they've just got to have right away. Half the people round here are working and the rest are unemployed and getting relief. The poor stand in the cheese lines for surplus government cheese, and you'll find that boys will sometimes rob old people of their cheese. It is hard being in business. I'm in sports goods and some big-name companies won't supply me because they say my business is too small. Recently, a man came in here and stuck a gun in my side and tied me up, and my assistant too, and took $700. If you're a businessman in Harlem people are sure you have a lot of money. Then this guy found out where I lived and came to my apartment with a gun but I chased him away. Now I lock the door of the store and you have to knock if you want to come and buy something. But for all that it is not too dangerous round here, and the people are good, and religious. If you're going to say anything about Harlem you can say that we're hanging on.

In the lobby of my apartment building I have just seen a gaucho in full fig – hat, baggy trousers and boots. It is the sort of curious sight that makes New Yorkers say with pride: Only in New York. I thought of asking the doorman how it was that a gaucho was so far from Patagonia; but I decided not to do so for fear of receiving a perfectly reasonable explanation.

6 The Onion Patch

Chicago and the Midwest

You are white –
yet a part of me, as I am part of you.
That's American.

LANGSTON HUGHES

'SAY,' began the taxi driver. He was built on solid midwestern lines and could hold the wheel in place with the bear-fat belly he had grown to protect himself against the winter winds which come snarling out of Canada. We were heading along the Magnificent Mile section of Michigan Avenue, the grand avenue of the keystone city of the American middle west. To be upon this breezy thoroughfare is to be invigorated, to be filled and enthused by a sense of Chicago's rugged style and power. Part of the river we were approaching used to flow the other way, carrying sewage into Lake Michigan; so Chicago, like Superman grappling with nature, reversed its direction. Chicago does not give itself airs and there is nothing dainty or flimsy about it, nothing *nouvelle cuisine* or pretentious about its food, its people, architecture, writing, business or politics. 'Here is a tall bold slugger set vivid against the little soft cities', wrote Carl Sandburg in his hymn to it. It is in all ways a big-boned and burly city and its muscular buildings stand in massive majesty like a row of wrestlers. It has three of the world's five tallest buildings, including the tallest, 1450ft, as befits the city that gave birth to the skyscraper. 'Yes,' a radio talk show host assured a caller, 'the Sears Tower is the tallest building in the world.' 'All right,' said the caller patiently, 'but is it the tallest building in Chicago?' The taxi driver made a broad and proprietorial sweep with his Popeye right arm. 'Say,' he said with a snorting laugh, 'what do you think of our town now we've kicked the Indians out?'

The Indians were shovelled away long ago. In its infancy Chicago was a frontier settlement and the Chippewas, Ottawas and Pottawatomies came here in large numbers to trade in furs, guns, whiskey and vermilion. Under a typical hustlers' deal, dignified as a treaty, they were dispossessed of land, paid off in cheap goods and whiskey and told to pack up and head west, out of sight, out beyond the pale of the Mississippi. In 1835 they departed, performing a final, terrifying, corybantic war dance in front of nervous pioneers, before trailing their thin shadows towards the setting sun. They had contributed to Chicago's early vitality and also provided its name: cheecagou was what they called the sharp-smelling onion that abounded in the swamps hereabouts, where the immense and fertile prairies met the vast inland sea of Lake Michigan. The city has retained a pungency and, from time to time, has given off a stink.

On this particular trip one of the people I planned to meet was Leanita McClain, the first black member of the editorial board of the *Chicago Tribune* and, by the by, recently named by *Glamour* magazine as one of America's ten most outstanding working women. Some months earlier she had written an extraordinary article in the *Washington Post* under the headline 'How Chicago Taught Me to Hate Whites'. It was an angry and distressed cry, quite harrowing in its bleakness, an anguished reaction to the dirty election war of 1983 from which Harold Washington emerged as Chicago's first black mayor. This was a clawing struggle for power, in which race provided much of the bile. White politicians played openly on white fears and whites were urged to vote 'before it's too late' for the white candidate. In her misery and confusion Leanita McClain concluded that Chicago was possessed by evil. 'Why is it this way? Why my beloved city, so vital, so prosperous, so exhilarating?'

Every morning during the campaign she listened to the radio. 'In what would become a standard bigot-in-the-street interview, the voice was going on about "the blacks". The blacks this, the blacks that, the blacks, the blacks, the blacks. *The* blacks. It is the article that offends. The words are held out like a foul-smelling sock transported at the end of an outstretched arm . . . '

She said she had been unprepared for the silence with which her white colleagues greeted Harold Washington's nomination.

I've been crushed by their inability to share the excitement of one of 'us' making it into power. [When Washington won] black strangers exchanged sly smiles on the streets. A jubilant scream went up, but it was a silent one, something like the high-pitched tones only animals can discern. The black man won! We did it! We had a feeling, and above all we had power. So many whites unconsciously had never considered that blacks could do much of anything. My colleagues looked up and realised, perhaps for the first time, that I was one of 'them'. I was suddenly threatening. Whites were out of their wits with plain wet-your-pants fear. Happy black people can only mean unhappy white people in this town.

I had put so much effort into belonging, and the whites in my professional and social circles had put so much effort into making me feel as if I belonged, that we all deceived ourselves. There is always joking about 'it' – those matching the suntans against black skin, or the exchange of dialect or finding common ground on the evils of racism. But none of us had dealt with the deeper inhibitions, myths, and misperceptions. Now I know that solving the racial problem will take more than living, marrying and going to school together and all of those laudable but naive goals I defend. Who was I to trust? How was I to know which whites were good and which were bad? This affair has cemented my journalist's acquired cynicism, robbing me of most of my innate black hope for true integration. It has made me sparkle as I revelled in the comradeship of blackness. It has banished me to nightmarish bouts of sullenness. This battle has made me hate. I've detested my colleagues at the *Chicago Tribune* who pretend to have immense racial concerns and knowledge but who don't know blacks other than me and who haven't come in touch with ordinary whites in decades. No white will ever be trusted again with the innermost me . . . At least I tried to extend my hand, which is more than most whites can say; they do not encounter enough blacks in their lifetime to try.

When I telephoned Leanita McClain's office a colleague said that she had taken her life a few hours before. She was 32 years old, idealistic and sensitive. Her unhappiness had many roots, but a black journalist said to me that she was deeply troubled by the prejudice of which she wrote and by the strains of being a rôle model, a successful black woman in a white world.

City newspapers were reporting that the figure of a saint in one of the city's Catholic churches had been seen weeping, and I reflected that it was not surprising. Chicago politics were at the civil war stage, with race the inseparable and complicating ingredient. Two-fifths of the city's three million people are white, two-fifths black; and the rest largely hispanic. Things had grown so bad that one of the city's aldermen claimed he was wearing a bullet-proof vest. The mayor's white opponents vowed they would never submit to a black-run administration. Unencumbered by integrity or a sense of civic responsibility, they laid siege and worked earnestly to smear and sabotage the new government, to bring down the mayor at any cost. It was deplorable and damaging, but this has always been a knuckleduster town, a political rough-house with a wafer-thin rule book.

Harold Washington was attempting nothing less than a revolution, the ending of Chicago's municipal oligarchy. In particular he was out to dismantle the Democratic party machine which had ruled here for more than fifty years. Many American cities have been run by similar authoritarian feudal networks. New York once had Tammany Hall and Philadelphia the Organization. Boston, Kansas City and Memphis had notorious machines, too. Bossism evolved in the 19th century as a seemingly efficient way of shaping fast-growing cities filling with immigrants of differing backgrounds. These people formed incoherent and shifting societies which accepted the systems they found and were content to have their cities' economies sliced up by barons. The bosses, little troubled by democratic notions, sought to manage efficiently and profitably. The machines were corruptions under the skin of American democracy, but democrats had to acknowledge their power for many years, finding it hard to swim against the tide.

Growing political maturity, a better press, demographic changes and public impatience brought about the demise of the oligarchies but Chicago retained the last of the great machines as an extraordinary anachronism. This ruled a patchwork of minor states, the city's neighbourhoods, through a complex hierarchy of command. The currency and leverage were jobs. The machine appointed judges, police chiefs, civil servants and the dustmen. It fixed business, banking, the labour unions and law enforcement. It made the trains run on time. It cut deals with property developers. It deployed its forces expertly to decapitate or incorporate new outgrowths of power. Many people liked the machine and the way that Chicago, in the words of the boss, was the city that worked. They liked the efficiency of being able to fix things down at the courthouse and city hall. Because of its ability to deliver votes in large numbers, national politicians, presidential candidates, came to pay respectful calls. The most formidable boss, Mayor Richard Daley, ruled Chicago for twenty-one years until his death in 1976. He was a big, ruthless, arrogant baron; and city hall, massive, grey and square, was his keep. He had an intimate knowledge of neighbourhoods and their politics, and of the weaknesses and ambitions of men. He had 40,000 jobs to disburse and dealt with the public through his chieftains, the ward chairmen and precinct captains, who had clout in their own manors and whose task was to keep the boss informed, to do his bidding, to work as hard as he and deliver up the votes at elections.

Spines shivered at Daley's growl. In the council chamber he had a sharp way with free speech, a switch to cut off the microphones of aldermen who talked too much. On St Patrick's Day, when the Chicago river was sentimentally dyed emerald, and Boss Daley, as the city's chief Irishman, took the salute at the parade, his subordinates and petty chieftains seemed to walk by the podium on tiptoe and stretch their necks as they sought to be noticed by him.

Harold Washington learnt his politics in machine-run Chicago and eventually became a US congressman for the city's south side, an established and stable black community of 800,000 with a strong middle class. Blacks had their place in the machine and accepted what it disbursed in jobs, housing and education; and it was not much. When Washington ran for mayor blacks saw their chance. In a significant eruption of political feeling and organisation they registered to vote in large numbers and the wave bore Washington into city hall. He made it plain that patronage and the carving up of Chicago were finished. This was a blow for the rump of the machine, the youngish, greedy and cynical men who had hoped for their turn at the carvery. It was a particular blow to the ego of Edward Vrdolyak, a millionaire lawyer in his mid-40s, the strutting leader and loud spokesman of the machine. He was annealed in the Chicago tradition and as sharp as a costermonger. His legal deals had earned him the name of Fast Eddie. The mayor called him 'the beautiful gambler, amoral and full of bull'. Fast Eddie said he was not going to have the new guy on the block telling him he was out. 'I don't go down easy,' he declared. 'I don't end up a nobody.'

The council divided on racial lines and the mayor, without a working majority, found it hard to get things done. Still, the council was liberated in the sense that it was no longer the machine's rubber stamp and had become a forum. The war was an unseemly spectacle, a rum way of running America's third largest city, but race was only a part of it. The machine was trying to wrestle the mayor to the ground, to get him to give up his reforming ways and go back to business as usual or get out. But the struggle was also one between past and future. Fast Eddie and Co. were dinosaurs roaring at the loss of role and dominance. Many of Chicago's whites were having to face the racial realities that those in the American south had learnt years before. Harold Washington's ending of the white ascendancy and machine dominance was part of the larger struggle and change in the United States, the politicisation and truer emancipation of blacks. As a crusader, though, Harold Washington wore armour that was not completely shiny and in his struggle to drag Chicago politics into the late 20th century he found himself hobbled not only by greedy diehards but also by his own streak of stubborn pride and carelessness. He was brilliant, but no great administrator. His sloppiness presented opponents with ammunition and exasperated his supporters. He had once been jailed for a month for failing to file income tax returns, although he owed little, and, naturally, his opponents made much of it. His prison mug-shot was shown on television and when he visited the local jail years later a television reporter described the event as a homecoming. A black writer said to me: 'Blacks feel let down by him. When he was elected he was a god. Now people are complaining. All blacks know that they have to be twice as good as whites in this city just to compete. It's a sort of code. But Harold has forgotten the code.'

When Washington was elected many blacks exulted: 'We want it all!' – which sent shivers through whites. There were excessively high expectations among people who thought that it was now their turn. The mayor improved the racial balance in city hall, but to save money he had to cut hundreds of city jobs, mostly black and hispanic, an action that caused dismay. He said he did not want to be the blacks' mayor: he wanted to be Chicago's mayor, if the bigots would let him.

Black mayors are a modern phenomenon. The first was elected in 1967 and by the middle of the 1980s more than 280 cities had black mayors, including major ones like Detroit, Atlanta, New Orleans, Newark, Philadelphia, Los Angeles, Oakland, Washington and Birmingham. In general blacks are elected when blacks form more than two-fifths of a city's people. Blacks migrated to northern cities in large numbers as employment declined in the southern cotton fields after the First World War. The proportion of blacks in city populations increased as whites moved to the suburbs and – in the 1960s and 1970s – to the sunbelt. While blacks saw the election of black mayors as evidence of advancement, the prizes were sometimes flawed. The major northern cities that had been the heart and muscle of industrial America, as steelmakers, manufacturers and car builders, fell into economic decline as the United States became less a strong manufacturing nation and more a service and high technology one, a trend that many Americans regretted, seeing it as the loss of a certain national virility and self-sufficiency. The old powerhouses of the north became characterised as the rust-

belt or rustbowl, losing jobs, factories, people and tax bases.
During the 1970s Chicago lost more than 123,000 jobs and more
than 360,000 people, a tenth of its population. Arson, decay and
demolition destroyed 60,000 homes and conditions worsened in
the slums and skid rows. So the challenge for new black mayors
was tough. Pessimists saw them as sextons for the cities. Optimists hoped they would be surgeons with a cure.

Of course, great cities do not crumble. Chicago has its problems but it remains a major business, manufacturing, food
processing, money, transport and wholesaling hub. It has huge
universities, a strong literary tradition and colourful tommygun
journalism. Its airport is the busiest in the world. Its neighbourhoods are lively. It is still the largest Polish-speaking city after
Warsaw – 'a mushroom and a suburb of Warsaw,' Arnold Bennett
called it. It has blue-collar brawniness and a blue-collar history.
With its background of pellmell growth, ethnic diversity, rivalries
and assertiveness it is the essential American city. Its black
culture is energetic. It has some of the top black businesses and is
a mainspring in black politics. It is a giant; and Harold Washington's victory was a political watershed. On the night of his election
Leanita McClain wrote that no black slept, and that 'there were
never so many bright black eyes as there were the next morning.'

Harold Washington became mayor of Chicago twenty years after
Martin Luther King stood under gaunt Lincoln's gaze in 1963
and cried out in impassioned oratory to the quarter of a million
people who had marched on Washington. His words sounded the
end of one age and the beginning of another . . . 'I have a dream
that my four little children will one day live in a nation where they
will not be judged by the colour of their skin but by the content of
their character.'

Shortly afterwards whites bombed a black church in Alabama
and killed four children. There was more bloodshed and cruelty
as Americans bent to the unfinished business of the Civil War.
There was the frenzied last stand of white supremacists, black

fury and burning cities, the murder of Martin Luther King himself in 1968.

During the 1960s idealistic whites stiffened the ranks of the small black middle class in the civil rights movement and played an important role. Many saw themselves putting right an immense social wrong. But in time the moderate civil rights movement, in which whites linked hands with blacks to sing *We Shall Overcome* began to wither as disillusioned blacks concluded it was better to jut an angry chin than offer a conciliatory cheek. Whites were perplexed and frightened by the bitterness of black revolt. Dr King's oration at the Lincoln memorial marked the peak of a movement acceptable to liberals for its nobility of purpose; but it also foretold that 'whirlwinds of revolt' would go on shaking the United States. It was a sombre warning as well as an inspiration. Whites found, like blacks, that slaying diehard southern dragons was not enough and that there were no easy solutions. They thought that fighting for civil rights would close a chapter; but the painful truth was that racism was not just southern: it was American and the racial problem was far more complex and poisonous than they had imagined.

In the first place, however, there was remarkable change, an ending of the old repressive system. The civil rights struggle was one of history's magnificent mass movements, a moral hurricane. It harnessed white sympathy, guilty consciences, recognition of injustice, the power of law and the practical desire to make the American system work properly. The south, which was economically and socially weakened by segregation, remains astonished at what has been accomplished in the two decades since Dr King said in Washington that he dreamed that the children of slaves and slave owners would sit together. Many young people in the south can scarcely believe that their parents lived under a system of apartheid. The battles to desegregate lunch counters and buses, to establish basic decencies, seem to them to be deepest history. But it was not that long ago that black soldiers, returning from Europe and the Pacific after the Second World War, reckoned that their fight for freedom began when they came down the troopship gangplank. They returned to be terrorised by white supremacists and lynch mobs. John Gunther's 1946 book *Inside U.S.A.* has a chart listing the states, their populations, incomes, number of telephones and cars – and number of lynchings. Most of the blacks lynched after the war had served with the forces.

The physical apparatus of segregation is literally in the museum. In the Museum of American History in Washington I saw signs, painted White Only and Colored Only, that were once affixed to lavatories and drinking fountains. In Atlanta, Leroy Johnson, Georgia's first black senator in the 1960s, recalled that cafés and lavatories in the state assembly were segregated and that in the first assembly session only four of fifty-two senators spoke to him. 'All that's finished,' he said. 'In that particular respect we've come a long way.' The mayor of Atlanta, Andrew Young, an aide to Dr King during the civil rights campaigns, and later the American representative at the United Nations, told me that when he was a student on his way home from college he was afraid to stop in Atlanta because he ran the risk of white harassment. 'Now I'm its second black mayor. Much of Martin's dream has been achieved and the social inequalities he fought against have gone. We don't have to march against brutal sheriffs any more. The police force in Atlanta today is 48 per cent black. But there is still oppression and discrimination and we have not been able to find ways of changing things rapidly enough.' When he first ran for office, Andrew Young had little support from the white community and the contest was a bitter racial one. Four years later, in 1985, he had improved relationships between blacks, who are three-fifths of the city's people, and the strong white business establishment, and won re-election by a landslide.

Among the relics of segregation in the museum in Washington there were also some Ku Klux Klan robes and a cross, built for burning. The Klan these days is a tattered, bitter and ugly remnant, a few thousand people divided into numerous factions, headed by 'imperial wizards' and 'grand dragons'. The original Klan was founded in 1867 by disgruntled ex-Confederate soldiers who saw their world turned upside down by postwar reconstruction. They took their name from *kuklos*, Greek for circle, and fashioned it into Ku Klux. Their brutality led their founder to disband it after two years. It was revived in 1915 by a preacher whose hate list included Darwinism, Catholics and Jews as well as blacks. It became a frightening force in southern life and politics and ruthlessly persecuted blacks by arson, lynching and beatings. In its terrorist heyday, 1920-25, it had about four million members, but its strength dwindled quickly after newspapers exposed its cruelty and corruption. Fragments of the Klan lived on, donning the white robes, burning crosses, part of the white terrorism of the civil rights years. Today it is penetrated by the police and FBI. Its various groups sometimes hold parades and, from time to time, commit acts of violence and intimidation. In 1983, for example, there was an echo of the old viciousness when two men in Mobile, Alabama, randomly selected a black youth of 19 from a street, took him out of town, strangled him and then drove him back into Mobile and hanged him from a camphor tree.

In his Washington speech Martin Luther King said: 'I have a dream that one day even the state of Mississippi, sweltering with the heat of injustice and oppression, will be transformed into an oasis of freedom and justice.' Whatever was happening in the rest of the United States it was worse in Mississippi, poorest state in the union. Its racism was brutal, embedded and legitimised. But today Mississippians look with some wonder on the change from the days when soldiers had to force the state's demagogic leaders to obey the desegregation law. Charles Overby, executive editor of the *Clarion-Ledger* in Jackson, the state capital said:

I remember the day that a gubernatorial candidate shook hands publicly with a black man for the first time. Shook hands! He knew it would cost him votes. It used to be fashionable to be racist – it was simply a part of our way of life. There was a great fear of the unknown in desegregation, but once the barrier was broken people saw that something good was happening. Everything here used to revolve around race, but no longer. Mississippi held out to the last on segregation, but now it is a model in race relationships. When you consider the last two hundred years of southern history we've made a great leap in twenty. The state legislature was a remnant of the white power structure, but it has at last passed measures to reform an education system that shut blacks out. When the *Clarion-Ledger* was owned by segregationists it called one of the early civil rights judgements a tragedy. Recently the paper reflected on the past twenty years and said: 'We were wrong, wrong, wrong'.

Southern newspapers used to doctor group photographs to prevent blacks appearing in print. Just as in the totalitarian states they affected to despise, America categorised some of its citizens as non-people. Miami's first black police chief, appointed in 1985, recalled that when he graduated from police college there were two official photographs taken of his graduation class. He appeared in one of them, but not the other. Segregation collapsed partly under the weight of the absurdity of its rules and bureaucracy, as well as its manifest injustices.

To all those who heard him that day in Washington, Dr King seemed to spin out a web of hope. There was a promise of deserved rewards after weary struggle, a belief that a better breeze would blow. The external manifestations of segregation were swept away. New laws helped to create a framework of more tolerant behaviour. Official pressures, the bussing of children to integrate schools, job quotas for blacks, helped to change attitudes; though not without controversy and doubts about their efficacy. In time there was the first black astronaut, the first black Miss America, black mayors and judges and police chiefs, 6000 elected black officials, the recruiting of thousands of black police officers. A black man ran for the presidency. Some of these events were symbolic but they excited the imagination of blacks, boosted morale and improved a sense of self-worth that had been crushed for centuries. Symbols have their important place.

But in the years after the civil rights victories blacks, and whites too, began to realise that these were only a beginning, only a partial fulfilment, that in the long and epic march of the black people of America it was another episode: and the road ahead was still hard. Hopes began to crumble.

In the 1970s the black grievance slid from stage centre as Vietnam dominated the national consciousness. During that war the bodies of a number of black American soldiers were refused burial in white cemeteries. In some cases parents obtained court orders so that their sons could be buried in cemeteries where blacks had not been buried before.

It was an example of the way old attitudes and superstitions lingered, an echo of the segregationist tradition of the American forces. Thousands of freed blacks fought in the Civil War, at a time when most blacks were slaves. When the United States entered the First World War in 1917 black units were loaned to France and fought under the French flag. When the Second World War started the forces operated a system of white supremacy and most black troops were in labour battalions – plantation battalions blacks called them – which built roads and airstrips. Many trained fighting men were kept at home. But with pressure increasing on white troops, General Eisenhower, once an opponent of desegregation in the services, told blacks they could volunteer for combat and many did; but they were not integrated. Black regiments and air force squadrons were formed; but most blacks in the navy were employed as stewards. In Britain and elsewhere black soldiers experienced the strange sensation of being treated with fairness and friendliness by whites, a stark contrast with their own country. It made them ponder. In the Korean war the forces continued to reflect civilian life and persisted with the absurdity of separate regiments, and separate officers' and sergeants' messes. It was not until the 1960s, and Vietnam, that Americans went to war with integrated units.

In the 1980s analyses of the black condition produced a balance sheet of the most dismal and pessimistic kind. It was true that blacks had gained a more prominent place in the mainstream. There were all those black heroes flying jets, being cheered in the sports stadiums and on political platforms, making good in business and the professions, earning their admirals' bars and generals' stars. But the debit side of the ledger showed that blacks were still far behind, hobbled by intractable difficulties. After one particular study a number of black academics decided that, 'it is difficult to be optimistic about the future of blacks in American society.'

They saw that blacks are economically mired, lacking boot-straps to pull on, at the bottom of almost every yardstick. Unemployment is twice as high among blacks as among whites. In 1955 three-quarters of young black men were working; now only half of them are. The black poverty rate is three times that of whites. In the mid-1960s blacks earned, on average, 55 per cent of the white wage average. They still do. More than two-fifths of black children depend on welfare assistance. More than two-fifths of the men in prison are black. Black juveniles are less than a fifth of the youth population, but they commit more than half the crime.

Life is harder in many ways. Blacks have a shorter life expectancy than whites, an infant mortality rate twice as high, and very high rates of divorce, separation and mental illness. It was only in the 1980s that blacks felt they could openly discuss a subject they had hitherto kept to themselves – the rapid corrosion of family life. Half of the black children born today are born outside marriage. Black leaders talk of an epidemic of illegitimate births. In some cities the proportion is as high as three-quarters. The number of female-led black families is growing rapidly and there is plainly a great decline in family and community responsibility, a huge undermining of a traditionally family-oriented people. More black girls bear a child in secondary school than graduate from college. A young woman hoping for a traditional marriage with a man who has a job is at a disadvantage: there are not enough men in that category. If young unemployed or jailed men are subtracted from the marriageable black male population there are far more single black women than men.

Educational standards are, in general, low, reflecting a wide-spread apathy. Half of the black pupils in Chicago high schools drop out before finishing their education. Almost half of black 17-year-olds are illiterate and blacks consistently score lower marks than whites in college entrance examinations. Although the proportion o blacks entering colleges rose in the 1970s, it began to fall in the 1980s. There is plenty of room for black lecturers in the leading universities and these establishments are anxious to have them; but they are hard to find.

There is another matter that some black leaders are reluctant to bring into the open, while others say it is concealed to the detriment of black communities: two-fifths of American murder victims are blacks killed by blacks. Murder is the leading cause of death among black men aged 15 to 24. A third of the deaths in this age group are murders. A white man stands a 1 in 186 chance of being murdered; a black man has a 1 in 29 chance. More than half of the killings in Chicago involve black victims and black murderers. Many whites have a strong fear of violent crime and believe that theirs is a very violent country. That is one of the reasons they arm themselves. But only one-twentieth of white murder victims are killed by blacks. It is blacks in the large cities who have good reason for fear, and the fear is ever present. They are more than twice as likely as whites to be robbed and attacked, and the poor suffer more than the better-off.

Newspapers carry numerous reports of casual and indiscriminate shootings on the streets and in schools. Young lives are snuffed out in casual playground shootouts. Many killers are in their teens and 8 per cent of murders are committed by juveniles. In some places it seems that guns are packed as routinely as school pencils. Police say that many young black killers feel no remorse and have no sense of the worth of a life, their own or anyone else's. They are brought up in poor neighbourhoods, with little prospect of a job, without hope and little self-esteem. They are conditioned by despair.

For both blacks and whites the legacy of slavery is shown to be more terrible and disappointing than they had ever imagined. They are witnessing an appalling disintegration. Civil rights promised so much, but did not deliver; and now people feel betrayed and embittered. 'We were slow to move from the protest movement into politics, thinking that passing a few laws was enough,' Harold Washington said. The 29 million blacks are about 12 per cent of the population of 239 million, but they hold only one per cent of elected positions. While more blacks progress in business it is harder for them to reach boardrooms and managers' chairs. Until the 1960s they were kept out of the American Bar Association. They are prominent in sport, but few get into management. Bigotry and fear help to push the scales to their disadvantage. The small middle class is doing well, but some unions still make it difficult for working class people to get jobs. The number of black businesses increased by nearly 50 per cent in the five years up to 1982, but their earnings fell, and those businesses are only 1 per cent of the total business sector.

Bishop Brookins, a leading Los Angeles churchman, said to me:

After all these years white Americans do not really know us, do not know how diverse we are. I feel frustrated that we have not come far enough and have not been able to make people understand our desire to be part of the whole. There is still resistance to black progress and white conservatives play on fears that black advance is at white expense. The job market remains segregated and the black man finds himself running to remain in the same place.

If there is one thing blacks earnestly desire from their fellow Americans it is their respect. It was in pursuit of this, and auxiliary goals of increasing the sense of black responsibility for their own development, and a deeper political awareness, that Jesse Jackson went on the road. I first saw him in Atlanta, before he announced his tilt at the presidency, and at that time there was no doubt that he was the most exciting man in American politics. Two thousand people packed the hall and women stood on chairs for a better view as he strode forward into the lights. An electric organ blasted a fanfare and he bounded onto the stage, detonating an explosion of cheering. He was introduced as a prophet of God and the crowd called out 'Yessir' and 'Right on!' Jackson fired people with the audacious notion that a black, the great-grandchild of slaves, could aspire to be president. He demanded that blacks should have their share of the American dream. 'We die in war together. We pay taxes together. Now we want to share power together. Hands that picked cotton will pick the president.'

His long and powerful oration had the cadences of the black church and rose in spirals of intensity, a sensational solo, while the sound of the crowd swelled like a great orchestra beneath him. 'Run for the courthouse. Run for the statehouse. Run for the White House. Run!' – 'Run, run, run,' chanted the delirious crowd as the organist pounded chords. Jackson abandoned his text and flew into evangelical fervour, all preacher, gasping for breath, his throat rasping. 'From outhouse to White House! Our time has come!' he cried in final exultation, and hands reached out to him as he fell, drained, into the embraces of his friends.

'I'm a catalyst,' he said to me later, 'trying to get people to take part in their own democracy, to register to vote, to use the vote. We have won freedom but we still have to reach equality.' At many meetings in the south, I watched him hammer the theme of self-worth. He spoke under pecan trees and in the churches that remain significant meeting places and places of solace for blacks. In the idiom of the church he told people, 'There's a freedom train a'comin.' Like a teacher, he made his audiences repeat constantly: 'I am somebody.' All black leaders have to give great attention to this fundamental inspirational work, the work of repairing the spirit of people long dishonoured. A large part of the true emancipation of black people lies in the recovery of the pride that was crushed out of them by slavery and the half-freedom that lasted to the 1960s.

Jackson's campaign to get people to register to vote was a battle against apathy. Having got the vote, blacks had not used it. Jackson and other leaders had to work for a wholesale change of attitudes among people who had no traditions of voting, a long history of exclusion from politics. The registration drive was also against prejudice, intimidation and the tangle of local registration rules creating difficulties for blacks wanting to register. Jackson's voter drive among blacks brought a response from white fundamentalist churches which ran their own registration campaigns, and most of the new white voters were Republicans.

Jesse Jackson's shot at the Democratic candidacy was also the culmination of a personal odyssey out of the pain and humiliation he endured as an illegitimate child in a racist society. He stirred in blacks a feeling that they count, and rallied people who knew that the civil rights tide had ebbed and felt that the Reagan administration was unfriendly to them. The government began a campaign to dismantle the civil rights policies on affirmative action, the use of racial preferences in jobs to help blacks get a firmer economic and social foothold. Edwin Meese, the attorney-general, to whom the destruction of affirmative action was a crusade, called the policies racist and discriminatory. To many blacks it seemed that the government was undermining blacks. They argued that preferences helped to ameliorate an historic wrong, gave the blacks a sense of their worth, built bridges into the mainstream and created the rôle models that inspire others. But a number of black intellectuals began to say that quotas and other remedies based in law are not necessarily the best way to meet the complex problems of the black poor. They contended that quotas are bad for the self-esteem of people who get jobs in this way: their white colleagues inevitably think of them as quota people, inferiors. These academics put a renewed emphasis on a traditional black theme, that blacks should take a greater responsibility for themselves and the emergency in black communities. They argued that it was pointless to wait for official panaceas. On the question of poor educational performance they said much of the difficulty lay in traditional black reluctance to compete, a legacy of racism and the negative image of blacks. They said blacks accepted the white characterisation of them as inferior, and rather than compete, they tended to withdraw. The answer was for blacks to reject imposed inferiority and take command of their problems. But millions of people have had hope wrung from them and it will be hard to restore it. Rudyard Kipling once noted that 'It is not good to be a Negro in the land of the free' – and today it can still be bad to be young, American and black. The black condition remains a crucial American question.

Plainly there are great dangers in neglecting it. Despair is
tinder.

One of the richest men in America is John Johnson, a publisher
and manufacturer. At the last count he was worth $160 million.
He started at the very bottom – a black boy raised in Arkansas and
in the slums of Chicago's south side in the bleakest years of the
Depression. His widowed mother was on the welfare rolls for a
time and worked in humble jobs to help get him an education. He
was fortunate to have a tough mother. 'She kept on telling me to
keep trying.' He has stayed in Chicago and now he has a fine view
of Lake Michigan from his luxurious office suite at the top of his
company's eleven-storey building; and his mother lived to see
him become prosperous. He does not conceal his pleasure at his
success, but also seems slightly surprised by it. 'I thought my way
out of poverty,' he said. 'I read Dale Carnegie's *How To Win
Friends and Influence People* fifty times.'

When he was 24, and working for an insurance company, his
mother borrowed $500 against the security of her furniture and
with it he started a magazine called *Negro Digest*. To get it
established on newsstands and to convince a white distributor
that there was a demand he persuaded friends to go around
asking for it. Within a year it was selling 50,000 copies a month.
Being black he had difficulties meeting prospective advertising
clients because he could not rent a room in large central hotels.
But he used to get a light-skinned colleague to register for a room
and he and other associates travelled to the meeting in the service
lift, mistaken for tradesmen. When he was buying his first
publishing building he had to get a white friend to act as a front for
him. In 1945, with the money he made from *Negro Digest*, he
started *Ebony* magazine, which was immediately successful. It is
the largest black magazine in the world, with a circulation of two
million. He also owns *Jet* magazine, two radio stations and a
cosmetics company which sells throughout the world. On his way
to becoming the most successful black businessman in the

United States he also became chairman of the insurance company where he started as an office boy.

Ebony is successful because it is glamorous, optimistic and runs stories of black success, of triumph after struggle. 'It promotes self-respect, shows the brighter side of black life in America,' Johnson said.

We operate on the principle that if someone is discriminated against he knows it and doesn't need to be told. *Ebony* shows people how they can succeed against all the odds. It reflects my own ideas of the importance of valuing yourself, of working hard, of never taking no for an answer. We show blacks making it. Every black mayor or police chief or successful businessman is featured. We are the journal of record of black progress in America. We try to inspire, to mirror black aspirations, to avoid bitterness and the politics of blame. We cover the important black figures and we were writing about Martin Luther King long before the white press discovered him. I gave money to Harold Washington's campaign and to Jesse Jackson – I was inspired by him.

Johnson seems, on the face of it, to bear no bitterness about the discrimination he has encountered.

Religion plays a large part in my life and some form of religion must have a part in the lives of minority people. You need the faith because so many things are going wrong in your life. Instead of getting angry I consider all the improvements I have seen. We used to be called negroes but we have come to terms with ourselves, have become emancipated in a particular way by acknowledging ourselves and calling ourselves black. But, for all the improvements, there is still discrimination. We are not given a fair chance to reach the executive suites in corporations. Although many of us are well qualified we are not on the right track to reach the top in white companies. We are not the right colour. We do not belong to the right clubs. We do not marry the right women or go to the right schools. The only power blacks have is political, not economic, and we still have to crack that economic barrier. There is so much to do. You have to believe in the prospect of change.

John Johnson and his company executives always fly first class as a matter of principle. Blacks, he says, have been going second-class for long enough.

Part of Chicago's theatre, during one of my visits, was the spectacle of a judge on trial for corruption, for taking thousands of dollars in bribes, fixing drunk driving cases and parking tickets, that sort of thing. The case stemmed from an investigation which led in the end to several other judges and more than a dozen lawyers being charged. Some of the courts seemed to be rotten with corruption and fixing, and the prosecution was talking of up to fifteen judges being in a bribery club. It all seemed perfectly straightforward: if you wanted an acquittal you just paid for it. If you were on a drunk driving charge $100 slipped into an envelope ensured that you left the court without a stain on your character.

Quite apart from the peddling of justice in Chicago, the American white collar was, in other respects, looking in need of a good wash. In 1984 and 1985 there were revelations and confessions of large-scale fraud by corporations and bosses, and American business found itself sweating under the spotlight, accused of shameless greed and falling moral standards. Newspapers had headlines telling of 'White Collar Crime Booming Again,' of 'The New Frenzy to Get Rich' and a 'New Permissiveness Eroding Corporate Morality.' There were reports on the 'Dirty Cash And Tarnished Vaults' of certain banks, and newspapers awarded 'Low Marks For Executive Honesty' and deplored 'The Age of "Me-First" Management'.

The blame was put on a decline in moral values, on increasing pressures on managers to be aggressive and to get results by hook or by crook. The Reagan administration, with its promises to get government off the back of business, was blamed for encouraging corner-cutting. An opinion poll reported that more than half the American people thought business dishonest. Certainly a number of major business institutions were found running some dubious or dishonest schemes. The huge General Electric organisation was discovered swindling the government of $800,000 by forging workers' timesheets on a missile contract. The company head, nominated by *Fortune* magazine as America's toughest boss, said he tried to make heroes of his company's risk-takers. General Dynamics, another defence contract giant, was found cheating the taxpayers. It billed the government for $18,000 so that one of its executives could join a golf club. Another executive charged the government $150 for his dog's board in kennels while he joined fellow bosses for a weekend at a resort, the expense of which was also charged to the government.

These were not isolated incidents. During 1984 more than 400 defence contractors were disqualified or suspended for irregularities; and between 1972 and 1982 115 of the 500 largest corporations were convicted of a major crime or had paid fines for serious misbehaviour. The venerable Bank of Boston was fined $500,000 in 1985 for breaking currency laws, and E.F. Hutton, a leading broker, was fined $2 million for systematically cheating 400 banks in a cunning scheme of overdrawing on accounts. As the firm was making $150 million a day on the scheme the fine was not even a pinprick. Some people in business said that the public's opinion of dishonesty in the corporate towers would have to be heeded because business crime was bad for business. The government talked of there being a few rotten apples in the barrel, but to many Americans it seemed that the whole orchard was blighted.

From Chicago I headed south-west across the prairie, the flat brown farmland of Illinois. This is what they came for in the last century – all those Germans, Scandinavians and Britons, trekking across land so immense and flat and treeless it made their eyes ache. And this is what they made, a landscape of the most productive farms in the world, handsome white clapboard houses, red barns, gleaming silos, spherical water tanks held aloft on towers and quiet little towns built from the basic formula of white wooden school, post office, garage, George's Diner and two or three churches to suit varying tastes. Here was created the American heartland – the prairies and the plough shaped the nation.

At the start of the century a third of Americans lived on farms. Today, although relatively few do so, the family farm is embedded in American consciousness, part of tradition and mythology. When President Reagan campaigned and talked airily of traditional values he used happy farming images in his evocation of a freedom-loving country of rugged individualists. But in the 1980s the farming heartland became racked by financial crisis. In the previous decade farmers were encouraged to grow as much as they could and to buy more land and machinery. They and the country banks bit off more than they could chew. The export market shrank because of the strong dollar. There was a farmland glut and land prices slumped. Farmers were paid by the government to grow less. Thousands were ruined, sunk in debt. Banks foreclosed on loans and newspapers were full of auction notices as farms were closed and their equipment sold. In some places bankers were hated figures. In Minnesota the son of a ruined farmer shot two bankers. Some bank men took to wearing bullet-proof vests.

The President's budget director said farmers were the authors of their own misfortune, but family farmers felt betrayed and said the government had encouraged overproduction and then pulled the rug out. All over the prairie there is despair. On a farm that had been in their family since 1854 I talked to a farmer and his wife whose anxiety was plain to see. 'The government lacks compassion,' the man said. 'People in politics get further and further away from farming and they do not see the connection between the agricultural economy and the whole economy. What I regret is that at the age of 61, when I was hoping to retire, I'm trapped in debt and face years of struggle. Farmers always have to be optimists, but I've never known such bad times.' A few months later he died of a heart attack.

On my way across Illinois I completed a sort of circle: I had earlier visited the deathplace of Wild Bill Hickok in Deadwood, South Dakota, and now I made a detour to see his birthplace at Troy Grove. The facts of Hickok's life are more extraordinary than most frontier fiction. He was a stagecoach driver, Union army scout and spy in the Civil War, gunfighter and marshal of Abilene. He worked for Custer in operations against Indians, and was killed, five weeks after Custer's death, while playing poker in a saloon, his hand holding two aces and two eights, known since as the 'dead man's hand'. A plaque on a granite boulder at Troy Grove records the birth in 1837 of the 'pioneer of the great plains . . . upholder of law and order . . . making the west a safe place for women and children . . . '

It was late by the time I reached the small town that was my goal that night. The only restaurant open for dinner was Haager's, a small and brightly lit place, with a war-bonneted Indian head painted on one of the walls and a ceramic banana coated with chocolate sauce mounted on another. A notice on the wall announced: I Sell Good Food, Not Atmosphere. Another said: Every Weekend Eat Till You Bust. The smiling girl behind the counter said the three-piece chicken dinner was $2.89 and the catfish $3.49.

People were arriving in pick-up trucks and coming in just for ice cream, large helpings with butterscotch and chocolate and cherry sauce, which they excavated in loving tongueloads. Many of the women wore polyester trouser suits in lime green, pink and turquoise, and were hefty in the hip and wobbled as they laughed. This was the heart of Crimplene Country, far from the skinny joggers of New York, the middle west where middle means something. The men had weatherbeaten faces and strong veiny hands and wore either western hats or bill caps which bore the logos of corn merchants and tractor manufacturers. Their good plaid-shirted bellies were reined by strong belts and their tongues stabbed the ice cream like seed drills. I ordered the chicken dinner with garlic bread and a Brownie Delite to cement it, and ate beneath a plastic chicken which dangled by its neck from the ceiling with a placard saying: Best Chicken in Fulton County – The Cluck Stops Here. I watched the people entertaining them- selves with their voluptuous ices and considered the notice on the wall which advised: The Human Stomach Can Only Hold So Much And You Can Stuff It At Our Place. This is the abundant land. Portions on a plate are majestic. The hamburger, the nearest thing to a national dish, is often huge and has to be bloodied with ketchup and grasped in both hands before being burrowed into. In the dining hall of a school in Iowa I saw the following notice: Second Lunch Menu – Monday, Hamburger and Fries, Tuesday, Hamburger and Fries, Wednesday, Hamburger and Fries, Thursday, Hamburger and Fries, Friday, Hamburger and Fries.

The hamburger, which requires no knife and fork and whose management inhibits conversation, the television watcher's tray meal and the retreat from parental responsibility are blamed for the decline in American table manners. In the mid-1980s there was an outpouring of etiquette books and the emergence of manners consultants. To their many other expenses corporations started to add the cost of hiring specialists in the handling of knives, forks, napkins and elbows to mitigate the oafishness of the thrusting young captains of industry.

I crossed the Mississippi bridge into Hannibal, Missouri, where Samuel Clemens, Mark Twain, spent his boyhood. He took the pen name from the cry of riverboat leadsmen calling two fathoms, and the town, the river, the people and his schoolmates gave him grist for *Huckleberry Finn* and *Tom Sawyer*. 'I can picture that old time,' he wrote of Hannibal, 'the town drowsing in a summer's morning, the magnificent and majestic Mississippi rolling its mile-wide tide along, shining in the sun.' Hannibal, St Petersburg in Finn and Sawyer, still drowses. And Jackson's Island, thickly wooded, the resort of boyish pirates, which lies out towards the Illinois shore, is still evocative, like the river itself. Hannibal contentedly makes a fair part of its living, about $40 million, from its association with America's greatest writer. There is a Mark Twain Motor Inn, the Tom n'Huck Motel, Huck Finn Shopping Centre, Becky Thatcher Restaurant, Twainland Tour Bus, Mark Twain Dinette – 'known for its onion rings' – Injun Joe Campground and the Mark Twain river steamer which serves a Becky Thatcher cocktail of rum and strawberries. The house where Sam Clemens lived for fourteen years is of white clapboard with dark green shutters and the fence alongside it is solemnly advertised as the famous fence Tom Sawyer persuaded his friends to paint. Inside the house is a plaque bearing the legend:

> This Great American Home
> is protected by Sears Paint
> as part of an ongoing effort
> to help preserve
> American Heritage

In the kitchen a taped commentary starts at the press of a button and ends: 'Thank you for your attention. Please drive carefully.' Upstairs the commentary bids: 'Goodbye and love to you all.' In the adjoining museum the hoard of Twainiana includes pipes, a typewriter, locks of the author's hair, Old Adjustable Spectacles Like Aunt Polly Wore, the author's head carved in soap and the gown he wore when he received his doctorate of letters at Oxford, along with Rudyard Kipling. Becky Thatcher, the 'lovely little blue-eyed creature' for whom Tom Sawyer fell 'without firing a shot', lived across the street and her bedroom is open for inspection. Her real name was Laura Hawkins and when she died in 1928 both names were inscribed on her tombstone. The house, now the Becky Thatcher Bookshop, is buttressed by a 7ft Coca-Cola machine. Every year a local boy and girl are chosen to be Tom and Becky to help the tourist trade along and actors come to read Twain's work.

Hannibal celebrates and profits from the Twain myth, the agreeable view of him as the moustachioed man in a white suit, the genial humorist and composer of picaresque tales which hymn carefree boyhood and evoke a vanished America. The literary reality, the fierce critic and bitter satirist, was long ago sacrificed to the myth. Twain loved America for its hope and possibilities as a new society and was disappointed by the establishment of new hierarchies of race, religion and class. *Huckleberry*

Finn was first published in London in 1884; the American edition was delayed until the following year because a mischievous engraver added a male organ to an illustration. It has been commonly misunderstood as an adventure story rather than a sustained attack on humbug, racism and greed by a satirist with a bleak view of mankind. These days it is held to be racist for its frequent use of the word nigger, as in:

> 'We blowed out a cylinder-head.'
> 'Good gracious! Anybody hurt?'
> 'No'm. Killed a nigger.'
> 'Well, it's lucky; because people sometimes do get hurt.'

The book was banned by a Massachusetts library on publication, as 'the veriest trash, more suited to the slums.' It remains one of the main targets of earnest school and library censors in the United States.

Parents and school boards restrict the book, and a black member of Chicago education board, complaining that it is 'one of the most grotesque examples of racism ever written', campaigns for its removal from school libraries. In 1984 a stage adaptation in Indiana was cancelled following protests. The most incisive attack on American racism remains misunderstood and widely unread.

Book censorship has increased considerably in recent years, according to librarians and teachers. J.D. Salinger's *The Catcher in the Rye*, Steinbeck's *Of Mice and Men* and *The Grapes of Wrath* are frequently the targets. William Golding's *Lord of the Flies*, Orwell's *1984* and Huxley's *Brave New World* have also been challenged and restricted. A dictionary was banned for having the word bed as a verb. Most school textbook publishers bowdlerise *Romeo and Juliet*. Sometimes the censors stumble: a school board banned, unread, a book called *Making It With Mademoiselle*, and looked foolish because it was a sewing manual. Anti-censorship groups identify their main enemies as religious or activist organisations on the far right, including the indefatigable Mel and Norma Gabler, Texans who for a quarter of a century have been running a group devoted to alerting Americans to what they believe are shortcomings in schoolbooks, and who, being strong creationist opponents of the theory of evolution, are in the thick of the impassioned battle in some parts of America over the teaching of evolution.

When I asked Mr Gabler about his work he said that many school books today are unpatriotic and unAmerican, and do not teach the work ethic, courtesy and moral values. There was a time when history books taught that Indians were the bad guys and settlers were good – now it is the other way round. One of the difficulties, he said, is that too many books are allowing American children to discover and decide values for themselves.

7 Following the Flag

I⁣T WAS canine graduation day in New York. Outside City Hall the mayor took his place on the bunting-decked dais. Below him a dozen newly trained police dogs lay in a row, panting gently, tongues lolling. There was quite a crowd leaning on the blue wooden crush barriers and a lot of policemen milling around, scratching their armpits and hitching up their hip belts which sagged with the cargo of revolver, handcuffs, radio, notebook, pen holster, Mace, torch and truncheon. Before the dogs and handlers were presented to the mayor a young black policeman stepped forward on the dais and began to sing the national anthem, his head thrown back so that his powerful voice seemed to project the words at the skyscraper counting-houses of Wall Street. The people shuffled to attention and put their hands over their hearts.

It demonstrated one of the differences between them and us. One could not imagine a young bobby singing *God Save the Queen* in such circumstances. It would seem bizarre and embarrassing. But a solo rendering of *The Star-Spangled Banner* is a feature of many public functions in the United States. Americans are serious about patriotic rituals. The flag is everywhere prominent, flown not only on public and business buildings, but also from numerous private homes, day in day out. Advertisements for a popular front lawn flag urge: Show Your Pride In The USA – Fly Old Glory. The National Flag Foundation, which exists to promote even more flag-flying and knowledge of the flag's history, says that 'because of our work more Flags are flown in America, the Flag is more often properly saluted, our resurging patriotic spirit is enhanced, new citizens are taught how to salute and youngsters better appreciate the priceless privilege of being an American.' The Foundation keeps a file of Patriotic Articulators who lecture about the stars and stripes. Children are instructed that to drop the flag is to desecrate it. Britons make pants and paper bags out of the union jack, but in the United States the vulgar use of the national banner is forbidden. The Statue of Liberty, though, has no such protection. Her upraised arm is a focus in a sales pitch for deodorants; she wears earphones and a teeshirt to promote a radio station; and her skirt is blown up around her thighs, as in the famous photograph of Marilyn Monroe.

During the 1980s there was significant growth in the $70 million flag-making industry and a surge in orders for giant flags 20ft by 30ft. When I arrived in Grenada, just after the American invasion in 1983, I was struck by the abundance of stars and stripes fluttering from newly dug gun positions and camps, like flags in children's sandcastles. It was as if groups of soldiers had re-enacted the famous and carefully photographed raising of the flag at Iwo Jima, a photograph that is itself a national symbol.

At the Republican convention in Dallas there was a frenzy of flagolatry which made the Democrats' large-scale flag-waggling in San Francisco seem a vicarage fête in comparison. Near the convention hall in Dallas a group of people making a political protest for the benefit of the cameras burnt an American flag. Out of a knot of spectators a man stepped forward. He knelt and gently scooped up the charred fragments in his hands, saying he would give them a decent burial.

American schoolchildren start their day singing the national anthem or hearing it played on a record. They recite the pledge of allegiance to the flag – 'and to the republic for which it stands, one nation under God, indivisible, with liberty and justice for all.' In Massachusetts in 1984 a girl of 17 caused outrage by refusing to join her fellow students in this ritual, saying the flag was only a symbol. She received a spate of abusive telephone calls and letters.

Flags and anthems have their place in all countries. But in

America the flag seems to possess the quality of a saintly bone. It is not surprising that it is so revered and discussed in the most grandiloquent terms. It is the symbol of the American accomplishment, of which these people are so openly proud; and the totem of a society, which, in order to remove the rivalries of tribalism, created the American tribe. Many other nations have long histories, race and religion to shape their nationhood and identity, and also languages, monarchies, customs, ancient institutions. Sometimes the close proximity of other cultures, or external threats, help to define them. But the United States does not have bedrock homogeneity. That is the wonder of it. It is the world in one meadow, a fusion of disparate peoples, predicted on the notion of being a new, consciously invented, nation of free people; an astonishing integration of foreigners, in a country so vast and varied that it is hard even for Americans to comprehend it.

Americans are immensely proud of the house they have built and have always been encouraged to consider themselves a chosen people. Their constitution, a magnificent proposition and creed, generous, progressive, classically liberal, is seen as a sacred tablet. Americans seem sometimes to claim God for their own; and, significantly, they affirm their trust in God on their money. William Gilpin, in his assertion of the idea of manifest destiny in the 19th century said: 'From nothing we are grown to be in agriculture, in commerce, in civilisation, and in natural strength, the first among nations . . . so much is our destiny . . . divine task! immortal mission!' Today Americans make the same point by punching the air and shouting: 'USA – Number One!' and sporting the same slogan on their bumpers. When they ask foreigners 'Ain't we great?' – and they often do – they reckon they have good reason for doing so and for expecting the answer 'Yes'. The American craving for praise has always grated on foreigners: Alexis de Tocqueville, the perceptive biographer of the United States, noted in the 1840s the 'irritable patriotism' of Americans. 'In their relationships with strangers the Americans are impatient of the slightest criticism and insatiable for praise. They are at you the whole time to make you praise them, and if you do not oblige they sing their own praises. Their vanity is not only greedy but also restless and jealous.'

It is one of the paradoxes of the United States that although it is one of the oldest of the democracies, and enviably stable, its people are sensitively aware of its youth and of a certain lack of solidity. In the background of many Americans is the experience or family memory of disconnection, of the discarding of old nationalities in the wholehearted embrace of America. Millions recall that their parents spoke German or Swedish or Polish or Russian, but discouraged their American children from doing so. Today, at a time of relatively high hispanic immigration there is an earnest debate about bilingualism: some Americans believe it would corrode their civilisation.

The American experience is of restlessness and movement, of constantly being refuelled by new blood. A century ago more than nine-tenths of immigrants came from Germany, Britain, Ireland, Italy, central Europe and Russia. Between 1960 and 1969 12 per cent of migrants came from Asia, 36 per cent from Latin America and 39 per cent from Europe. After 1980 nearly half the migrants were Asian, 35 per cent Latin American and 12 per cent European. Until 1965 there were restrictions on the flow of Asians; now they are the new yeast in America. Their academic and economic success marks them out as model migrants, standard bearers of the American dream, starting from scratch and becoming prosperous through hard work. They are having their turn at America.

Thus there are always plenty of new people to be inducted into the tribe, to salute the flag and adopt the American way. America is always being added to, its flavour changed. Apart from inflows of newcomers there are great internal currents of migration, the movement of blacks out of the south after the mechanisation of cotton picking, the rush to the suburbs, the spilling of the mighty cities, the filling of Florida, Texas and California, the sudden peopling of Alaska, the growth of the hispanic population in the south and west.

To these kaleidoscopic changes in American demography in the 1960s and 1970s were added political and social turmoil. Having emerged from the Second World War powerful, victorious and hugely enriched, America feasted gloriously upon the fat fifties. People filled enormous and absurd tailfinned cars with cheap petrol and smoked without fear. The young wore suits and short hair and did not demonstrate, and rock and roll was yet to be. They were an apathetic younger generation on the whole, and their teachers were appalled by their lack of curiosity about the world and their own society. They seemed to lack the energy that brings about change and creates leadership. Students were portrayed in cartoons as empty suits. On the quiet campuses these safe and stodgy young people were not much interested in the way that the witchfinder-general, Joseph McCarthy, the blacklisters and the spiteful and corrupt inquisitors of the House Committee on Un-American Activities – that Orwellian name – spread fear and corroded America. The pendulum, of course, swung wildly. Dissidence and disenchantment swept the campuses, and the young and the parental generation grew apart in the disputatious 1960s and early 1970s. The civil rights movement dislodged the American axis. Cities burnt. Americans queued for petrol like the black and brown peasants they saw on their television screens queuing for water. There were political assassinations, criminality in the White House, the doubt and torment of the Vietnam war.

Ronald Reagan arrived at the confluence of many streams. Liberalism and dissent were in retreat, the Democratic party heading for collapse. Hair was shorter. Jane Fonda was long back from Vietnam and was making money in a leotard, undress uniform of the young affluent. The civil rights tide was ebbing and people felt that they had contributed to reform, that money had been thrown at problems in great quantities, that the required social engineering had been done. The better-off were looking for their turn and the political weather had turned conservative.

Pain and shame were draining from the memories of Vietnam. For years after that defeat it was as if Americans agreed not to talk about it, the family scandal. Now a catharsis was under way. The Vietnam veteran emerged from hiding. Ronald Reagan said the war was noble. It was typical of the way he went straight to the American ache, meeting a fundamental need for emollient. The 1960s and 1970s had confronted Americans with hard choices and the labyrinthine complexities of a world in which they found themselves challenged and, here and there, hated, envied and reviled. It was suddenly dangerous, in some places, to be simply an American. Reagan, who had a sure instinct for saying what people wanted to hear, snatched up the fallen flag and set it flying. He pressed the pride button, simplified everything, restated the basics: America great, Russia bad, economy booming, happy days here again. He was himself a simple, personable man and looked authentic.

To an extent Americans see in their presidents a representation of themselves, a diary of their fortunes. Kennedy was cut short, Johnson broken, Nixon besieged, Carter troubled. The images of these men were a shorthand for difficult and disappointing years. But Reagan was optimistic, and optimism is like a vital chemical secretion to Americans. They feel they deserve good things: their Declaration of Independence holds the pursuit of happiness to be an inalienable right. And while 'Have A Nice Day' is phatic, it has an edge of American optimism to it. Reagan's gift was to communicate the optimism in a strong and physical way, and to package it brightly on television. It was his television presence, style over substance, that earned him the label of 'great communicator'. Certainly he had no skill as an extempore speaker; he was no orator and was inarticulate and even incoherent without a script, though he could read one tolerably well. He never said anything memorable or original. He liked to relate anecdotes to illustrate his points or to quote lines from films. He understood instinctively the theatre of politics and the presidency. A Republican woman from Nevada remarked to me that 'It's not a bad thing that we have an actor for president. Only an actor knows how a president should behave.' It reminded me of the television commercial for a medicine in which a man in a white coat says: 'I'm not a doctor, but I play one on television' – and then recommends a drug.

Reagan was a canvas on which Americans could paint themselves. His slogans were comforting and sentimental. 'America is back, standing tall . . . ' He hailed 'the new patriotism . . . what a change from a few years ago when patriotism seemed so out of style.' During the 1980s this became a commercial as well as a political theme. An advertising spread for a new car showed an upraised fist with the slogan 'The Pride Is Back . . . The good feeling about Made in America is back.' Bumper stickers, the American tomtoms, beat out 'Proud To Be American'. American newspapers chronicled a resurgence of patriotism. 'America's Upbeat Mood,' reported *Time*. 'Once again, people feel good about their lives and their country.' 'America's Mood: Still Finding the Silver Lining,' said *U.S. News and World Report*. At the Olympic Games in Los Angeles there was such an outburst of mafficking that the event seemed at times an exclusive celebration of America. To foreigners it was like watching a grossly obese man stuffing himself at a laden table.

Critics thought the President's inarticulateness and limited interests – a *Washington Post* columnist talked of 'the space between Reagan's ears' – would tell against him. They were wrong. It was true that gaffe-control was an adjunct to his election campaigns and his presidency. Assistants followed like sweepers to mend and re-order his sentences, explaining that 'the President misspoke'. His campaign handlers kept him away from the press because, as one said to me, 'we don't want him to screw up.' He was a poor debater, lacked a command of issues and detail. Once, when he received a tough question at a meeting, an aide thoughtfully disconnected the microphone. His mistakes and tall stories, presented as facts, were described by an associate as parables.

None of these shortcomings mattered much as far as the President's popularity was concerned. The President is head of government and head of state and Reagan skilfully disconnected himself from the former role and concentrated on the latter. He shrewdly built his bridge directly to Americans by way of television and other image-building conduits; and in this pact with the people his authority was based upon his standing as a popular hero: he was like a king declaring himself the people's champion against oppressive government. In all this the blunted press had bit parts. At White House press conferences, a piece of the presidential theatre, journalists were little more than a chorus. They endured the frequent humiliation of having to shout questions through the roar of the presidential helicopter as the President and his wife waved over their heads to the cameras. The helicopter arrivals and departures, and the grin and the wave, events which had no news value whatever, became the most familiar newsreel clichés of the presidency. On the whole, Americans were pleased to see the press reduced in Reagan's time, for they believed that journalists had grown too arrogant and presumptuous. The press was associated with the unhappiness of the 1970s, particularly the debacle of Vietnam, and reporters were judged by many to be guilty of the gravest American offence, failing to support the home side. When the press complained about being kept out of Grenada it did not get much public sympathy.

Reagan was plain and people could understand him. He did not have many ideas, but people thought they knew what he stood for. Much of his popularity lay in his presidency being a repudiation of the immediate past and his appeal as a repository of hope. He talked frontier, free enterprise and 'traditional values', sizzle rather than steak. He suggested that Americans could stop worrying about the poor, and channelling money to them, because in America everyone was free to make it to success, to swim as well as sink. He himself was an American success story, had reinvented himself and taken the second chance. In 1964, the year he made his last film, *The Killers*, in which he played an underworld figure, he switched from the Democrats to the Republicans; and two years after that he was Governor of California. Reagan drew on the strong sentimental strain in his countrymen and encouraged them to believe that as well as remaking themselves as individuals – the frontier dynamic – they could also remake themselves as a people – America is Back. It was the people who gave him his magic armour. They had had enough of presidents being broken, humbled and disparaged, for it was their own self-esteem which suffered. This man was granted proof from criticism. His mistakes and stumbles did not matter. When he fumbled for an answer it was his interlocutor who looked ill-mannered. His abject performances in the debates with Walter Mondale, his opponent in the 1984 presidential race, were irrelevant; and the debates themselves were beside the point. The election was a referendum on his leadership. Most Americans thought the emperor's clothes looked fine. He seemed charmed. His age was a factor in none of his election campaigns and he looked in tune with American determination to conquer the years, the obsession with youthfulness. In the old westerns the hero was often 'winged' by a bullet, and bandaged by the adoring heroine; Reagan, too, survived a shooting, and his wife was invariably photographed gazing at him in adoration. He was operated on for cancer and came out laughing. He had a robustness and an appearance of indestructibility. In a purely physical way he came to represent the happy qualities of survival and luck.

Debate about the Vietnam war reached a certain peak in Reagan's presidency. The main national focus of remembrance and feeling, the memorial in Washington, was dedicated in 1982. It is a place of poignant pilgrimage, a place like no other in America. Thousands come here every day to contemplate the wall of black granite slabs which bear the names of 58,000 dead. It is highly polished so that the people see their own reflections through the names of dead sons. People run their fingertips over the carved names in the manner of the sightless touching a face. They photograph the slabs and make pencil rubbings, and leave teddy bears, letters and small flags. The inclusion of the middle initial helps give the names their distinctive American rhythm – Willard

A Philson, Dan T Washington, Ulysses S Burroughs. The creation of the memorial by veterans of the war marked a turning point in American thinking about the first war the country had lost. For a long time it was too raw an injury to examine. Thousands of men had returned from the fighting to find themselves despised. To have fought, to have been a part of defeat, was a matter of shame. Many former soldiers are still being treated for mental breakdowns. The building of the memorial represented the re-emergence of the veteran. Instead of guilt it was all right to feel pride in service. In the same way that European writers and poets spent years trying to confront and explain the First World War, Americans began exploring, in films, plays, a spate of books and a long television series, what once seemed unapproachable. But ten years after the fall of Saigon two-fifths of Americans questioned in a poll could not say which side America had been on in the war. A young soldier questioned by a reporter was surprised to learn that his country had lost.

Many in the Vietnam generation remained tormented by the war. Because of Vietnam they had lost faith in government, generals and journalists, believing that the war was mismanaged politically and militarily. They were left painfully educated about the limits of power and the price of ignorance. The arguments surfaced again, in a curious manner, in a libel action against CBS brought by General William Westmoreland, who commanded the American army at the height of the war. The general, like Reagan, thought the war a good cause. He said he had been 'lynched' in a programme about the war and asked for $120 million – sums demanded in American lawsuits are monstrous and seem to mock the value of money. The general's celebrated action was more than a fight for an old soldier's honour. In its way it was a refighting of the bitter political and social war behind the shooting war. Many shared the general's view that American withdrawal had been forced by public opinion which was swayed by vivid reporting, particularly on television. Many in the services never forgave the press, blaming it for America's humiliation.

The general was said to be a front for conservative interests, exploiting the new climate in the country, trying to refight and legitimise the war and rewrite history; and also to get back at, and intimidate, the press. The general lost, but a screen hero who refought the war did not. Rambo offered the fantasy of another chance. 'Do we get to win this time?' he demanded before smashing the Vietnamese and Russian enemy while audiences chanted 'Kill, kill'. A man wrote to *Time* that 'I found the cinema full of other bearded 35-year-olds hooting and hollering as Rambo blew away half the North Vietnamese army. Childish perhaps, but there is vicarious satisfaction for us Vietnam vets in seeing Rambo win where we were not allowed to.' The film, it was said, filled a national need to reshape Vietnam into a winning experience.

In many ways the United States felt itself reshaped in the 1980s, more at ease with itself than it had been for twenty years. Reagan was a peacetime and good-time president, for there was neither external nor internal war. After years of self-criticism Americans settled for a long spell of being satisfied with what they had. Reagan was the beneficiary and stimulator of a mood in which America celebrated itself. President Carter had talked of America's malaise; but Americans had had enough of bleating and, wherever America had been, they were glad that America was Back. Big cars came Back. Executions came Back and, until the novelty wore off, mobs of young people cheered outside jails as murderers were put to death. Fundamentalist churches were Back, perhaps because they offered simplicity and a return to unambiguous basics in a complex world. Swaggering television preachers assumed themselves licensed by the more conservative climate to become political busybodies. Government hardliners sought to undo civil rights measures that had strengthened the country and had brought opportunity to weaker people. The poor were squeezed harder. Certain conservatives, mistaking the conservative wind for a gale, were disappointed that the President was not more assertively right; but Reagan was in office because he held the broad middle ground and he was checked by a Democratic House of Representatives.

Young people were at their desks, not demonstrating; joining the forces, not burning draft cards. They were the most conservative younger generation since the 1950s. Some teachers complained that there was little inspiration among students – they did not question, they seemed satisfied. To some of their elders it seemed that the empty suits were back. The middle-class young expected to become rich and they had heard President Reagan say that his greatest hope was that the United States would remain a country where someone could always get rich. The well-off young were likely to remain conservative to protect their interests. They could see that under this regime the country was heavily in debt and storing up aches for the future. Unemployment was high and likely to remain so. Many Americans were living below the poverty line. Reagan failed to build a bridge towards the poor and the gap between the wealthy and the poor widened. In that sense the country became less united. America, which once made many things, produced less, but manufactured more lawyers and public relations men. A modern symbol was the yuppie, the young urban professional, acquisitive and striving to remain young. He gave the impression that Americans were fitter, but a survey in 1985 showed that school-age Americans were fatter and less fit than they had been a quarter of a century earlier. The one-parent family became a commonplace. The traditional family with a father working and a mother at home bringing up children became the minority.

Reagan's lack of curiosity reflected and even encouraged a limited world view, legitimized ignorance. There was an uncertain and incoherent foreign policy. The obsession with the Russians was intensified rather than mitigated. Americans remained extraordinarily susceptible to crazes. A television melodrama about the aftermath of nuclear war raised such an uproar that the secretary of state had to go on television to calm the hysteria. Americans played into their enemies' hands by becoming neurotic when terrorists took hostages. The television networks, the excited outgrowths of the national nervous system, helped to stoke the frenzies. The so-called new patriotism sprang partly from fears and uncertainties, though it had its uses as a balm. But its stridency suggested not confidence but a lack of confidence, as well as – on occasion – an uglier sort of nationalism. It was part of the mood of conformity in which the vital grit of dissent could not easily work. It suggested that criticism itself was disloyal. It was intimidating. It was, as exploitation of patriotism often is, a cloak for humbug, fear and cheap sentiment; a diversion, a piece of packaging. It made the flag a carpet under which difficulties were swept away. Of a great people it demanded very little.

Index